For Rob, Liz and Family –

Love and Many Happy and precious memories!

Marjory xxx

Destiny Obscure

Marjory Wroe

authorHOUSE®

AuthorHouse™ UK
1663 Liberty Drive
Bloomington, IN 47403 USA
www.authorhouse.co.uk
Phone: 0800.197.4150

© 2018 Marjory Wroe. All rights reserved.

No part of this book may be reproduced, stored in a retrieval system, or transmitted by any means without the written permission of the author.

Published by AuthorHouse 09/22/2018

ISBN: 978-1-5462-9533-4 (sc)
ISBN: 978-1-5462-9532-7 (e)

Print information available on the last page.

Any people depicted in stock imagery provided by Getty Images are models, and such images are being used for illustrative purposes only.
Certain stock imagery © Getty Images.

This book is printed on acid-free paper.

Because of the dynamic nature of the Internet, any web addresses or links contained in this book may have changed since publication and may no longer be valid. The views expressed in this work are solely those of the author and do not necessarily reflect the views of the publisher, and the publisher hereby disclaims any responsibility for them.

Contents

Chapter 1 1
Chapter 2 13
Chapter 3 24
Chapter 4 33
Chapter 5 49
Chapter 6 57
Chapter 7 68
Chapter 8 74
Chapter 9 83
Chapter 10 92
Chapter 11 103
Chapter 12 109
Chapter 13 120
Chapter 14 127
Chapter 15 136
Chapter 16 155
Chapter 17 173
Chapter 18 180
Chapter 19 196
Chapter 20 210
Chapter 21 225
Chapter 22 235

Chapter 23 250
Chapter 24 258
Chapter 25 264
Chapter 26 278
Chapter 27 289
Chapter 28 295
Chapter 29 306
Chapter 30 312

Chapter 1

The atmosphere in the car was tense and Tom's frustration was intensified by the bright rays of the morning sun blinding his eyes. "Have you got your sunglasses with you?" he demanded of his wife who was poring over the map.

"Yes,` I'm wearing them", surprised that he hadn't noticed, "Do you want them?"

"Either that or you drive", was his sullen reply.

"What's the matter, Tom? We're almost there now—at least it's a lovely day and the scenery's fantastic".

"Oh is it? Well I can't bloody see it. I can hardly see the road!"

Jenny sighed, handed him her sunglasses and hoped that this mood would not last. It wasn't like him to be like this. Please, please don't let this be a waste of time. They were on their way to see a 10 acre farm on a remote hillside in North Wales. It had been her dream for a long time to escape from suburbia and live somewhere 'far from the madding crowd'. A place where she could keep her beloved horse, a few chickens and grow her own vegetables. Somewhere away from traffic noise and pollution, an environment free from the dangers of drugs and petty crime. Tom on the other hand could not see how it could work out. He had recently been promoted to Head of English in a very good secondary school and doubted that he would be able to get a job at all in North Wales, particularly as he didn't speak Welsh. He cursed himself for giving in to her yet again! She always got her own way, not by nagging as most women were supposed to do, but by withdrawing into herself, shutting him out, making him feel guilty and selfish. He loved her so much that he couldn't bear to see her unhappy. He dreaded losing her, but he couldn't see how they were going to resolve this problem.

He glanced across at her and she grinned up at him transporting him back to the first time he saw her. Fresh from university he had just started teaching and had been persuaded by Jack, his friend and colleague, to join the local Tennis club. Jenny was sitting on the side of the court leaning against the wire fence and breast- feeding a baby.

"Meet our opponents for this evening", said Jack airily, "This is Jenny with baby Jo, and this is Jan, my girl friend"

Jenny had given him that same grin and his heart lurched. She was the most beautiful girl he had ever seen.

"Won't be long—she's almost done".

She put the baby in its pram, grabbed her tennis racket and sprinted onto the court, slim and agile, her light brown hair tied back in a ponytail, not a trace of make-up and barely twenty years old.

They had a great game, closely fought with lots of fun and banter. Tom was surprised at her fitness, especially as she was a fairly new mother and still breast feeding. He had a lot to learn about Jenny and the emerging generation of young women capable of working alongside men and competing with them without rancour. These young women cast aside and rejected the old prejudices that they were the weaker sex which needed patronising or mollycoddling. They were the new generation of 'womens' lib'--not the old 'bra-burning' brigade! There were some aspects of this feminine uprising which were not easy for a conventional 'gentleman' like Tom to accept. Emotionally she was much stronger than him and he could not shed his inbred instinct to cherish and protect. This meant that she usually got her way. He couldn't bear to see her unhappy. This trip to bleakest Wales was yet another testimony to his weakness.

He sighed deeply and jerked himself back to reality "How much further?" he demanded. "I'll bet there isn't a petrol station for miles!" The latter observation was said almost petulantly.

Jenny feeling his rancour and realising that he felt backed into a corner, gently placed her hand on his thigh and squeezed gently, "Please cheer up love. Thank you for coming. I just want us to have nice day together."

He glared at the road and said nothing. He could not understand why she wanted to give up a modern house in a smart suburb. Most women would love what she had. They had lived in harmony in their modern semi for nine years Tom adored Jo as much as if she had she had been his own child. Life had been good. Jenny was happy working at Beechfield Riding Centre, teaching and competing, and all was well. True, she didn't like the the neighbours in the middle class cul-de-sac. She had nothing in common with them, particularly the next door neighbour, Mrs. Snell, a self-righteous interfering middle-aged snob whose greatest delight was defamatory gossip. Jenny however, disregarded her threats and insults about garden weeds and noisy dogs. Instead, she got on with her own life and had as little as possible to do with any of them. But now things were changing! Liz and Brian had decided to give up Beechfield where Jenny had worked for the past ten years and to sell the land to a property developer who had made them an offer they couldn't refuse. It was this hammer blow that had sparked off Jenny's desire to leave the town and move to what she hoped would be a rural idyll. Tom had a different outlook. He had been secretly pleased that Jenny would not be working at the stables any more. He wanted her to stay at home and have *his* child. Preferably a son. Yet here they were, off on a jaunt to see some hillside hovel. He shuddered and cursed himself for having given in to her yet again!

Tom's reveries were interrupted by Jenny's shout," There's the church. Turn left at the next junction!"

"Thanks for the warning!" he said sarcastically as he swung the car into the narrow lane. Jenny ignored him and felt a mounting excitement as she realised they were almost there.

The lane rose quite steeply and was flanked on either side by dry stone walls whose crevices had become filled with hosts of mosses and wild flowers. The great granite boulders were cemented together by vigorous growth of blackberry and ivy intertwined with columbine. Bluebells and mayflowers grew in abundance on high grassy banks interspersed with hawthorn, blackthorn and holly. Jenny was entranced as they twisted and turned their way up the steep hillside.

"Look at this", she sighed, "It's so unspoilt—so natural".

Tom, however, was in a different state of mind as he steered the car up the narrow lane which in places barely afforded sufficient space for even one vehicle,

"This is a sod of a road" he retorted bitterly, "Bloody impossible in winter! How much further is it?"

"Hard to say from the map. Less than half-a mile, anyway".

A buzzard rose noiselessly from its boulder perch and glided towards the woodland, hovering, watchful.

"Look at that!" Jenny gasped, "They're quite rare now!"

"Common as muck here I should think. Plenty of rotting sheep carcases for them to feast on", was Tom's bitterly facetious reply. Jenny ignored it. She was taken aback by the natural beauty of it all. No tractors had raped this land, grubbing out hedgerows, massacring trees and defaecating fertilisers everywhere. Looking at the giant oaks and elm trees whose branches interlaced with their neighbours on either side of the road, she had an uncanny feeling of being able to reach back in time and share the hopes and aspirations of those who had lived out their lives in the small tumbledown cottages which nestled here and there in the nooks and troughs of the rolling hills.

The sunlight sparkled and danced, kaleidoscope-fashion, through the woody canopy. Jenny was utterly entranced. To her the entwined branches were in a fond embrace forging love, peace and tranquillity. "Look Tom," she said earnestly, "It's like the trees are cuddling each other across the road, giving strength and hope." Tom scoffed at her naivety. It is true that mood reflects the way we feel about things at any given time, for to him, the branches were competing for space and choking the life out of each other. His mood was black, full of melancholic foreboding. Typically, he quoted lines from literature and mumbled almost inaudibly, *"I begin to feel some rousing motions in me which dispose to something extraordinary in my thoughts"*

"What's that, love? What did you say?"

"Nothing--just a line from Samson Agonistes. I'm doing it with the sixth form for A-level and it just crept into my mind." He shuddered, then continued," It's the atmosphere around here. "The way the trees are blotting out the sun. The sad discarded dwellings-----------"

"Say it again-- the Samson Agony thing!"

Tom repeated the lines slowly and deliberately.

"What do you mean?" she said, shuffling in her seat and regarding him worriedly, "Tell me about your thoughts"

"Strange and scary really. As if I've been here before. As if ghosts from my past and future are all around. A kind of dread foreboding."

Something in his demeanour frightened her and a cold chill clutched at her heart. She immediately dismissed it as a ploy on his part to put her off the whole idea of living here. She gave a little laugh.

"It's the incredible age of these trees that makes you feel weird. They must have been around since the Napoleonic wars, when my ancestors were battling against yours!" They both considered this in silence then she jumped in her seat and and cried, "Whoops! There it is. Stop here and I'll open the gate!"

A short rough track led up to a cobbled farmyard surrounded by stone outbuildings in various states of decay. They were struck by the large number of holly trees standing sentry at the front and sides of the buildings.

"That's how it got its name, Bryn Celyn---Holly Hill, in English!" exclaimed Jenny.

To Tom, the holly trees were not attractive. The shiny leaves, sharp prickles and blood-red berries seemed to spell a warning, 'Keep Away!" He shuddered.

The farmhouse itself was two storeys high, of simple design, reminiscent of a child's drawing—two downstairs windows with a door in the middle, three upstairs windows and two chimneys rising from a slate roof. The whole construction was of granite blocks, no doubt quarried locally. The wooden window frames were rotten, likewise the door-frame which gave way with the first push, yielding entry to the interior.

The first thing they both noticed was a large inglenook fireplace supported by a thick lintel of curved oak. The original ovens were still there, on either side of the large and black-leaded grate and the hearth comprised a solid block of polished local slate with a brass fender tarnished by age. Above the fire was a sturdy mantelpiece, also of polished slate. The whole effect was splendid, notwithstanding the thick layers of dust and grime and the stench of neglect and decay.

"No signs of vermin." commented Jenny, "Just a few spiders."

"They'll be back," muttered Tom grimly, "Just as soon there's something to for them to eat."

Jenny ignored him. Her imagination ran riot as she thought of the potential the place offered. She loved the sturdy oak beams stretching the length of the room effortlessly supporting the structures above. They symbolised strength and eternity. The floor was of red and black quarry tiles laid on earth and this, coupled with the small windows and rotten wallpaper peeling from the walls, made the atmosphere cold and dank, crying out for some warmth and loving care.

"Look at that, Tom! She enthused, seizing his arm, as they entered the erstwhile kitchen. She indicated another huge open fireplace "Perfect place for an Aga. Can't you just imagine it?"

Tom could well imagine it but did not comment as he felt himself once again backed into a corner.

Jenny, excited and entranced ran up the rickety stairs.

There were three fair sized bedrooms, each of which had its own small fireplace with more sturdy oak beams supporting sagging ceilings.

Tom wrestled with his feelings— a strange opposing mixture of romanticism and pragmatism, and his emotions jumped from one side to the other. "Yes", said the romantic side, "This could be made into something extra special!"

"But how are you going to finance it?" said the practical side. "Come on, be realistic! It would cost thousands, which you haven't got and even if you sold the semi in Primrose Close, how are you going to commute to work every day? And this place is far from being habitable. You'd have to live in a ruddy caravan, and how would you get even a small one up that darned lane? No chance. Forget it!"

"But it is special—look at that fireplace-- and making love snuggling close in a softly yielding bed with the red glow of a real fire and the wild elements battering at the window- Mmm lovely!"

Lost in his own thoughts he hadn't been listening to Jenny's rapturising prattle, but now she seized him by the arm and urged him to look at the view from the window. It was breathtaking! A panoramic vista over the rolling valleys to the Menai strait and Anglesey with its beautiful beaches and quaint lighthouses perched on rocky shores.

"Wow! That is superb! Come on. Admit it!" She cuddled closer to him appealing to his romantic side, but he kept silent, still loath to show any weakening of his intransigent resolve.

However, the black mood which had crept over him in the car began to fade away as he gazed out at the lovely countryside intent on renewing itself as it revelled in the warm Spring sunshine. Humour coupled with pragmatism initiated his next remark, "Great, but where's the bog?"

Jenny paused for a moment then giggled, "Why, anywhere you like. Take your pick! There is a privvy outside but we could have two more—one upstairs and one downstairs. Come on Tom! Admit it. This is a very special place."

"A great place to have a holiday, but entirely impractical as a permanent home," he grumbled.

Jenny, sensing that he was softening, continued excitedly,"Let's go and look at the land. According to the blurb there's about ten acres altogether including four acres of ancient woodland. I'll bet there's loads of wildlife there. Come on!" she almost fell down the stairs in her excitement.

They walked up the gently sloping fields over the tussocky grass and alongside a stream which wound its way along the boundary fence.

"This is handy", enthused Jenny, We won't have to carry water to the livestock and we can even keep ducks!"

Tom shrugged but said nothing. "She's behaving as if we've already bought the bloody place", were his bitter thoughts, yet he too, in spite of himself, was enraptured by the environment and the dream of living there, but that was all it could be as far as he was concerned—a dream.

The land was divided by dry stonewalls into eight paddocks of varying size, the largest being a wild woodland of some four acres comprising holly, ash, sycamore, beech, birch and oak. The gnarled and twisted shapes of the most ancient gave them a venerable air and once again Jenny experienced a deep captivating nostalgia. She felt that if she listened hard she could interpret the soft whispering which seemed to pass between them and thereby learn the secrets of those who had lived and loved here in previous generations. Tom for his part noticed the unwelcome invasion of hawthorn and blackthorn competing for space amongst the larger trees but today, Springtime prevailed and their dense shape and prickles were hidden by their beguiling blossoms. They encapsulated his mood. "Don't be fooled by face-value." He reminded himself as he sighed and followed Jenny as submissively as a child.

The floor of the woodland was carpeted by bluebells, thousands of them and their heavy perfume pervaded the air. As Jenny inhaled it, she was a little girl again, laughing, running and dancing through the trees. Tom watched her for a moment then in response, began to chase after her, as he too threw aside all his usual adult inhibitions and his negative forebodings. Breathless and laughing excitedly they ducked and dived through the trees until he caught her in a clearing, pulled her down onto a bed of bluebells and kissed her.

They lay close, inhaling the heady perfume, both conscious of their own and the other's heartbeat.

"I love you Tom", she whispered.

"Me too", he said teasingly, and they both giggled and cuddled closer together.

They lay like that for a while, warm and close, soaking up the peace and tranquillity. All tensions and differences faded away as they cuddled close. The circumstances of their lives had hitherto prevented them from ever being alone in an environment such as this. Little Jo was always with them, and so they had missed a teenage-type courtship. Also, it was very rare for town dwellers to find such a spot where they knew they could be completely alone for as long as they chose. Jenny was the first to break the silence,

"Being here like this makes me feel very lyrical", she mused as she snuggled even closer to him. I can remember some lovely poetry I learned at school, which seems just right for here. Do you want to hear it?

"Go on then", he replied, light-heartedly.

She took a deep breath and very softly, trying her best to put the right expression in her voice, whispered,

> *"Through primrose tufts in that green bower*
> *The periwinkle trails its wreaths*
> *And 'tis my faith that every flower*
> *Enjoys the air it breathes.*

Tom's response was not what she expected. He chuckled, quite spoiling the moment for her.

"That's Wordsworth." She said, somewhat miffed. "I liked him at school"

"Wordsworth—Turdsworth" scoffed Tom teasingly.

"Is that what your horrid little pupils call him?" she said, trying not to laugh but failing, in spite of herself.

"No, not at all. That's what his contemporaries, Keats and Shelley called him. They thought he was shallow, snobbish and entrenched in religious beliefs. I don't share that view, but he's not my favourite poet."

"Well *I* like him! At least I can understand him. You are such an intellectual snob!" she said petulantly.

"Wordsworth, Turdsworth, Wordsworth, Turdsworth," he taunted teasingly, rolling her over and over while she tried, not very hard, to free herself.

"You feel lyrical, well I feel bestial, my coy mistress-

> *'Let us roll all our strength and all*
> *Our sweetness into one ball,*
> *And tear our pleasures with rough strife*
> *Through the iron gates of life-------'*

He pinned her down, holding her arms above her head, and looking deeply into her hazel eyes. She shivered and sighed deeply. He felt her whole body melting beneath him.

He leant down over her and they kissed. There was no one else in the world. The sky was their eiderdown, the bluebells and the yielding grass their bed. Nothing else stirred. Only the waving branches whispering their approval.

Chapter 2

Not much was said on the journey home. Each was tussling inwardly with the problem of how to proceed. Jenny knew if she started to hassle him, she would, in effect, provide him with ammunition to strengthen his negative resolve. He, in his turn, knew if he reiterated his arguments for the sheer impracticality of the upheaval, this would spark off a bitter quarrel and the memory of that perfect pleasure they had both experienced and wished to preserve, would in some perverse way become fragmented into contentious missiles which they would hurl at each other thus strengthening the barrier which was growing between them. Jenny studied Tom as he drove morosely with almost robotic-like movements, deep in his own thoughts. Why had she fallen in love with him-- if it was love? It certainly wasn't the kind of exciting carefree feeling she had experienced with Joe. It was more a feeling of admiration and respect. Plus he had given her the stability and security she had never had as a child-- a sense of belonging to someone you knew would never let you down, who would always be there for you. Their childhoods had been so different. Tom's parents had been killed in a car crash when he was only four years old. He found out later that his father, an alcoholic, had been the cause of a tragic accident resulting in the loss of innocent lives. Tom's sister Julie, eighteen years old at the time of the accident, had been given custody of her young brother, a responsibility she had taken very seriously. In fact she had dedicated her whole young life to Tom making sure that he had the best possible upbringing and education. This meant that she had missed out on the social life so important to a young person eligible for the marriage stakes. All the money they had received after the accident had been used to ensure that Tom received the best education. After Grammar school he had entered Oxford from where he graduated with first class honours in English—a credit to Julie's care and encouragement. She basked in the reflected glory which she felt was just reward for her sacrifice and devotion. Whilst Tom was at Oxford, Julie had married a man much older than herself but it was a loveless marriage made worse because he, Desmond, turned out to have less money than she thought he had led her to believe. Tom remained the most important thing in Julie's life. She expected total loyalty and fealty from him and had never forgiven him for marrying Jenny whom she regarded as a slut. Tom tried hard to keep the peace with Julie, after all she was the only mother he had known and she had given him love and security in abundance. Now however, as far as she was concerned, it was payback time. She still wanted to govern his life. Poor old Desmond could not fill the void she had experienced when Tom left so she remained embittered, hating Jenny and blaming her for taking Tom away. Dismal Desmond was a mild-mannered doormat of a man and Jenny felt sorry for him and wished he would stand up for himself instead of creeping around the house with his, "Yes dear" attitude.

Jenny mused on, studying Tom's features and analysing her feelings towards him. He certainly wasn't a doormat. Neither was he a bully. He was forthright in his opinions but accepted differing views and relished discussion. Excellent qualities for a school teacher. What was it that bound her to him? Was it the security and stability she had lacked in her childhood? He was utterly dependable and she felt that he would always be there for her. The complete opposite of Joe—wild unruly devilishly good-looking Joe! He had swept her off her feet. To Hell with ambition and conformity! Live for today! This devil-may-care attitude no doubt contributed to his tragic end. She shivered and contemplated Tom again.

Physically he wasn't a handsome man, nor did he possess a great physique, but his blue eyes were soft and gentle and he was a man of great tenderness. Above all, she admired his intellect. His greatest loves were literature and poetry. He sought and gained comfort and inspiration from passages and quotes he remembered from the great literary masters, much as some people do from quoting passages from the bible. Jenny had no qualifications save mediocre results in GCSE's and A-levels. Her skills were confined to physical and sporting prowess. Tom had opened up a whole new world by introducing her to literature, poetry, classical music and the theatre. These had enriched her life and raised her self-esteem which had hit rock-bottom when she left university, an unmarried mother with no prospects whose only skill was that she was a good horse-woman. Now what was going to happen? Without Tom she had no chance of buying Bryn Celyn. Would he burst the bubble of her dreams? If so, would she, could she, ever forgive him? She felt empty and miserable on that droning journey back to the cheerless semi in the dismal cul-de-sac.

Tom, on the other hand, was reliving their conversation on the night he had proposed to her. They had been sitting outside the bar at the tennis club enjoying the cool evening air. They had known each other for less than three months and their meetings had been largely confined to playing tennis with Jack and Jan and sometimes sharing dinner with them.

He knew little about her background but already felt that she was someone with whom he wanted to share his life. He decided to ask her about her family and was fascinated to discover how unconventional her upbringing had been.

"I know nothing about your past," he had commented. "I have told you about mine. All I know about you is what other people have told me."

So she began to relate the facts about her early life.

Her parents had met in Chamonix. Her Irish father, Mike was a mountaineer and her French mother, Danielle, a ski instructor. The birth of Jenny had been a shock and surprise to both of them. This unplanned responsibility had brought them to the Peak District in Britain where Mike worked as an Outdoor Pursuits Instructor and Danielle taught French.

"They were great parents. When I was a little girl we had exciting holidays walking and camping. Dad carried me on his back for miles. I loved it— even in the bitterest weather. He and mum were restless, always craving adventure. I remember when I was seven I wanted a pony. They had no interest whatsoever in horses but they took me to Beechfield.

Destiny Obscure

I loved it and that's where I spent all my time whilst they went off on their various expeditions. Liz and Brian were my second parents and their daughter, Jan, my best friend, was like my sister."

Jenny had said this with fond nostalgia. Tom had listened gravely and wondered if she had ever been hurt by the unaccountable loss of her parents. 'Missing presumed dead?' Would she ever give up hope of their return?

She had a faraway look in her eyes.

"So," he mused, "It was all skiing, mountaineering and climbing at first. What got them into sailing?"

"Well, it was something they had both always wanted to do---the only outdoor sport they had never tried. One of dad's clients invited them to crew on his boat in the Irish sea. They loved it so they became bitten by the sailing bug." Another deep sigh, and a faraway look before she continued, "Mike and Danielle never did anything by halves so they decided that their next big challenge should be sailing round the world. Just like that! Typical!"

Tom gasped and Jenny smiled. "It was no surprise to anyone who knew them. The world was their oyster. Anyway, they read a book about the first British couple, Eric and Susan Hiscock, to sail around the world in the 1950's and this inspired them to do the same.

She swirled the beer round in her glass before taking a sip, "It was also no surprise when Mike said he was going to build his own boat, designed along the same lines as the Hiscock's boat, Wanderer 111. It was a very small wooden boat, about 30 foot long. Mum helped him of course. They financed it by working from dawn 'til dusk. Again Liz and Brian helped to make it possible by giving them a huge empty hay barn where they could build it. They called it 'Vagabonde' which is French for wanderer."

Tom had remained silent trying to imagine all this and the effect it must have had on their only child. They really were an incredible couple! And they produced Jenny. No wonder she was determined, courageous, ambitious and er, selfish, too-----!

"Anyway," she continued, "When the boat was finished they decided to take her on a maiden voyage over to Ireland and around the Isle of Man and they wanted me to go with them. I did and I hated it. It just wasn't for me. They were very disappointed but they understood. They always understood. They were never judgemental." She hesitated again and Tom discerned a slight smile of affection tinged with pride as she reminisced. She continued, her tone changing from admiration to slightly critical, "Typical of them they refused to rely on satellite navigation or ship-to-shore radios. They wanted to be utterly self-reliant, like the Hiscocks and all the other old sailors, and navigate by the stars. Dad used to say, 'You're buggered if your battery fails'. Some truth in that I suppose." She raised her eyes to the sky with a deep sigh and he sensed what she must be thinking--- maybe things would have been different if they had succumbed to electronic aid.

Intrigued, he had taken her hand impulsively whilst she composed herself to continue.

"I was eighteen when they set sail on this crazy adventure. They both hugged me and dad said, 'follow your dreams girl-----'"

She had kept squeezing and releasing his hand as if pumping more strength into herself to continue. A habit she still had when she was stressed or worried.

"Anyway, I was ready to start university. That's where I met Joe. He was wild too—a bit like mum and dad and---," She gulped and squeezed his hand harder, "He killed himself on his motorbike!" Her hitherto calm voice broke as she added almost breathlessly, "He never even knew of the existence of baby Jo. Neither did I at that time. I was barely two months pregnant."

"How awful for you. How did you cope?"

"I had to, for baby Jo's sake. Liz and Brian took me in and were towers of strength. I don't know what I would have done without them."

He had absorbed all this thoughtfully

"Your mum and dad were amazing people!"

"*Are*, please! It's only a couple of years since they left and I haven't given up hope."

"Sorry, I didn't mean it like that. You must miss them."

"No, not really. I'm so used to them going off on their adventures."

She had sighed deeply and looked down at a struggling butterfly splashing in a puddle of spilt beer.

Deeply affected by all this Tom had been consumed by an overwhelming urge to give Jenny something which he felt she had always lacked— constancy, security and dependability. He had taken her hand in both of his and gazed into her downcast eyes.

"Jenny, I love you. Will you marry me?"

She had looked up at him, expressed no surprise, and whispered, "Yes." Then typically and light-heartedly she had swept away any pretext of romantic slush by adding with a grin, "I thought you'd never ask."

They had both laughed.

He remembered all this from nine years ago. Their quiet uncluttered Wedding Day spent in a quiet uncluttered village in Derbyshire, the very place where Jenny had been born. Their only guests had been the Johnson family, Brian, Liz, Jan and best-man Jack, Tom's tennis friend now married to Jan. For a wedding present Tom had commissioned a painting of 'Vagabonde' from a photo taken on their maiden voyage to Ireland. This became Jenny's most treasured possession and had pride of place on their bedroom wall. Often, before they went to sleep they would look at it and remember the beginnings of their love. Sometimes too, Jenny would sigh and whisper, "Good night mum and dad, wherever you are."

So that was it. Two very different characters with very different upbringings. They had lived together in harmony for almost ten years, Jenny working at Beechwood, Tom teaching and Jo growing up in the security of a loving home. However, things were moving on. Beechwood had been sold and Jenny would soon be out of a job and separated from her beloved horses. This change in the status quo is what had sparked off the impending upheaval in their lives. Reminiscences, reasons, results! What next?

Tom's whole being was possessed as he drove mechanically through the death throes of the dying day--- sunlight, twilight, dusk, pitch dark.

It was past midnight when they arrived home at 2, Primrose Close. They were greeted by loud barking from inside the garage and when Tom opened the door, Lulu, their exuberant Irish Setter, hurled herself upon them with loud ecstatic yelps. Tom grabbed her and tried in vain to silence her.

"Oh God", he groaned as the bedroom window of the next door neighbour opened and the shrill voice of Mrs. Snell shrieked,

"What time do you call this! Shut that rotten animal up—some of us have to get up for work in the morning!"

"Sorry", shouted the distracted Tom, "Lulu, shut up, good dog".

He tried to hold her jaws together, but she thought it was a game and tore herself free, bouncing and leaping around them making more noise than ever.

Mrs. Snell renewed her onslaught, "I'm sick of that stinking dog! I'll see to it that you have to get rid of it. It does its mess in my garden - a health hazard for my children. I've had enough now! I'm going to make a complaint to the Council. See if I don't!"

Jenny lost control. She and the Snells had never got on.

"You're a liar, Smelly!" She yelled back. "My dog has never shit in your garden. Your bloody cat is always digging and shitting in my veggie patch!"

Mrs. Snell's furious screech could be heard all over Primrose Close and more bedroom windows opened, "Just listen to the dirty-mouthed slut! Veggie patch indeed! A few ugly potato plants and caterpillar-infested cabbages! And you've no right to bring that dirty horse down here— showing off –pretending to be something you're not – and leaving its muck for someone else to clear up. That's another thing you'll be reported for. We don't want your sort here---get back to the slums where you belong!"

Jenny's temper snapped. She seized a handful of earth and gravel and hurled it at the window, "Stick that in your mouth you embittered old bitch!" Her voice had risen to a scream and she bent to grab more gravel intent on silencing her adversary by forcing her away from the window. By this time yet more windows had opened and more angry voices joined in. Tom had released the dog in order to restrain Jenny who was still struggling and swearing when the police car approached. The whole scene took on a surreal quality –twisted faces ugly in their anger-- Snell screeching and screaming hysterically; bellowed protestations from those households outraged at being so rudely awakened and throughout all this madness, Lulu leaping joyously and barking gleefully, blissfully unaware of her part in unleashing the simmering hatred now erupting over this middle class neighbourhood. PC—Primrose Close whose normally Politically Correct residents would not dream of being part of any public disturbance now gave full vent to their hitherto repressed rage as they flung foul language from one to another. Tom, poor Tom, completely out of his depth amid this chaos, took a deep breath closed his eyes and in an effort to preserve his own sanity recited Kipling's immortal words, *"If you can keep your head when all about you are losing theirs—"*

And now, the silent sleek arrival of the flashing blue light.

Jenny ran. She ran wildly through the gardens, scrambling over fences heedless of the brambles seizing and clutching her as if trying to arrest and detain her before the police did.

She ran to the sanctuary of Beechwood.

Breathless and bleeding she climbed the perimeter fence and stumbled across the sand arena to the stable block. The contented chomp of the occupants enjoying their evening hay nets brought a semblance of sanity after the madness of her encounter with the residents of Primrose Close. She approached Bella's box quietly and stroked the silky muzzle evoking a soft whicker of gentle greeting. She began to shiver uncontrollably and feeling weak and dizzy, crept into the box and buried her hands under the soft mane feeling the comfort and warmth of the mare's velvety neck. "Oh Bella, what am I going to do?" Sobbing quietly, she poured out the whole story to the bemused yet patient animal until overcome by exhaustion, she crept into a corner and fell asleep on the thick bed of straw.

Chapter 3

She was awakened just after dawn by a familiar voice, "Bugger me—what's this? Bugger me!"

Old Bert had worked at Beechwood Riding Centre for donkeys' years. Nobody could remember him ever having a day off sick and even during official holidays he would usually pop in to see his beloved charges. Unmarried, he had lived with his widowed sister until her death and now he was alone the horses and Beechwood were all he had left in the world. Bert, however, was no moper, and as he worked around the yard mucking out boxes, driving the tractor, shoving wheelbarrows, painting, mending fences or doing any of the seemingly endless tasks on a busy yard. He was always cheerful. He enjoyed teasing the stable girls and they responded by giggling and mock admonishment which amused and pleased him making him feel part of the happy family atmosphere on the yard. He was well loved by all who knew him and was referred to affectionately, as 'Bugger-me-Bert' because his stock response to everything shocking or surprising was, "Well, bugger me!" Sad or happy situations evoked, "Poor bugger", or "Lucky bugger" with the appropriate intonation. Seeing Jenny huddled in the corner of the stable his tone was one of shock and consternation. "Hey up! You OK? Bugger me!"

Upon hearing this familiar voice full of surprise and concern, Jenny broke down in tears and related the whole sorry saga as they trudged together towards the farmhouse lured by thoughts of welcoming arms and the irresistible smell of egg and bacon.

Liz, busy at the stove as always, wiped her hands on her pinafore, gave Jenny a warm hug and listened to her outpourings. Then in her usual common-sense manner said, "Don't let those petty Primrose Close people upset you. You need to get away from there. The farm sounds lovely, right up your street. What's holding you back?"

"Tom reckons we can't afford it and he doesn't want to commute, even at weekends, but I can't ever go back to Primrose Close, especially not now after last night's fiasco! I hate the place and even if I did want to go back I probably couldn't as that bitch Julie Snell will more than likely be seeking an injunction to stop me. I love Tom, but we don't seem to want the same things any more and I can't bear the thought of spending my life in some snobby suburb surrounded by Snells. What am I going to do, Liz?"

The anguish in her voice increased and Liz put a comforting arm round her shoulders and said gently, "Well, you can always come to New Zealand with us, you know".

"I know, and you've always been more of a mother to me than my own mother but I don't want to leave Britain—not yet anyway, and besides, I've fallen in love with 'Bryn Celyn'."

Liz released her and became business-like again, "Come on, have some breakfast and give me time to think about it.

Most problems have a solution. We just have to be patient. After breakfast, can you work Freddy for me? Someone's coming to look at him this afternoon. She sounds really nice and I'd love him to go to a good home".

"Me too," agreed Jenny, He deserves it."

She showered changed her clothes and put the present irksome problems to the back of her mind as she occupied herself with the endless daily chores on the busy yard.

Liz, meanwhile, was clattering away in the kitchen clearing the breakfast dishes so immersed in thought that she didn't hear Brian come in.

"What's up love—you look worried. Any chance of a cuppa?"

Liz looked around furtively, wiped her hands and closed the kitchen door. "Sit down, I want to talk to you about something"

Somewhat puzzled by her attitude, he pulled his chair up to the table and sat down.

"What's up, love?" he demanded.

She related Jenny's circumstances then waited, studying his reaction.

He supped his tea thoughtfully, his large rough hands cupped around the pint pot. Then he said slowly, "Well, I suppose we could always lend her the money. We've done pretty well out of this place".

To his huge surprise she flung her arms round him and kissed him ignoring his protests and the slopping tea.

"Steady on, love. Steady on. What's all this about?"

"It's because I love you and no wonder we've been married for forty years—forty wonderful happy years. I knew that's what you'd say because that's just what I thought we could do. "We'll tell her when she comes in for dinner. She'll have to stay here tonight. I've phoned our Jan and Jack to fetch her things from Primrose Close."

"What about little Jo. Where's she at?"

"Staying at Tom's sister's—under protest—she hates her auntie Julie. No doubt she'll be staying here too 'til things sort themselves out. Strange, the two most hated women in Jenny's life share the same Christian name—the Snell woman is a Julie too! Funny too that all their names start with the same letter, Jan, Jack, Jenny, Julie, Jo. The tenth letter of the alphabet. I wonder if there's any significance in that."

"Is there heck! It's called coincidence. You women are always looking for obscure meanings in things—luck, chance, destiny. We can't change these things."

"Course we can!" she rejoined, "We've changed our destiny by planning to go to New Zealand."

"Not yet we haven't. We're not there yet. Anything could happen between now and when we actually leave."

"Yes, I can see that, but what if the plane crashes and we're all killed. By deciding to go we've altered our destiny. If we decided to stay put we'd have a very different destiny."

"Not necessarily. Death is our ultimate destiny—cancer or some other dread disease could be round the corner and ready to strike us wherever we are. We can't ever completely control our destiny. We can try, as you said we are doing, by going to live on the other side of the world, but our real destiny is obscured."

She sighed and wiped her hands on her apron, "That's enough of that---it doesn't do to think too hard about it," she replied resignedly. "It's best to take every day as it comes and live it to the full. Look! Is that Tom I can see out there----and little Jo?"

Jo started calling to her mother who was busy preparing 'Freddy'. To distract her, Bert took her arm and suggested that they went to see 'Dinky', Jo's pony, so she skipped off in front of him towards the stable block with never a backward glance.

Jenny was in the arena putting 'Freddy' through his paces for the prospective buyer, a middle-aged woman smartly dressed in the latest equestrian gear. She was watching Jenny and 'Freddy' intently and gave Tom no more than a cursory nod and smile as he approached. Tom watched his wife jumping the big powerful horse with apparently effortless ease and he noted, not for the first time, that she was a natural and gifted rider. He also realised as he watched her that he could not expect her to give it up for him. She would never be happy and things would not work out between them.

Liz approached and greeted the prospective buyer who was obviously impressed. Jenny jumped off the horse handed him to Liz and faced Tom for the first time since the debacle of the night before. Tom looked pale and strained and the resolve to cold-shoulder him for what she saw as his unmanly lack of support melted away and she seized his hand as they walked towards the house. "Where do we go from here?" There was a catch in her voice but she swallowed back her emotion. To weep now and cause a scene was the last thing she wanted to do.

Tom sighed deeply, "I don't know. I really don't know but I do know that it would be hard for you to come back home."

Jenny released her grasp, "Hard! Hard! More like bloody impossible! It's never had the 'homely' feel of a real home—not like here. There was a catch in her voice as she turned away from him. Then anger and frustration took over, "I never ever want to set foot in that stinking suburban shithole again!"

Tom winced and looked around nervously to see if anyone else had witnessed that vulgar outburst. Luckily they were alone. Jo had gone off to brush her pony and Liz and the posh lady were in animated conversation outside the arena. On an impulse, Tom grabbed Jenny's arm and pulled her round to face him. He could see that she was very near to breaking point so he softened, and put his arms around her trying to soothe and comfort. She pushed him away to stop herself from giving vent to the pent-up emotions which were welling ever nearer to the surface. Suddenly the deadlock was broken by a shout from Brian, "Hey you two—come in for a cuppa!"

In the warmth of the farmhouse kitchen, seated around the large wooden table, tensions evaporated. Bert came in muttering to himself as usual and joined them. Brian and Bert had heard the tale of the fiasco at Primrose Close before from Jenny but it was clear that they wanted to know more. It was also clear that to them, it was no more than a storm in a teacup, a comical one at that, and they were guffawing and bugger-me-ing when Liz came in looking rather pleased with herself.

"She's bought Freddy. No haggling—she's given me what I asked which I never dreamt he was worth!"

"I'm not surprised," said Tom, "You should have seen the way he was going for Jenny!"

The delighted Liz hugged Jenny, "You're a marvel! We're all going to miss you—but let's not go there. We have something else to talk about."

She looked enquiringly at Brian, wanting him to take over. He cleared his throat,

"We have a proposition to make but first of all we'd like some input from Tom. "What did you really think about the little Welsh farm?"

Tom looked surprised. He guessed that Jenny had told them all about it. Got her oar in first!

"Er, well, it is a great place—lots of potential, and well priced for the amount of land but there are problems associated with it. He hesitated and glanced at Jenny who, disconcertingly, was staring fixedly at him.

He continued much in the same vein as he did when he was explaining something to his pupils. "Well, the first consideration is, of course, financial. We have to be quite realistic about this. Even if Number 2 were to sell quickly at a reasonable price, then the residue left after paying off the mortgage would not be sufficient to pay for the deposit and necessary improvements to make the place habitable let alone comfortable." Another pause, "Even if that were not true, the other insurmountable problem as I see it would be the question of my job. There's no way I am prepared to spend three hours commuting to and from work every day, er-- that's six hours in total."

He sighed and looked at Jenny who averted her gaze to look down at her tightly clasped hands and replied. "Well, that's your point of view, here's mine. There's no way that *I* can ever go back to Number 2—absolutely no way! You know that as well as I do". She struggled hard to control her emotions.

Liz spoke up, "Forget the problem of the money. Brian and I have discussed it and we are happy to lend you the deposit and whatever you need to pay the mortgage until you've sold Number 2."

They both looked up quickly and were about to protest when Brian intervened. "Don't argue! We'd do the same for our daughter and you Jenny, are like a daughter to us and the yard would not have thrived as it has done this past ten years without you."

Jenny blushed and looked down but said nothing

"Also," continued Liz, "We do feel that we have rather left you in the lurch by selling up, but we are both ready to retire and, well, the Supermarket made us an offer we can't refuse---so please don't argue any more about the loan. Don't feel bad about it. Remember it is just a loan. An interest free loan and you can pay us back when you get back on your feet. It's the very least we can do for you."

There was an uncomfortable silence as Tom and Jenny searched for the right response.

The tension was evaporated by Bert who had remained silent throughout save for the slurping of his tea, "Bugger me, Tom and Jerry" he teased, "That's a good offer! This Bryn whatd'yercallit sounds like a bit of heaven compared to that snobby cul-de-sac. Number 2—that sums it up, that does. Number 2—rhyming slang for pooh!" Everyone laughed, then Tom spoke up. "Thank you both," he said humbly. "That's a great offer, but it doesn't solve the problem of how I'm going to get to work every day."

Jenny spoke up eagerly, "Tom, it's only a couple of hours away and there's no traffic. Some poor devils have to spend that time commuting in heavy traffic every day and you should be able to find a job teaching English even if you don't speak Welsh. Not many teachers have what you have to offer—a first class honours degree from Oxford! "she paused, "Anyway, I can't live without my riding- it's all I can do, and Jo will want to keep her pony no matter what."

Silence. All faces turned to Tom. He shrugged and sighed resignedly. So, it was all settled. Jenny was jubilant and ran to hug him, "I know you won't regret it. We'll live happily ever after!"

He released her, shrugged again, then said, "Where's Jo?"

"With her pony, of course--she'll be ecstatic when we tell her!"

So there it was-- a new life in a new place—a new destiny!

Chapter 4

During the school summer holidays that followed, Tom and Jenny with the help of a local builder set about making Bryn Celyn habitable. They were determined to keep the essential character of the place and by the winter they had a weatherproof and comfortable home. They had never been happier. Jenny was pregnant with a child conceived during that rapturous romp in Bluebell wood. Tom was coping with the commuting at weekends and staying at his sister's during the week. He longed for the lengthy school holidays and constantly applied for jobs in the North Wales area which did not require fluency in Welsh. Jo too had settled well in her new school although she lacked a friend who was interested in horses.

The opportunities for hacking out in the surrounding area were very good and Jenny was making the most of it before her pregnancy prevented her from riding. All in all, they were settling nicely into their new life. When Jenny found out she was pregnant she decided to put Bella in foal--a good idea for two reasons, firstly, she knew that with a new baby she would have much less time to ride and secondly, it would only be a matter of three or four years before Jo would outgrow her pony and need a horse. Perfect if she inherited a baby from Bella!

One misty, murky day in early November Jenny was riding Bella down the narrow lane when she heard a vehicle approaching. She stopped and waited as there was little room to pass. A small red car appeared round the bend and upon seeing her the driver stopped and wound down the window.

"Excuse me", he said politely, could you tell me where 'Pen y Graig' is?

Jenny paused and pondered the question She noticed a Jack Russell asleep on the back seat. "Pen y Graig---er—wait a minute –yes---"

That was as far as she got. The dog opened one eye, spotted the horse and hurled itself at the window, snapping and snarling.

The startled horse whipped round and lashed out with both back feet.

There was a loud and sickening crash as metal connected with metal then Bella reared, leapt forward and bolted back towards home. Jenny could do nothing except hang on desperately whilst trying in vain to regain control of the terrified animal who did not stop until she reached the safety of the farmyard. Jenny jumped off the snorting, shaking mare and checked the hind limbs for any visible signs of injury. Luckily there were none. Jenny was trembling as much as the mare and an overdose of adrenaline made her feel sick and faint but she pulled herself together, removed the tack from Bella and groomed her gently, hoping that this would have the effect of helping both of them to relax.

By the time she had finished and put on the stable rug, Bella was happily munching hay, apparently none the worse for the experience.

"What now?" thought Jenny, still in a state of shock, as she sipped a comforting cup of tea in the cosy kitchen, "Bella must have done a lot of damage to that car----supposing he comes here causing trouble----who's to blame? Thank God I'm insured! I'd better ring the company and tell them what's happened. That way I've at least covered myself."

She decided not to relate the incident to either Jo or Tom. She knew that Tom would be worried about the possible consequences to the child she was carrying. She searched her own conscience about whether or not she should still be riding at all so near to the birth. Was it fair to risk your own life when in so doing you put the life of someone else in jeopardy?

The son they had both waited so long for was now a reality. Surely she could and should stop now for all their sakes! But this argument could go on forever. She would still be risking her life and also risking ruining the lives of her family if she started riding again after the baby was born! At least though, it *would* be born and Tom could look after it until it could fend for itself and make its own decisions. She pondered on her own childhood—had her parents ever considered her needs when they disappeared on their jaunts? She saw a parallel between their behaviour and that of many animals, who, when their offspring are ready to fend for themselves shed the responsibility—'We've done our bit—we've given you life—now go and get on with it!'

Was this really how her parents were? Had they cared about her at all?

The truth of the matter is that they had not actively planned to have a family and when they found themselves lumbered ---yes, lumbered, they dealt with the situation in the only way they knew how. True, they were more than happy to let her share their life as soon as she became old enough, but by this time she was her own person and capable of making her own decisions. Being uprooted from everything she knew and cared about, which was Beechwood and her beloved horses, to be thrown into some wild adventure had no appeal. She sighed remembering their last farewell. They'd hugged her and Mike had said, "Follow your dreams, girl!" They looked so fit, so young, so happy. She felt very proud of them. They were very different from all the other kids' parents and during her teenage years when parents were so often regarded by their offspring as being boring, the exploits of Mike and Danielle set her apart from the rest and made her feel special. She knew they loved her – they were just unconventional. They believed that once you discover what you want out if life, you should strive to obtain it and not be driven into conformity and end up in an embittered old age full of regrets. She gave a deep sigh and studied the dregs in the bottom of her cup, remembering how her Irish grandmother used read fortunes in the patterns of the tea leaves. The tea bag had burst but Jenny could interpret nothing in what she saw but destruction and confusion. She wondered yet again where her parents were and what they were doing at this very moment. How would they react to being grandparents? Would they ever be content to settle in one place and lead normal lives? Jenny doubted it. Like a lot of adventurers their destiny would probably lead to their Nemesis in some far-flung place and they would fade in to obscurity as they entered 'That bourne from which no traveller returns'.

Two weeks after the bolting incident Jenny decided to go for one more hack on Bella and make this the last one before the baby was born. It was a bright fresh day and as she rode along the quiet country lanes she felt a deep inner peace. She knew it had been the right decision to move here and she felt that Tom did too but he never said so. The autumn colours were truly beautiful, reminding her of a weekend at Tarn Hows in the Lake District with her parents. They had camped by the lake and walked for miles surrounded by majestic mountains carpeted with extravagant hues of gold and russet brown. The trees which had given up this glory stood stark, their bare branches reaching down towards the rich store of compost they were leaving for the next generation. Jenny was no more than five years old but she could still relive and relate the gentle sway as her father walked with her in the papoose on his back to what she felt now on Bella. Strange, she mused, why lately she should be thinking so often of her parents. Perhaps it was because she was pregnant. She was again carrying their genes forward into immortality. It hadn't been the same when she was carrying Jo. Her pregnancy had been a shock to her and she was sure that Joe would not have been pleased-- neither of them was prepared for parenthood. Then came his fatal accident leaving her alone and devastated. She would have to cope with becoming a single parent. She had fretted over the loss of her first love and wondered how she would manage. God bless Brian and Liz! What would she have done without them?

Jenny's reverie was rudely interrupted by Bella's head shooting up violently as she stood stock still, quivering, ears forward, staring fixedly. "What's the matter, silly?" said Jenny experiencing the familiar shot of adrenaline and the instinctive tightening of her hands on the reins. Looking around for the source of Bella's fear she spotted two large dogs in the garden of a nearby cottage. As she was leaning forward to pat the horse and reassure her, she noticed that both dogs were towing car tyres attached to their collars by chains, no doubt to stop them from jumping out. When they saw the horse they bounded towards the fence barking loudly, the tyres and chains bouncing and scraping behind them with a fearful unfamiliar racket. This was too much for even the most laid-back of horses. Panic-stricken, Bella bolted. There was a red car coming towards them some fifty yards away and it took all of that distance for the horse to come under control. Breathless and shaking, Jenny raised a trembling hand to apologise to the driver, who got out of his car full of concern. Jenny went cold as she recognised him. It was the same man whose car Bella had kicked just two weeks ago.

"Are you all right? He sounded concerned.

"Er, yes, I think so", she felt flustered and embarrassed.

"Is your horse OK after kicking my car---it was you wasn't it?"

Surprised that he should be more concerned about the welfare of the horse than the damage to his car, she stammered, "Well yes, er she's fine thank you, but if she damaged your car, don't worry, I'm insured and I reported it as soon as I got home"

He smiled, "Don't worry about that. It's only an old banger and I've got a scrapper at home. I took the door off that one. Anyway, it wasn't your fault. It was Rambo, the wife's Jack Russell, being stupid. I was worried that the horse was hurt and that you might have fallen off too. By the way, I'm Bob, Bob Longton."

"Jenny Weston", she replied, warming to him instantly as she reached down to shake his hand.

During the conversation that followed Jenny learned that that Bob and his wife Jean, had recently bought a property in the area and had just moved in with their grand-daughter, Emily, who was the same age as Jo.

"Emily is horse-mad – that's one of the chief reasons for moving here. My wife, Jean, has always wanted to live in the countryside and now we've both retired we can do it. We've bought a cottage with a couple of acres. It's good that I've met you as you'll be able to put us in touch with local Pony Clubs. We've brought a pony with us that we bought for Emily from her club."

That's marvellous!" said Jenny. "We haven't lived here that long and my daughter too is pony-mad and will love having a friend to ride out with".

They exchanged phone numbers and parted, each eager to become friends and neighbours. How fortuitous! She had a good feeling about Bob, and to have found a potential friend for Jo too—great! She felt happy and uplifted as she hacked home singing to the rhythm of Bella's eager trot.

That very evening Jenny rang Bob and Jean and the following weekend they came over for dinner with their grand-daughter, Emily. Jo was so happy to have a pony-mad friend and the adults too were pleased to have found good neighbours. After dinner whilst the adults chatted over coffee, Jo and Emily went outside to see the horses. The night was dark and still. They crunched their way over the gravel and a soft whicker greeted them as they entered the stable. "This is Bella mum's dressage horse. Her real name is Meribel. She is called after the ski resort in France where grandma and grandad met, but her stable name is Bella." Jo announced proudly. "She's in foal at the moment. The foal will be for me when I've outgrown Dinky."

"She's beautiful!" breathed Emily as she caressed the mare's silky coat. "When is the foal due? You lucky thing!"

"Sometime in March after mum's had my baby brother."

Emily smiled. "Where's Dinky? Can I see her too?"

They left the stable and walked across the yard to the gate. Jo placed her fingers to her mouth and gave a shrill whistle. Dinky lifted her head and came galloping up to them.

"That's so cool. What a super pony! Will you teach me how to whistle like that?"

"Yes, if you want. It took me a while to do it properly. I was taught by an old man who worked at the stables where mum worked. He said girls shouldn't do it 'cos it wasn't lady-like. He used to say, 'a whistling woman and a crowing hen will frighten the devil out of his den'!" They both giggled, "He was a real character was old Bert. We called him Bugger-me-Bert 'cos he was always saying, Bugger this and Bugger that and Bugger-me!"

Emily laughed, "Well, can you show me how to do it?"

"OK, Watch!" and she began to demonstrate the technique. "You put your fingers like this, then press down and blow hard."

She emitted another piercing whistle. Emily tried to copy her but all that she achieved was a lot of spittle. They both laughed.

"Just keep on practising" urged Jo, "You'll get it in the end. It took me a while."

As they walked back to the house the conversation centred around ponies and they began to warm to each other. They were so different in looks and character but each had attributes which attracted the other. Emily was smaller than Jo with bright blue eyes fair skin and shoulder length blonde hair which was tied back accentuating high cheek bones in a very pretty oval face. Her smile was warm and slow but often erupted into an infectious giggle. Her normal expression was soft and demure. Fiery-tempered Jo wondered if Emily ever got angry or sulky. Emily, for her part, felt slightly in awe of Jo's confident, even bossy, demeanour but felt instinctively that she was someone she could trust.

Back indoors the adults were relaxed and happy, so pleased to have made acquaintance. Jenny reflected on the strange coincidence which had brought them together and which could have had such awful consequences. She smiled and thanked her lucky stars.

True to her promise to Tom, Jenny decided not to ride again until until after the baby was born and during the ensuing months she steeped herself in domesticity for the first time in her life. To her surprise, she enjoyed tasks she had previously considered to be alien to her nature –cooking, cleaning--ironing--even knitting! Perhaps this new-found interest owed a lot to Jean who became her friend and mentor. The cottage kitchen became like the one at Beechwood, the true heart of the house, cosy, warm and suffused with welcoming aromas of freshly baked bread and cakes.

A warm friendship developed between Jenny and Jean even though in many ways they were different. Jean was the product of an older generation where men were accepted as the bread-winners and natural leaders in society and the role of women was to ensure their home comforts and to defer to them in most decisions affecting their lives, whereas with Jenny, the relationship was based on absolute equality. Jean and Bob were lovely people. To Jenny they were very like Brian and Liz, honest, uncomplicated, salt-of-the-earth people, always ready and willing to give help and support in a crisis--- friends for life. Typically, Brian and Liz had insisted that Bert accompany them to New Zealand. They knew that they were the only family he had left and couldn't bear to leave him behind, alone in the world. Jenny missed them all terribly and often talked about them to Jean. After all, they were like her only family too, especially when she tried to come to terms with the fact that she may never see Mike and Danielle again. Once more she was saddened to think that they may never see nor even realise the existence of their grandchildren.

Jean noticed Jenny's lapse into melancholia, "Cheer up, love!" she said, as she placed the hot mince pies on the kitchen table, "Christmas is round the corner! Shall we go and get some holly and start decorating the house before Bob collects the girls from school?"

So they donned warm coats, wellies and gardening gloves, grabbed secateurs and braved the bitter weather to collect sprigs of holly resplendent in bright red berries. There were at least twenty holly trees lining the dry stone walls, most of them covered in berries.

"You can see how this place got it's name, 'Holly Hill'. I wonder who planted this lot", remarked Jean.

"God, probably!" laughed Jenny with a touch of irony.

"Whoever said, 'Red and Green are seldom seen' was obviously a Townie or a Twit!" rejoined Jean.

"Or both!" agreed Jenny and they giggled, feeling close and Christmassy.

The porch looked warm and welcoming with bright sprigs of holly bursting with red berries lining the window sills and walls. This was how Jenny had dreamed the house would look when she first saw it. She smiled with a deep sense of satisfaction. She glanced skywards and murmured, "My dreams are coming true mum and dad."

"This holly will ward off witches and evil spirits", laughed Jean as she tied up a robust sprig.

"I thought you needed garlic for that." bantered Jenny.

"Well, if you see or sense any evil we'll get garlic as well."

"Why not go the whole hog!" Jenny giggled. "There's a a bay tree too near the gate so that's yet another deterrent. Ghoulies and ghosties and long-leggity beasties not welcome at Bryn Celyn!" They both laughed feeling a secure inner warmth, safe and sheltered in each other's company.

They used the rest of the holly to festoon the aged beams in the lounge and kitchen. The effect was festive, warm and welcoming.

"'Bryn Celyn' inside and outside now", smiled Jean.

Emily and Jo clapped and laughed excitedly when they saw it and begged to be allowed to collect more holly to take to school.

"Help yourselves!" laughed Jenny. And they did, collecting armfuls, shrieking as the thorns pricked their fingers, laughing and comparing the colour of the drops of blood to the vivid red of the berries. They began singing lines from the well known carol, 'The Holly and the Ivy' ----

"The holly bears a berry, as red as any blood", sang Jo, and Emily completed the verse, "And Mary bore sweet Jesus Christ, for to do us sinners good." They were in rapturous mood, captivated by the special carefree spirit of Christmas.

"All we need now is snow!" "Please God," begged Emily, "Send some snow---

lots and lots of it so they'll have to shut the school!"

"Yippee!" shrieked Jo, "I'll second that!" and they dumped a pile of holly in the porch and ran excitedly into the warm house.

Meanwhile Jenny and Jean were preparing a meal for everyone. As it was Friday, Tom was coming home for the weekend so there were six for dinner and the sumptuous smell of Steak and Ale pie pervaded the kitchen and the hungry youngsters and Bob were shooed out as they crowded the cooker, sniffing and salivating and pestering about how much longer they would have to wait. Jenny's speciality as a non-cook was to prepare the dessert, fresh fruit salad and ice cream. Jenny wished she could cook like Jean. "It's only practise", Jean told her, "If you can read, are able to buy the freshest ingredients, learn by your mistakes, oh, and don't forget the most important ingredient for whatever you are cooking", she paused then added emphatically, "Love!"

Jenny thought about this for a moment, gave her friend a hug, then agreed wholeheartedly.

Tom arrived at 6.30 to a warm welcome from family, friends and an ecstatic Lulu, bouncing and barking and slipping on the tiled floor.

"Back in the Madhouse!" he laughed as he hugged Jenny and Jo.

Everything was such a contrast to the clean and clinical atmosphere at his sister's semi where law and order prevailed-- meals were always on time, everything was spick and span, warm and draught-free but there wasn't much laughter. Scorn and self-righteousness epitomised Julie whilst her poor down-trodden doormat of a husband, Dismal Desmond, crept around and suffered in silence, or so it seemed. In comparison, Tom felt it was lovely to be home in Bryn Celyn where he could relax and not have to worry about causing offence with even the slightest transgression. One of Jenny's quips made him smile-- 'at Julie's house it was much better to suffer stomach ache than to fart!' How secretly glad he was now that the decision to leave Primrose Close had been forced upon him. He had led such a closed-in and sheltered life that he had been unable to experience or conceive of anything different. This slightly chaotic humdrum household, this 'hovel in the hills', was very different and he loved it.

They laughed and joked as they ate together in the large farmhouse kitchen with the log fire crackling and spitting in the Inglenook and bunches of holly winking and twinkling in the dancing firelight. They felt close, secure and very happy.

Next morning, Jo and Emily went to Pony Club together and as she waved them off the postman arrived with an official looking letter addressed to Tom. He wandered downstairs and collected it casually. It was from the Estate Agent. He tore it open eagerly then gave a whoop of delight, "Jenny, Primrose Close, it's been sold-- for the asking price too! Whoopee-- What a great Christmas present!" Jenny came tearing out of the kitchen and flung herself into his arms and they danced around like demented dervishes.

"We'll be able to pay back Brian and Liz, now", said Jenny excitedly, "And I can have a new dressage saddle and we can buy a trailer and a four-by-four to tow it and plan more improvements to this place and---"

"Steady on girl. We haven't got the money yet and we have a new baby on the way; Thomas William Weston," he added proudly

He stroked her stomach gently, "Won't be long now. Six or seven weeks?"

"Seems like an age to me", she sighed, longing to be able to ride again and to work hard on the property alongside Tom and Bob who both regarded pregnancy as an infirmity and absolutely refused to allow her anywhere near where they were working.

Jo had stayed overnight at the Longton's as she and Emily had been to the Pony Club Christmas party. This gave Tom and Jenny a whole day to themselves.

Jenny, thrilled and energised by the good news of the sale of the dreadful semi knowing that she would never again have to live alongside the self-righteous snobbish Snells seized Tom's hand, "What shall we do today? Lets make the most of being on our own." she hugged him and added, smiling, "No romps on the yielding grass of Bluebell wood though. It's too darned cold!"

"I can wait for that until after Thomas William, our little Billy, is born." He cupped her face in his hands and kissed her gently."

It was bitterly cold and had started to snow. Jenny longed to go for walk. Just the two of them and Lulu. It was ages since they'd done that. Tom agreed so they donned their warmest clothes and boots and walked to the mountain track through their own fields feeling pride and gratitude that fate had made all this possible for them. The snow settled gently on the trees round Bluebell Wood and Jenny thought of the child inside her and how he owed his very existence to that spot where she and Tom had experienced such profound love and empathy. They walked on in silence encompassed in mutual love as they gradually gained access to the open boulder strewn space which sheltered and dominated Bryn Celyn. Jenny smiled as she recalled that a local ex-serviceman had likened this mountainside to the Falklands--nothing for miles but scrubland with sheep instead of penguins! The snow was falling more thickly now and transforming the whole landscape into a beautiful seasonal paradise. Lulu beserked in the cold white feathers, leaping and rolling and snapping at the falling flakes. She could not contain her boundless energy and joy. Tom and Jenny realising again how enriched all their lives had become, linked arms and felt so at peace that neither spoke a word yet each shared silently the other's thoughts and feelings. The snow continued falling freely from thick grey clouds and showed no signs of abating. Now their feet were crunching through a thick cold carpet of virgin snow and well-known landmarks were becoming obscured.

"We'd better make tracks back", said Tom somewhat reluctantly, "You okay love?"

"Never been better," sighed Jenny then added, "I hope they get back from Pony Club without any problems".

"Don't worry. They'll enjoy hacking back in the snow and if the roads are bad, Jo will stay at Emily's again tonight."

Tom put an arm around her shoulders and whispered fervently a few lines from Mary Lathrop's poem, 'Snow',

> *Soft as the fall of a beautiful thought*
> *Or a leaf on the stream,*
> *White as the robe by purity wrought,*
> *Bright as the flow of a dream,*
> *Calm as a sleeping infant's breath -----*

He paused, overcome by emotion, and placed both his hands reverentially on her swollen belly.

Jenny shivered feeling vulnerable yet protected and loved as she clung to him. They were in a trance-like state as they began the homeward trudge, back to the warmth and welcome of Bryn Celyn, with the gentle snowflakes caressing their cold faces and clinging to their jackets whilst Lulu leapt and snapped and rollicked ahead, showing them the way.

Chapter 5

Jo and Emily broke up from school five days before Christmas and were soon in a truly festive mood helped enormously by the snowy conditions which transformed the whole area into a winter playground. They built snowmen, pelted each other and the adults with big soft balls of snow, did roly-polys in the deepest parts emulating the horses. Then they swooshed, shrieking, down the fields on home-made toboggans. The days were short but action-packed and ecstatic. After dinner they thawed out in front of blazing log fires writing cards, wrapping presents, making decorations and singing traditional songs and carols accompanied by Tom, somewhat rustily, on his guitar.

The DVD's of choice for the youngsters that first Christmas at Bryn Celyn were, 'The Snowman', '101 Dalmations' and Charles Kingsley's, 'The Water Babies', especially the latter, and they skipped and danced around the house and up the lane leading from the village singing 'Hi Cockolorum' at the tops of their voices. All who heard them smiled, and became infected with their youthful enthusiasm and joy as they remembered and re-lived their own carefree days unencumbered by propriety.

"This is going to be the best Christmas ever", sighed Jenny who had never been happier, "Shall we go to the village church on Christmas Eve? Some of the parents I met at the school Carol Service said it's really nice and helps to get everyone into the Christmas spirit. Apparently the vicar does it instead of Midnight Mass as it means all the family can attend and the local WVS supplies mince pies and sherry plus soft drinks and biscuits".

"Sounds like a good idea to me", said Tom, "What time do we have to be there?"

"It's four 'til six"

"Ideal! I just hope it doesn't snow any more or we won't be able to take the car down to the village".

"We'll walk if that's the case," then sensing his opposition to this added somewhat defiantly, "Tom, I am not an invalid. I am eight months pregnant and walking is good for me!"

Tom pulled her close and whispered, "I know darling, but I have waited so long for a son of my own that I couldn't bear it if something went wrong".

"Neither could I. I love you so much Tom and I want this baby just as much as you do. I understand that it's worse for you, being on the outside as it were, but honestly, I feel wonderful and all the pre-natal checks have been very positive".

She bit her tongue just before revealing that she had asked Manon, the midwife if she could have a home birth and Manon had agreed that she could provided that nothing changed between now and the due date. She knew that

Tom's fertile imagination would conceive of everything that could go wrong. Poor Tom. The very thought of it would ruin his Christmas and drive a wedge between them which might be even worse than the leaving of Primrose Close affair. If necessary she would deal with this perceived problem later when the time was ripe!

Christmas Eve dawned bright and sunny albeit bitterly cold. Tom stoked up the kitchen fire and Jenny spent the day preparing vegetables and making mince pies, a first for her as previous Christmases had been divided between Beechwood and Tom's sister Julie where she had never felt welcome. Well, they were going to have a lovely family Christmas this year. When Tom told Julie she was most put out about it, 'How could you, sniff, sniff. I have no-one else in the world--and whinge, whinge'. She refused, thank goodness, their invitation for her and down-trodden 'Doormat' to spend Christmas in that 'hovel in the hills'. She had never visited Bryn Celyn even though Tom had tried his best to persuade her. She was adamant in her opinion that Tom was utterly dominated by Jenny and had been crazy to give up a lovely semi in the suburbs for a damp and derelict dwelling which should have been left as a sheep shelter which, she surmised, was all it was fit for. Knowing all this and that she was blamed for everything, Jenny did try to understand her animosity, even tried to feel sorry for her, but she had been treated by Julie from the outset of her relationship with Tom with such frigidity and disapproval that she could not. They had agreed however, that Tom should go to Julie's for New Year whilst Jo and Jenny would celebrate with the Longtons. This prospect delighted Jo as they had decided to go the Draghounds New Years Day Meet on Anglesey to see the horses, meet the Masters and the Field and hopefully watch them galloping and jumping over the ditches and dry stone walls.

Jo helped Jenny with the mince pies but soon got 'cabin fever' --Tom's term for being cooped up inside-- so she grabbed her Wellies and warm coat, not unnoticed by Lulu who leapt up from her basket by the Aga, seized Tom's jumper and began shaking it growling excitedly. Tom yelled," Hey, stop it! I can take a hint!" and he dropped a potato he was peeling and donned his jacket and hat. The three of them went out, beckoned by bright sunlight and shining snow. Watching them and hearing their laughter as they threw snowballs for Lulu which splattered in her face as she tried to catch them, Jenny sighed, feeling blissfully happy.

"May it last forever", she mused and she turned on the radio and hummed along happily to the timeless tunes of traditional seasonal music.

Meanwhile, Tom and Jo sang along too as they scrunched through the snow accompanied by a yelping Lulu who stopped from time to time to dig vigorously, showering them with snow! It was good for Tom and Jo to spend some time together. There was so little opportunity with Tom working away and the weekends being filled with Pony Club activities. Jo, happy and excited, seized Tom's hand and began to swing it backwards and forwards as she skipped along singing 'Jingle Bells'. Tom felt totally fulfilled but his natural reserve prevented him from outwardly showing exuberance so he strode along with the happy child and the delirious dog until they reached the forest fence. They paused here to regain their breath then they looked out over the hillside clothed in purest white like a beautiful bride. Tom's poetical nature, inspired by this natural beauty, recited the last verse from Mary Lathrop's lovely poem,

> *Falling to gladden the hearts of some*
> *With the joys it has in store,*
> *Falling to chill in the hovel home*
> *The souls of the suffering poor,*
> *Melting to pearls on the brows of the glad,*
> *Melting to tears on the cheeks of the sad,*
> *What gladdens the one drives the other mad,*
> *Oh! Coldly beautiful snow!*

Jo looked at up at him, obviously moved and bewildered. "That's sad and happy. Do people still live in hovels?"

"Not so much now. "People like us buy them and make them into comfortable homes". He smiled inwardly then added earnestly, "What it really means is that when you're sad and life kicks you hard then everything gets you down--even things that you previously enjoyed. You have to find an inner strength and conquer your troubles and fears--put them behind you and look ahead to the future, for the past has gone and is engraved in history for ever. You cannot change it. If you torture yourself and those around you by dwelling on it, then your life becomes a misery and you are no fun to be with any more. I think these next few lines sum it up perfectly--the philosopher, so we are led to believe, Omar Khayam, is likening 'Time' to a moving finger which writes indelibly----

> *The moving finger writes*
> *and having writ moves on,*
> *Not all thy piety nor wit*

> *Shall lure it back to cancel half a line*
> *Nor all thy tears wash out a word of it*

Jo shivered and squeezed his hand, "You're so clever Daddy--you know everything!"

"I don't know about that," he laughed, "but I do know that I'm hungry now and it's time we went back. Come on, Lulu!" and back they trudged side-by-side through the coldly beautiful snow.

Bryn Celyn was as warm and welcoming as ever, embracing them as soon as they entered the door. They shook off their snowy coats, kicked off their boots then sat round the large pine table, mugs of tea, hot mince pies and brandy butter warming their bodies and souls whilst Lulu plonked herself contentedly in front of the glowing open fire.

"I love our comfortable hovel", sighed Jo.

Jenny looked surprised so Tom explained their conversation and she smiled, pleased that Jo was getting from Tom what she had gained, a love of language and literature.

At three o'clock they left for their walk down the lane to village. The scene which confronted them was reminiscent of a traditional Christmas card with groups of villagers, young and old muffled up in the snow, laughing and talking in Welsh and English as they congregated outside the small and beautiful church with its graveyard and monuments shrouded in an eiderdown of softest snow turning yellowish grey in the growing gloom.

Jean, Bob and Emily had already arrived so the two families entered the building together each emotionally moved by the utter peace and tranquillity as they stared in awe at the beautiful stained glass windows, the choir-stalls and the pipe organ in the chancel. At the front, on the right hand side stood an ornately impressive pulpit which seemed to tower above the pews as if subjugating them into silence and submission.

Tom surmised that the wealthy owners of the slate quarries which abounded around the area had paid for all this to save their own souls and salve their consciences for exploiting the poor 'hovel dwellers' who laboured outdoors in often dangerous and appalling conditions. Perhaps these same smug Squires and self-styled 'Pillars of the Community' assumed that the poor would find peace, solace and hope in this beautiful and cherished church and would continue to base their hopes and aspirations for the future on 'life-everlasting' in Paradise. Prayers and preaching would indoctrinate them with religious beliefs which would deter dissatisfaction and rebellion. Wasn't this what the scriptures taught?

'The rich man in his castle,
The poor man at his gate,
God made them high and lowly
And ordered their estate'

'Blessed are the meek for they shall inherit the earth'.

He shuddered as he thought of historical repression justified as religion and pedalled by the rich and powerful to subjugate and pacify the poor. Bollocks!

He jumped suddenly as the organ struck up with, 'Oh come all Ye Faithful" and the occupants of the pews struggled to their feet to sing lustily. He smiled, squeezed Jenny's hand and joined in, politics for now, forgotten.

It was a lovely Service with readings and hymns in both Welsh and English. The vicar, Matthew Jones, was warmly welcoming and his sermon although pious, was not devoid of humour. Tom warmed to him and although he described himself as a non-believer, finding the word 'atheist' too strong, maybe even confrontational, especially if admitted to confirmed Christians. To say he was agnostic was too easy a 'cop-out'. Nevertheless he felt that he would like to get to know Matthew better.

After the Service they chatted to acquaintances and strangers quaffing sherry and scoffing mince pies whilst the youngsters laughed and joked about Santa and Christmas stockings. As the gathering grew smaller and darkness descended Jenny was anxious to get back so she called Jo and looked around for Tom and saw that he was in animated conversation with Matthew, the vicar.

As they trudged back up the hill through the scrunchy snow Tom told her how happy he was to have found a 'soul-mate'. Matthew too, had studied at Oxford and gained an MA in Theology. He was also a keen Chess player and had invited Tom to visit the vicarage for a game. Jenny squeezed his arm and smiled, glad that he too had now found a friend locally, someone he could relate to, an intellectual equal who shared one of his favourite hobbies. Since their move it seemed that everything was going right for them. Fate was on their side. All they needed now was for Tom to find a job somewhere in the area.

Chapter 6

After Christmas the days grew longer and dusk descended a little later each day. Jenny felt tired and heavy as the birth drew nearer. One cold blustery day at the beginning of February she was standing up after tending the fire in the lounge when she was seized by a spasm which was followed instantly by a gush of warm liquid running down her legs. She gasped, realising instantly that her waters had broken! She picked up the phone and called Manon, the midwife, who told her not to panic and that she would be there in less than half-an-hour. Jenny took a deep breath and switched on Radio 4. It was 'Woman's Hour'. The calm reassuring, almost smug voice of Jenny Murray pervaded the room adding a touch of normality so she no longer felt completely alone and helpless. Nevertheless she was glad that the guest being interviewed was not one of those 'Wonder-women' who do the most amazing things such as giving birth in the jungle or the Antarctic completely alone, pontificating about it being such a wonderfully easy and natural thing notwithstanding man-eating tigers and perilous polar bears prowling nearby! She giggled at her outrageous imaginings.

How inadequate she would feel being nervous and frightened in a warm comfortable environment with help at hand. She wasn't afraid, just alone and needing a confidence boost that she could have this baby unassisted if needs be. After all, it was her second child. Perhaps Tom was right—she should have booked a hospital birth. "Ouch!" too late now as a severe pain swept through her. She stood up and grasped herself hard between her legs feeling the pressure against her hands as she tried to to hold the baby where he was.

"Wait, wait a bit longer, Billy, please!" she implored. "Come on Manon! Where the hell are you?" She lay back on the makeshift bed feeling that gravity would accelerate the birth if she remained standing up.

Minutes later, Manon bustled in, smiling and relaxed, "Hello Jenny. Let's have look at you. Good, good. Won't be long---the little chap's ready. Now deep breaths and push when I tell you!"

In less than twenty minutes Thomas William Weston was born, yelling lustily.

"What a lovely little chap!" enthused Manon, "Perfect. Well done you! Shall we have a cup of tea now? You feed him while I put the kettle on".

As the the squirming baby suckled enthusiastically Jenny reflected upon how much easier and pleasanter this birth had been to the austere clinical one she had experienced in hospital with Jo. There she had felt pressurised. The hospital staff were busy and she was in a queue of other mothers in the throes of giving birth. She had been given an injection to speed up her labour and in consequence the pains had increased greatly in strength and regularity. A mask of gas and air had been thrust onto her face and after more screaming and pushing, Jo was born. That was not the end of it. "You just need a couple of stitches where the wall of the vagina has given way. Just relax, it won't hurt." Jenny shuddered at the memory and vowed never again! Wonderful experience? No way—more like a hellish nightmare! Here, at home, it was so much more the natural and fulfilling experience it was meant to be. Her earlier initial tribulations she dismissed now as foolishness. Manon, ever cheerful and efficient, tucked the sleeping infant into his crib and began to tidy up. Jenny, now refreshed and relaxed, rang Jean who promised to come at once. She decided to text Tom as she guessed he would be teaching and that his mobile would be switched off. Much better that he should call her after school and be assured that all was fine. As she gazed at the pink snuffling infant, she considered how all their lives would be affected by this new member of the family but she knew instin ctively it would be for the better.

Manon stayed until Jean arrived then she left, bustling out as she had bustled in and calling, "See you tomorrow. Call me if you need anything before then!"

Jean came straight up to Jenny and hugged her. Then she gazed at the sleeping baby and reached down to touch his cheek. Large tears welled up in her eyes and she lifted her head and wiped her hand across her face, "I'm sorry", she said, choking back her tears. Then to Jenny's surprise, her body began to shake, convulsed with emotion. Jenny realised that this was not the normal feminine 'Aw isn't he lovely' emotion, but something much deeper so she waited for Jean to regain enough composure to explain her unusual behaviour. Jean clenched and unclenched her hands, seized a tissue and between sobs, recounted the tragedy she and Bob had suffered. Jenny listened, appalled at what she heard.

"We were only blessed with one child in spite of years of trying and praying, A lovely daughter, Rachel." She hesitated, and buried her face in her hands, took a deep breath and continued. "She was lovely child, never any problem until she became a teenager. Maybe we had stifled her, given her too much, expected too much from her. We wanted to be the centre of her universe as she was of ours.

When just sixteen, she seemed to have no close friends. When she did go out, she told us she was going to the Youth Club. She seemed to cut us off from her private life. We thought it was a normal teenage phase so we did not press her. Then, out of the blue, she told us she was pregnant! We were astounded! We couldn't—didn't want to believe it!." Jean wrung her hands and stared at Jenny as if waiting for some response, some comfort. Jenny remained blank, she didn't want to hear this now. This was *her* time. Jean composed herself and continued, "She refused to name the father and we had no idea who she had been seeing. We assumed it must be either a married man or a 'one-night stand' but we never discovered his identity and Rachel became angry and hysterical when we pressed her for details. We were upset, shocked and ashamed. We felt guilty too, as if we had somehow driven her into this." Maybe we were a bit hard on her. Bob was very hurt and angry and we just couldn't understand why she had let us and herself down in this way. We tried to find a reason or a cause and began to wonder where we had gone wrong as parents." She choked back another sob, "We loved her--she was all we had."

The last words were torn out of tears and it was some time before she could continue. "Anyway, she left school and Emily was born in hospital. We didn't know what to do. We thought about adoption but couldn't go through with it. We were so angry and upset and confused. When she came home from hospital she was so miserable and depressed. We were both working too so she was alone a lot. I know now that we should have given her more support instead of thinking of our own shame and hurt and shattered dreams." She hesitated and wiped her nose vigorously on a clean paper towel proffered by Jenny. Then, composing herself, continued in a louder matter-of-fact tone, "Oh yes---we had big ambitions for our only child! She was going to go to university to be a doctor or a lawyer and she had thrown all this away". She snivelled and wrung her hands and it was as if her voice was somehow detached from her body as she continued, "Emily was just three weeks old. It was a Saturday morning, raining and windy, a really horrible day. Rachel asked us if we would look after the baby as she wanted to go for a walk. We tried to dissuade her but she became angry and said she had been cooped up for so long that she had to get out." She paused again and drew a sharp intake of breath. "We never saw her again. We don't know if she's dead or alive ---or anything----! She took nothing with her—she left all her clothes and possessions behind. It's the not knowing which is the hardest thing to bear. We pray for her every day---if anything has happened to her. If she's dead—we know she will be with God and that we will all be together again one day".

Her body engulfed in great gulping sobs Jean buried her face in the duvet covering Jenny's bed and it was a long time before either spoke.

Eventually the anguish of the emotion subsided.

"You poor, poor thing," sympathised Jenny, stroking the greying hair still damp from the rain.

"I'm sorry, I really shouldn't be upsetting you at a time like this. It's very selfish and stupid of me," she gulped. "Please, please forgive me!".

She was about to give vent to more sobbing emotion but Jenny interrupted her.

"Jean, there is nothing to forgive! What you've been through is unbearable and very upsetting for anybody, but I must admit I did wonder about Emily's mother. Look, the best thing for us both now is to put it behind us. Nothing can change it. Cloud it over in your mind as you must have done for so many years. Just think of the future which is looking rosy for all of us since we altered our destiny and came to live here in this rural paradise. Come on, pull yourself together and make us both a cup of tea!"

Jean, shoulders slumped and still trembling with emotion, put the heavy-bottomed kettle on the Aga. Jenny felt very sorry for her but wished she would go home. She did not want Tom's first meeting with his new-born son to be over-shadowed by Jean's wretchedness. As if reading her mind, Jean handed her a cup of tea and said she had better go to get the dinner ready for Bob and Emily. They hugged, and she was gone.

Jean's outpouring upset Jenny and she wondered how anyone could cope with such tragedy. The hurt and deep sense of loss would endure for ever but were salved by deep religious beliefs. Jean and Brian were genuinely good people who could gain comfort and relief from prayer. When they felt despair they donned the armour of their religion and were shielded until their strength returned.

With a deep sigh, Jenny gathered up the gurgling infant and cuddled him close whilst he squirmed and suckled contentedly. She studied him intently for the first time and tried to see likenesses in his features to Tom, herself or her own parents, Mike and Danielle, but could find none that were obvious. He was just like any other baby---pink and wrinkled. She smiled and whispered softly that he would in time become as handsome and strong as grand-dad Mike and as clever as his dad. Again she found herself wondering about her parents. If only they could see and get to know their grandchildren. If only she could see them again. She thought she had come to terms with the situation but she was again consumed by a sense of loss and longing, no doubt surfacing as a result of her own motherhood. Her thoughts then turned to Brian and Liz, who had always been surrogate parents and to Jan who had been as a sister and best friend. They will be delighted with the news, she thought, and wouldn't it be wonderful if they could come for a holiday! Who knows, maybe we could visit them in New Zealand when our financial situation improves, but that was all in the future--so many more dreams to fulfil before then-----

She was startled back to reality by an excited shout as Jo rushed in.

"He's here! Can I see him? Wow, hasn't he got a lot of hair--he looks just like dad!"

Jenny smiled. Tom would be here soon and she couldn't wait to hand him his long-awaited son. Tom did arrive about twenty minutes later but unlike Jo, he crept in and took the child almost reverentially. With a trembling voice he whispered, "He's beautiful. Thank you darling, thank you. Welcome to the world little Thomas William Weston!"

A tear rolled down his cheek as he cuddled the newborn miracle.

Spring came with a burst of beautiful crocuses and daffodils, their splendour rewarding Jenny for her efforts in the cold and blustery days of Autumn. Bella too was blossoming. The foal was due almost any time now and Jenny was watching her carefully for imminent signs—the bulge moving nearer to the back end, the teats waxing up. The mare was happy and contented in herself waddling around in the field and lying flat-out in the sunshine. Jenny hoped that she would give birth outside. It was far cleaner, more natural and safer as she had much more room to spread out and move around and grass was far more forgiving than concrete should she drop the foal whilst standing. Would it be a filly or a colt? At this stage Jenny's prime concern was that all would go well and mother and baby would bond and be happy and healthy. Jo and Emily were excited about it too and every afternoon when they arrived home from school they brought Bella into her box and brushed her.

"What are we going to call it, Mum, if it's a colt?"

Oh I don't know—I thought I'd see what it looks like first and then give it a name. Anyway, it might be a filly. Let's wait and see. Shouldn't be long now—two or three days."

"That's weekend. Come on Bella---save it 'till Saturday so we can be here to watch you!" and the two girls laughed and patted the lovely mare.

Jenny too hoped the foal would born soon as the weather was warm and gentle—perfect conditions to induce birth and to welcome a new life into the world.

"I love May", sighed Jenny as she cuddled baby Thomas William and looked at the trees their buds bursting into blossom. Life beginning anew --birth and rebirth- a never-ending cycle, revitalizing hopes and aspirations. Here at Bryn Celyn, a new baby, and soon a new foal – all positives for assuring a wonderful life close to Nature. Feeling totally at peace she settled down under the huge old chestnut tree and day-dreamed about what the future would hold for them. The baby suckled vigorously as she sang softly, 'The folks who live on the Hill' wondering if the villagers would give them that title ---'Jack and Jill' who would become 'Darby and Joan' in years to come. She hoped so.

At 9 o'clock that evening the weather became wild with blustery wind and belting rain, too wild for a foal to be born outside so she brought Bella into her stable for the night and noticed that her teats had waxed up. "Won't be long now, my lovely Meribel." she whispered as she gently stroked the patient mare. She banked up the bed with fresh clean straw then went indoors to settle the children down. She missed Tom during the week and hoped and prayed that he would be able to find a job nearer home. That was the only drawback, the only blot on an otherwise beautiful landscape. She settled comfortably on the sofa and picked up her book. Dusk began to settle as the sun disappeared into the sea and the brilliant red light faded into pink and ebbed away so that the hillsides and nestling cottages became as one. "Bodes well for a better day tomorrow," Jenny sighed as she relaxed on the sofa. Two hours later she woke up feeling cold and cramped. She switched on the light surprised to see that it was midnight! She must have fallen asleep. She grabbed her coat and boots and hurried across the yard to check on Bella. To her amazement the foal was born and already struggling to get to its feet whilst Bella whickered, licked and nuzzled. Jenny watched quietly. All seemed well. The afterbirth lay intact on the straw. Bella and her baby looked well. They didn't need her. Best to leave them to form that important bonding. She would pop back later to check again. Trembling with emotion she returned to the house. No use to wake up Jo or phone Tom. She checked Billy then lay on the sofa and set the alarm for two hours in case she fell asleep again.

At 2am. the strident beep-beep sent her hurrying across the yard. Bella and baby were fine. This time she did go into the box. She removed the afterbirth and checked the sleeping foal. It was a colt with identical markings to his sire, the lovely and talented 'Lloyd George', dark brown—almost black, with a white star and snip, perfectly central on his muzzle. "You little beauty!" she whispered as she gently caressed his velvety neck. We're going to call you 'Lloyd George Junior' after your Dad. If you've inherited his temperament and talent you'll be all we could wish for!"

Little Lloyd George strutted into the field next day behind his proud and protective mother and the sun shone brightly welcoming him into the world.

Jo and Emily were made up with him and already discussing his future as a champion Show Jumper, Dressage horse or Eventer or whatever they wanted him to be. Jenny, listening to their girlish banter, smiled and felt deeply contented, reinforcing yet again the feelings she had about their move having been the best thing possible. Nothing had gone wrong—nothing could go wrong. All their hopes and aspirations were being fulfilled. However, as she watched Emily running around with Jo, so carefree and happy, she thought of the dreadful shadow constantly haunting Jean and Bob and she shuddered. Let things stay as they are—live for the present. Digging and delving into the past, regretting, recriminating is completely self-destructive. Bury the bad things in Hell! Plant your dreams and watch them come to fruition in Heaven. Look upwards to the sky for a bright future. She shrugged-off the shudders and revelled in the carefree joy of Bella with her brand new baby and the delight of Jo and Emily. She martialled her emotions and looked upwards at the changing sky. Did she discern darker clouds gathering in an otherwise bright eternity?

Chapter 7

Their second summer at Bryn Celyn was even busier than the first had been—new baby, new foal, new friends. Tom threw himself wholeheartedly into DIY on the house ably assisted and advised by Bob. Jo and Emily rode the ponies and joined in the many competitions and rallies organised by the local Pony Club. Jenny divided her time between caring for them all and bringing Bella back into work. Matthew was a regular visitor and he and Tom tackled some of the local peaks and in the evenings did battle with their intellects on the chess-board. Tom, the hitherto bookworm, had never felt so fit and well. However, for Jenny, one thing was missing—she had nowhere to adequately school Bella and she began to dream about building an arena. She mentioned this one evening over dinner to Tom. He already felt pressured financially with the mortgage and the cost of materials for the renovations which still needed doing. He stopped eating, sighed and placing his knife and fork crookedly on his plate said, exasperatedly, "Jenny, one thing at a time. We have neither the money nor the resources at the moment"

Destiny Obscure

"I know that but I'm thinking ahead. If we had an arena then I would be able to ride at any time and train the horses too. At the moment I can't hack out or go anywhere because of Billy. Also Jo could exercise and train 'Dinky' after school and it won't be long before she becomes too big for a pony and takes over 'Georgie Junior'. An arena would make backing and breaking him so much easier and quicker---and safer!" She emphasised the last word as she knew how dangerous he thought riding was and this plug for safety could possibly help in getting him to look more favourably on this latest enterprise.

Tom felt trapped again, much as he had when Jenny first suggested the move to Wales. He knew that she would continue to apply pressure, persuasion, even coercion, to get her own way. An arena would no doubt be great but not yet. She would have to wait until their financial situation improved and that was that! He would stand firm this time. He was about to get up from the table leaving his meal unfinished when she said, "Tom, I will not go against you on this I promise, but it's not just a whim. I've given it a lot of thought. I feel guilty that I'm not earning and contributing—no--don't say anything until you have heard me out—If we had an arena I could take in horses for breaking and schooling and I could teach too. I've already been asked by local riders and Pony Club parents and to break and school a youngster costs around £500 and this is something I've been doing all my life. An arena, as well as being an asset to me and Jo, would bring in money and pay for itself in less than a year and we have the whole summer ahead of us to do it and manpower too! Please, just think about it and we'll go over the finances and other practical problems tomorrow. If it isn't feasible then I'll put it to the back of my mind I promise!." This rush of enthusiasm left her breathless and Tom speechless. He left the table without a word and went outside to seek comfort and reassurance from the warm red glow of the setting sun as it sank slowly, almost cautiously, into the sea.

Jenny cleared the table and swished her hands in the warm sudsy water in the sink. She washed the dishes slowly and mechanically somehow gaining comfort from this mundane task. She'd upset him again she knew. He's a born worrier, she thought, and hates taking risks of any kind financial or physical. She remembered his alarm and amazement when she told him of her parents sea-faring adventure. He would never take to sailing unless it were on a placid boating lake no more than five foot deep with life jackets and life boats at the ready! And now he was afraid of too much debt. The absolute opposite of my parents, she mused wryly. For them, life was all about taking risks. She wondered who Jo and Billy would take after? And sighing deeply, she thought yet again about her parents and their possible fate.

Evening chores completed, children checked, snug and sleeping in their beds, she ventured outside to join Tom.

He was sitting on the bench under the stalwart branches of their favourite elm tree. She sat down beside him and reached for his hand. He withdrew it and gestured towards the sea.

"You've missed a most beautiful sunset", he murmured.

"Yes, I was washing up". This practical peremptory response caused them both to laugh spontaneously and any ice that may have formed between them began to crack and melt away. She sought his hand again, this time more gently, more cautiously and spoke questioningly,

"Now, where were we---the pros and cons of building an arena-----"

They spent a long time in the darkening shadows of that mellow summer evening calculating the financial implications that extra borrowing would encumber them with. They then attempted to offset these with the possible remuneration which could be generated by Jenny breaking and schooling young horses and coaching riders. Another important factor was that psychologically, Jenny would never be satisfied by total immersion in domesticity. Tom knew this only too well. She was ambitious and competitive and needed to fulfil these needs.

In the end, Tom gave in. The decision was made. Jenny had won again!

So, that second summer was deliriously busy. Mud and machines clanking, digging, and scraping all day long and when dusk fell so did silence as the diggers and dumpers like everyone else who had worked so hard, rested and recuperated in readiness for the next onslaught.

The arena was finished and fenced before the start of the new term and Jenny began to plan and dream about bringing Bella back into training. Bella was an eye-catching animal with very good natural paces and Jenny planned and dreamed about taking her as far up the dressage ladder as she could go.

Her first ride in the new arena fuelled her ambitious enthusiasm even more as she walked, trotted, and cantered on the firm yet yielding surface.

"This feels so good!" she enthused to Jo and Emily who were watching.

"Wow! She's like an equine ballet dancer," breathed Emily, "Look how she leaves the ground! It's as if she's floating on air."

"Like this", quipped Jo and she began to leap and spin around.

"No way!" laughed Emily. "You're more like a ruddy cart-horse!" and she ran off with Jo in hot pursuit.

The girls had spent almost every day day together during that busy summer riding their ponies and playing in the fields. They were out from dawn 'til dusk, happy and carefree making their own adventures revelling in each others company and the freedom of the countryside.

They were happy and excited too about the prospect of starting Secondary school. To them it was the beginning of growing up. The bonds of dependence and childhood were beginning to weaken.

They would soon be teenagers, young adults, able to make their own decisions. The prospect was attractive.

On the first morning of the new term, proud and yet self-conscious in her new uniform, clutching a new satchel, Jo set off down the lane to catch the school bus. Jenny walked with her carrying baby Billy on her back. The mood amongst the pupils at the bus stop was noisy and excitable, especially amongst the older pupils. Jo hovered in the background, not yet confident enough to be part of the 'in-crowd'. The pupils surged forward and claimed their places next to their friends, shouting and laughing. Jo bided her time and was amongst the last to board. Jenny knew that it would only be a matter of time before Jo asserted herself and pushed her way forwards like the other bolder types. She did wonder about Emily though but was sure that that Jo would stand up for her gentle sensitive friend against bullying. As she trudged back up the hill she mused over how quickly time flew. Jo already almost a teenager. Would it pass as quickly for Billy? She determined to savour all the stages of his development. He had a better start than Jo, or herself, for that matter. His birth had been planned and longed for and he had a far more stable background. Thank goodness for Tom. He adored Jo and could not love her more even if he were her natural father and now, at last, he had his longed-for son. How lucky Jenny felt to have met him twelve years ago this summer. Who would have dreamed then that this could be their destiny------

Chapter 8

The days grew shorter and summer faded into autumn. Jo and Emily seemed to be settling well into their new school but when questioned about the lessons or the teachers the epithet was usually a non- committal, 'Ok', as if they just wanted to put it all behind them until tomorrow. No complaints, no enthusiasm. It was as if school was just a routine commitment. However, they did come up against authority. They were running around in the field at weekend when they found a store of conkers under the huge spreading chestnut tree.

"Look at these beauties! Let's collect them and take them to school tomorrow.

We can play Conkers at break."

"And challenge all-comers to take us on!"

They scrabbled around selecting the some of the largest toughest specimens and after hardening them in the Aga, threaded them on strings.

Next morning during break-time they selected their biggest conkers and encouraged by their classmates they were having great fun playing the age-old game of 'Conkers'.

Suddenly, a whistle shrieked and a loud voice shouted, "Stop that at once! Give me those conkers! That game is forbidden on school premises.

Their least -favourite teacher, 'Auntie Bitch', strode up, one hand outstretched.

"Oh Miss," pleaded Jo, "We're having fun and mine is a 'Twentier' already!"

"Don't be so childish and stupid! That game is dangerous. You could get splinters in your eyes and nasty bumps on your head. Do as you are told! Hand them over at once and collect them after school."

They reluctantly handed over their precious conkers and agreed that the nick-name, 'Auntie Bitch' applied to the austere Miss Owen was well-earned and justified as she strode stiffly away ignoring the scoffs and giggles of the bystanders.

However, Jo was not prepared to let it rest there. Emily listened to her plan and giggled her agreement.

The following day they took their riding hats gardening goggles and gloves to school and thus kitted out began their conker game again. They were soon surrounded by a group of laughing fellow pupils who thought their ploy hilarious and were cheering them on. Inevitably, Miss Owen, hearing the racket, pushed her way through the throng and confronted them with a furious shriek, "What do you think you are doing! That game is forbidden in school. I thought I made myself clear yesterday."

"Yes Miss, but you said it was dangerous so we are just trying to make it safe ----- Honest!"

"Don't be impertinent! Come with me at once! We'll see what the Headmaster has to say about this deliberate defiance!"

She marched them away to the slow-clapping and cheers of their fellows.

Mr. Thomas, the Headmaster, remembering his own conker-playing days but beleaguered by the stringent rules of 'Health and Safety above All', told them simply but sternly that they must never play conkers on the school premises again—Even in suits of armour! The two girls looked so funny standing before him in their riding hats gloves and goggles that he had to suppress the urge to laugh even though he was well aware that they had done this as an act of defiance and mockery.

"Remember that school rules are made for your own safety so no conkers, no snowballs, no sliding! This was said with a touch of ironic humour and he paused clenching his jaws as he forced himself to regain his dignity and authority, then snarled, "Now get out!"

This incident was not reported to their parents and earned them a few brownie points in the eyes of their classmates. However, the humourless 'Auntie Bitch' never forgave them and regarded them with gimlet eyes every time their paths crossed as if hoping for an excuse to punish and chastise.

They collected their conkers after school and handed them out to their classmates because all they wanted to do when they arrived home was to jump on their ponies and ride. Everything for them centred around Pony Club and events coming up at the weekend—Competitions, Rallies, Training Camps. Jenny understood and encouraged their enthusiasm. To her it was far better for them to be active outdoors rather than watching TV or twiddling on the computer. Tom too, settled into his committed routine, teaching all day, dining and sleeping at his sister's house, and every weekend commuting back to Bryn Celyn.

As for Jenny and Jean they met almost every day and Jean tutored Jenny in the art of making jam and chutney from the fruits yielded in plenty during that 'season of mists and mellow fruitfulness'. It was a good time for the two women and another plus was loving and caring for baby Billy who was a happy and contented child.

The foal, 'Georgie', was now six months old and maturing so fast that Jenny decided to castrate him and then wean him after he had got over the shock of the operation. This was duly done and Jenny warmed to the vet, a cheerful and kindly man who had a genuine concern for his patient's physical and mental well-being.

"Don't wean him for another month. Keep him with his mum. That way the shock will be reduced and he'll get over it much better".

Jenny thought about this, "Yes, I was going to do that to comfort him", then added, "Will he feel bereft?" She felt rather stupid as soon as she said it.

He laughed, "Who knows? Let's hope not. They do say that what you never have, you never miss." He smiled to himself as he collected up his instruments. Did she detect a touch of irony? He continued, "Seriously though, the biggest danger is infection but it's unlikely at this time of year and he's strong and healthy. Ring me in a week's time and let me know how things are going."

"Will do. Thank you", and she waved him off.

She rather hoped that Jo would one day be a vet. It had been a dream for herself. Too late now. Circumstances had prevented it even if she had been clever enough to gain the necessary stringent qualifications. Her destiny, had thus far, brought her here to this perceived rural paradise. So be it. No regrets.

As autumn progressed, the leaves took on a splendour more striking and beautiful than in spring. Rich reds and russet browns interspersed with bright yellow and gold seemed to glow with an inner warmth even as they died. Jenny with a feeling of deep nostalgia was transported yet again to Tarn Hows, swaying gently on her father's back. She had unknowingly yet instinctively absorbed forever the incredible beauty of the landscape, even though she was only five years old.

It wasn't long though, before the wind, the weather's most powerful destroyer, unleashed its force and ripped and tore the hitherto lovely leaves from the grasp of their mother branches and blew them into untidy heaps where they fluttered helplessly until inevitably, they rotted in the wet mire of winter. Jenny, looking at these sad heaps remembered what her father had told her, "They don't die in vain. They make compost which is a rich food for the next generation. Nothing lives or dies in vain".

Nothing lives or dies in vain. This is a maxim worth remembering.

November gave way to December and Christmas was upon them again. Jenny and Jean absorbed themselves in the busy, happy ritual of Carol Services, cooking and decorating, choosing and wrapping presents, writing endless cards, some with a promise well-meant but seldom kept-- to meet in the coming year--whilst Brian collected and chopped the dead branches from Bluebell Wood and stacked them ready for the winter fires. Would there be as much snow as last year?

Well it didn't matter as long as they could keep warm and well-fed. As usual they bought a rooted Christmas tree from the nearby Garden Centre so they could plant it afterwards and watch it grow.

"Lovely tree! Can we decorate it?"

Jo and Emily loved sorting out the baubles, arranging the lights and flinging bright tinsel for the final effect so they set about this annual ritual with enthusiasm.

"Mum, what do you think? Does it need more tinsel?"

"No, it's perfect. Beautiful. Well done!" and she gave them both a cuddle and a mince pie.

Tom, jubilant to be home with his family for two whole weeks, burst into the kitchen laughing and hugging everyone. Jo and Emily danced around the lounge singing their favourite carols and Christmas songs. The fire crackled and sparkled in the hearth adding its warmth to this precious family festivity. Even the horses, seemed infected with the Christmas spirit as they charged and bucked joyfully around the field.

Lulu too loved Christmas—delicious smells, warm cosy fires and the promise of long walks on the mountain. She rolled over on the hearth rug and gazed adoringly at her beloved humans.

They were all together again, family and friends, filled with the warmth of yuletide and looking forward to the festivities yet to come. Jo danced around the house with Billy in her arms. It was his first Christmas and she was was sorry that he was too young to be immersed in the Santa-down -the -chimney legend. Next year—yippee!

Three days before Christmas the weather was bitterly cold and the stark brown branches of the trees glittered with frost.

"Look Dad—all the trees outside are decorated too! Shall we go for a walk on the mountain with Lulu?"

Donning boots and scarves they set off with an ecstatic Lulu. The sky was still and grey as they made their way through the fields heading towards the wild and rocky moorland. They saw each other so rarely now that it felt good to be able to walk and talk unhindered and uninterrupted. She opened up to him about school, told him what she liked and didn't like, what they were doing in different subjects, friends she'd made and enemies too, good and bad teachers, interesting and boring lessons. The saga of the conkers made him him smile. He listened, adding comments, asking questions and noticing how she was maturing mentally and socially. She was already forming strong opinions about people and society in general. All this at barely thirteen years old. What would she be like as an adolescent? He changed the subject. "It's so beautiful and fresh up here and I never tire of the view or the walks because it's always changing. Today it's cold and bracing. In spring it's bright and promising. In summer er, warm and wet". He smiled as he said this remembering sodden days he had spent with Matthew.

"I like it in winter best, when it snows", enthused Jo, "It's more beautiful and exciting then".

"I like all the seasons. They all have their purpose in ensuring that life in nature continues as we know it. I have a friend who worked for years in Brunei. He loved it there but said that what he missed most was the changing seasons—falling leaves, snow, log fires".

They walked on in silence, pondering this and watching Lulu snuffling around rabbit holes, intent on doing her own thing, seemingly unaware of their company.

Eventually they arrived at their favourite resting spot in the shelter of the dry stone wall. They got out the sandwiches Jenny had prepared for them then sat on their rucksacks and marvelled at the seeming stability of the many massive rocks littering the mountainside. They both imagined the utter destruction and devastation should they ever be disturbed and tumble down into the valley!

"It's a good job we don't have violent earthquakes here." Tom mused quietly thinking of the death and destruction these caused in other parts of the world.

Jo remained thoughtful, studied Tom's face then asked, "Are you glad we came to live here now?"

Tom stopped chewing and turned towards her in surprise. Strangely enough no-one had asked him this question so directly before. Jenny probably assumed that he must be glad but saw no point in discussing it in case it opened up old wounds or reinforced his uncomfortable belief that she was the dominant one and made all the decisions-- the arena being the latest one! His sister never tired of strengthening this belief by accusing him of being 'under the thumb'. Rather ironic he thought. But was there a parallel here between him and 'Dismal Desmond the 'Doormat?' He preferred to dismiss the comparison. Hardly good for his self-esteem!

He swallowed hard and sighed deeply.

"Well," pressed Jo, "I know you were dead against it before".

"Yes I was, for purely practical and selfish reasons. I hate being away from you all and having to commute every weekend. Also, I'm missing seeing Billy growing up. I feel like a stranger to him sometimes. However, it makes me happy to see how happy you and your mother are and I'm lucky to have the long school holidays with you".

"Do you know what the best Christmas present would be for all of us? She said assertively, then paused. Tom looked at her, wondering what was coming next. She grabbed his hand and burst out, "That you get a job round here then we can all be together like a proper family."

Tom sighed. "Well it's not for want of trying. All I've had is one interview at the university and heard nothing yet. Fingers crossed eh!" He packed the remains of their lunch into the rucksack. "Come on, lets make tracks!" And they stumbled and slipped over the frosty tussocky turf as they made their back with Lulu bounding before them.

Amongst the cards delivered on Christmas Eve was a brown envelope addressed to Tom. Probably a bill, he thought sardonically—nice timing! He opened it, stiffened, re-read it, then gave a great whoop of joy!

"Jenny! Jo! It's the Christmas present we all wanted! They've offered me the job I applied for at the Uni. Starting next September. Lecturer in English Lit!"

"Yippee---fantastic! What a brilliant Christmas present!" Ecstatic hugs all round. Another dream come true.

Now it seemed they had everything.

Chapter 9

During the spring Jenny brought Bella back into serious work and was delighted with her progress. She also managed to earn some money backing and training young horses which came in useful towards the expenses of shoeing, hay and feed and helped to justify the expense of the arena.

One thing she missed about Beechwood was the competitions. As well as being fun they provided a useful yardstick to measure progress and monitor achievements. It was out of the question at the moment because her life was so full with domestic chores and caring for Billy, who was now walking. Also she would need a horse trailer and a four-by-four to tow it as most of the competitions were held far away. A trailer would be useful too for Jo and Emily. They had to cadge lifts if they wanted to go anywhere out of the area. She told herself to curb this must-have acquisitive feeling which seemed to be an intrinsic part of her nature. They had huge debts. They had borrowed a lot of money for the arena plus renovations to the house and they had a sizeable mortgage. Never mind, she thought---they would have more money when Tom started at the university. Could they manage more expenses? Well, you only live once and much better to have the things you long for when you are young enough to enjoy them. She was naturally impulsive and impetuous. No doubt traits inherited from both her parents---risk-takers-- who knew what they wanted and went for it. Where were they now? What had happened to them? It had been so long---they must be dead. Why was she thinking about them so much recently? She shuddered and turned her thoughts elsewhere. A trailer! That would complete her 'must-haves' at least for the present. How could she persuade Tom? Get him in a good mood. She pondered this for a while then smiled as she thought again about that most memorable and precious first encounter with Bryn Celyn---the aromatic bluebell bed where their dreamed-for son had been conceived. "That's it, she thought excitedly—I'll go there now with Jenny and Billy and we'll collect armfuls and have them all around the house when Tom gets back later".

She convinced herself that the sight and smell of these beautiful wild flowers would reawaken blissful memories and help to make him more agreeable to this latest 'must-have'!. Poor Tom, she knew she could twist him around her little finger if she went about it the right way. She began to feel guilty and selfish but made a promise to herself that this would indeed be the last thing she would ask for. She did need a trailer if she wanted to fulfil her dream of getting to the top of the dressage ladder and she believed that she and Bella were capable of achieving it. Also it would mean that Jo and Emily could join in far more activities with the Pony Club. No Tom. I don't want fur coats and fancy jewellery. Just a trailer and a four-by-four!

Tom was out walking in the hills with Matthew. He always returned from these walks physically and mentally refreshed. He would be happy and hungry after a long strenuous day revelling in his new-found health and fitness. Just the mood she wanted---Good!

She gathered Billy into her arms, put him in the carrier on her back then called Jo to come and help. Hand-in-hand they walked past the bubbling stream stopping for a while to watch the frolics of the newly-hatched baby frogs.

Bluebell Wood was so special to both she and Tom and it was coming close to the third anniversary of that incredible union which had created a new life--- the precious gift of their son.

The bluebells were prolific and glorious and their perfume pervaded the soft spring air so that as she inhaled, memories of that rapturous closeness were awakened. The effect was sobering, relaxing and poignantly nostalgic. She walked to the very same spot where she and Tom had rolled, laughed and loved. She set Billy down and invited Jo to sit beside her.

She took her daughter's hand and said softly and reverentially, "This place is very special to me and Tom. When we first saw 'Bryn Celyn' we actually frolicked here like two kids and-------." She paused, sighed deeply, then added," We sometimes come here now to be alone together to talk and to count our blessings and typical of Tom, he found a poem about bluebells written by Anne Bronte. She began reciting the poem softly, unable to disguise the emotion in her voice:

> *'There is a silent eloquence*
> *In every wild bluebell*
> *That fills my softened heart with bliss*
> *That words could never tell'"*

"Oh Mum, that's lovely!" she held her mother's steadfast gaze, then added almost inconsequentially, "I didn't know Anne Bronte wrote poetry too"

"Neither did I." This was said almost dismissively before she continued earnestly, "Now Listen, love, I don't want to sound morbid but this place is so special to us that we both want to be buried here, in this exact spot, covered with and surrounded by bluebells". She paused, took hold of Jo's shoulders so they were facing each other, then in a firm and steadfast voice she said," When we get around to making a Will, that request will be written into it. Jo squirmed,

"Mum, you are being morbid. Why talk about such horrible things now?"

"No love, it's not morbid or horrible, just practical. Please listen to me. I can't see us ever leaving this place and the fact that we will be *here* together in this very spot for always will sustain us in our final years." Promise me that you will see to it."

Jo took both her mother's hands into her own and sighed deeply, "That is so lovely and so romantic, Mum," then in a matter-of-fact voice added, "And you are right. It isn't morbid because we are all going to be here together –happy ever after--for a very, very, very long time". She smiled reassuringly, "But don't worry, whenever, whatever, I'll see to it that your wish is carried out."

"Thank you, darling." They cuddled close and laughed at little Billy who was also cuddling close to an unprotesting Lulu.

They walked back to the house in silence, cradling armfuls of aromatic bluebells.

> *'A fine and subtle feeling dwells*
> *In every little flower,*
> *Each one its own sweet feeling breathes*
> *With more or less of power'.*

"Now Bluebells," whispered Jenny, "Work your *magical* power on Tom!"

She and Jo arranged the bluebells on the window sills and tables and Jenny saved some which she placed carefully on the dressing table in their bedroom. She looked around to see the effect. She didn't want it to look too obvious—just subtle enough to evoke precious memories of their first union with Bryn Celyn.

She closed the window and turned up the heating to encourage the flowers to give off even more perfume. "That's a better aphrodisiac than Viagra!" she chuckled to herself. Then she lovingly straightened the picture of 'Vagabonde' and whispered, 'My dreams are coming true mum and dad and will be complete when you come back and cuddle your grand-children." She really believed that their return was inevitable. After all, they were immortal!

Tom and Matthew returned happy and exhilarated after their walk and both commented on the sight and smell of the lovely bluebells. Matthew, after a a cup of tea and a chat, went home to the vicarage where his mother, Megan, had prepared dinner.

After their family dinner and the usual bedtime stories, Jo and Billy were tucked up in their own beds and Jenny and Tom relaxed by the fire and enjoyed a glass of wine whilst they talked about the present and the future. Jenny picked her moment then, swirling the rich red wine as it reflected the golden glow from the fire, said musingly, "Bella is coming on so much in her dressage. She could go to the top, I'm sure." She paused, lifted the glass, then continued, "The problem is, there aren't enough competitions around here for her. I would need to take her to some of the qualifiers which are all about two to three hours away and without transport it's not possible." She blew out her breath in a long sigh. "If only we could afford our own trailer". She gave another deep sigh then added, "It would be great for Jo and Emily too. They can't go to Pony Club competitions out of the area which is a bit frustrating for them as well."

Tom yawned, sipped his wine and said nothing.

"My dream, which I've treasured for years, is to qualify for the National Championships at Olympia". She paused then added, almost aggressively, "I can't do this unless I can travel to bigger competitions."

She waited for his response. He yawned again.

She took his hand and said, gently, "I can see you're tired love, after your long walk with Matthew. Let's go to bed."

They snuggled down in the softly yielding bed. Tom held her close whilst the aroma of the bluebells seeped into his spirit re-awakening once more the blissful memories of that rapturous closeness in Bluebell wood which they had occasionally equalled but never bettered. He sighed, released her and leaning on his elbow looked down and studied her for a long moment. Those beautiful bewitching hazel eyes! Then he said gently but earnestly, "Jenny darling, I'll do anything I can to make you happy but when you have fulfilled this dream, what will be the next one?"

She sensed and understood his underlying emotions so she thought carefully before she answered. "My next and dearest dream, Tom, is to have another baby, your baby, then to devote myself entirely to caring for you and helping you to fulfil *your* dreams."

His face softened as his whole being became suffused with love and tenderness. He drew her closer to him and murmured, "You fulfilled my dreams when you married me and bore my son."

They kissed, deeply and tenderly, their feelings encouraged and enhanced by the heady perfume of the bluebells. How lucky they were to have each other. How could they deny each other anything.

> *Thy love is such I can no way repay:*
> *The heavens reward thee manifold, I pray*
> *Then while we live, in love let's so persever,*
> *That when we live no more, we may live ever.*

The following morning at breakfast Tom, looked around at his family and thought again how rich his life was. So what if they borrowed a bit more money to buy a trailer! So what! To Hell with parsimony!

He smiled, shook cereals into his bowl and announced in a matter-of-fact voice, "Jo, I've been thinking about what to buy your mother for her birthday next month."

He paused. "Something *you* could share too." Then added almost flippantly, "How about a trailer?"

Jo dropped her spoon in surprise and it clattered on the floor causing Billy to laugh and respond by clattering his spoon on his bowl.

"Daddy, that would be awesome!" and she jumped up from the table and hugged him.

Jenny, hearing all this clatter, came downstairs. "What's going on here?" she asked, sensing the excitement.

"Daddy said we can have a trailer--soon---for your birthday!" shrieked Jo.

Jenny threw her arms around him. "Thank you darling". She held him close feeling and relishing the roughness and warmth of his stubble against her cheek then she added softly and earnestly, "I promise that there won't be anything else now. Not for *me* anyway."

That evening during his drive back to Ashbridge, he had time to contemplate about how he could afford to pay for a trailer *and* a towing vehicle. At least he would be earning much more money in September as a lecturer at uni. "Ah well", he thought, "You only live once!"

The farm responded to the onset of summer with yields of lush grass which was duly cut, dried stacked and stored. Plenty for their horses and a surplus to sell. Fledgling birds fell from their nests as they strove to fly and Jenny was relieved that they didn't have a cat. Thankfully Lulu ignored them. The trees displayed their leaves to the bright sun and used its power to grow and to store food. Insects and animals awakening from hibernation busily scurried and flurried around ensuring continued existence for themselves and other species. Bees back in work after their winter hibernation buzzed around hoping to fill their empty pollen baskets. Flowers opened up their petals slowly, sensuously to tempt and welcome them. What a wonderful time to rejoice in the infinite kaleidoscope of life itself!

The days grew longer and the evenings gave the opportunity for activities outdoors. Jenny and the girls hacked on the mountain, the horses got fitter and stronger and the time for Tom to be home for good grew near. They had everything to look forward to. No-one ever can or ever wants and should never try to envisage consequences other than positive ones which may result from simple everyday decisions. Yet these are the stuff that accidents, happy and tragic, are made of. Live for the moment. Tomorrow is another day.

Chapter 10

In the middle of July Tom bade farewell to the school where he had worked since leaving university. He felt saddened but not regretful. He had been happy there at least until the move to Bryn Celyn and he had good relations with most of the staff and the headmaster yet ironically, it was the pupils who seemed the most affected and sorriest to lose him. He pondered upon this. Was it because they genuinely liked him or were they thinking of how their futures would be altered by having to adapt to another teacher. He preferred to think it was the former.

Julie and the Doormat were not happy to see him go. They tried to extract promises of regular visits which he gave although he envisaged that such visits would be made through filial duty rather than pleasure. He knew that he must put the past thirteen years behind him, shrug off any forebodings or regrets and face a new and promising future, together at last with his family.

There were whoops and cheers and celebrations when he arrived at the farm. Jean had cooked a special dinner, Matthew had brought champagne, Bob had made a solid table for outdoors and Emily and Jo had made a poster for the door with 'Welcome Home, Dad!"

They ate, drank and laughed together sitting outside on that warm soft July evening watching the sun go down in a crimson glow over the darkening sea.

The following days found them all making plans about how they would spend their time during the long-awaited summer holidays. Tom and Matthew decided to try more challenging routes on Snowdon and the Carneddau. Bob and Jean planned to landscape their beloved garden. Jenny determined to continue training Bella whose dressage was improving greatly. Jo and Emily were to join in all the activities planned by the Pony Club. A happy and fulfilling time lay ahead for all of them. Hectic fun-filled days in which there is no room for boredom. This is how it should always be in an ideal world.

Emily practised and practised the art of a strident whistle and one warm sunny afternoon as she and Jo were sitting cross-legged on the grass watching Dinky grazing contentedly, she succeeded. A loud and piercing whistle rent the air and Dinky raised her head, neighed, and came trotting towards them.

"Yippee! I can do it!" yelled Emily leaping to her feet and repeating it again and again.

"Bet mine's louder than yours!" challenged Jo and she too gave vent to a raucous shrill whistle. The pony, confused and excited began to gallop and buck around the field. They laughed and whistled again and again for all they were worth until at length, out of breath they agreed to call it a draw and collapsed on the grass revelling in the warm sunshine and each others company. Emily began painstakingly to make a daisy chain and when it was finished she turned to her friend and said, "Here, for you, a necklace for my very bestest friend." She placed it carefully round Jo's neck and their eyes met. Neither said a word but each felt an inner glow. The warmth and love of true friendship.

Eventually they walked back to the stables to continue with the endless chores of clearing and sweeping the yard. Jo let out a sudden yell, "Ugh—look at that!" as a large black beetle scurried across the concrete. She was just about to squash it under her foot when Emily cried out, "No--Don't kill it!"

"Why not!" demanded Jo, "I don't like dirty ugly creepy-crawlies!"

"They aren't dirty and they don't do us any harm. He's probably got a family of baby beetles waiting for him."

"Don't be daft! They aren't like us. They don't think and feel like we do".

This was said sarcastically.

"Maybe not, but they do run away from danger. They do want to live. Like us, life is all they've got. We shouldn't kill them for nothing."

Jo looked at Emily's earnest face and the appeal in her beautiful blue eyes and she knew her friend was right. She hugged her on a sudden impulse then smiled and said with exaggerated benevolence, "Go little black beetle, back to your wife and family."

The two girls giggled as they watched the small creature scurrying away seeking refuge under the stable wall. Jo, a little chastened sighed and thought to herself, "Emily is so tender-hearted and she's right--we should all have a reverence for life and never kill indiscriminately."

It was a Sunday morning and Jo was, as usual on Sundays, at a loose end as Emily was always at church with Bob and Jean who were devout Christians.

"I wish they wouldn't make her go." she complained to Jenny, "I'm so glad you don't believe in God. It must be so boring sitting there with all the old coffin dodgers desperate about dying and trying to book a place in heaven--- as if there is such a place!"

"Now Jo, that's not a very nice thing to say", chided her mother "How do you know there's no heaven? What might seem boring to you is fulfilling and comforting to other people and I'm sure that Matthew's sermons are far from boring. I find him most interesting and stimulating and so does your dad, so let's not have any more silly criticism and comments about something you know nothing about. Anyway, to change the subject, what have you got planned for next week?"

"The Pony Club has organised a Fun Ride for next Wednesday It's a ten-mile ride over the mountain and into the next valley. It sounds really good. We have to take a packed lunch. Can I go? Emily's going to ask her Gran if she can go."

"Yes, 'course you can. Sounds fun! Can parents go too?"

"No, it's just for Pony Club. Louise is taking us. She's a great instructor and such a good rider. We'll have a brilliant day if the weather's good."

"Fingers crossed for that then, you lucky things!"

On Wednesday morning Jo set off early to meet Emily so they could ride together to the meeting point. As she rode away Jenny noticed that she was looking rather tall for 'Dinky' and came to the conclusion that she would soon have to get her another horse or let her share 'Bella', at least until 'Georgie' was broken in.

The two friends met in the village full of happy anticipation as they cantered to the farm which was the staring point for the ride.

Their guide, Louise, was an instructor well-known to all of them and when all twelve riders had arrived she gave them a brief talk on how they must behave in order to ensure the safety of themselves and others.

Some of the ponies were quite excited at first to be on the mountain in a wide open space and were bucking and dancing, anticipating the first gallop which they invariably did up a fairly steep hill. Louise hoped that this first strenuous gallop would 'take the wind out of their sails' and make them more controllable afterwards. It worked and after the exhilarating gallop they jogged and trotted on, ponies and riders bouncing in joyous harmony over the springy turf towards the river where they planned to stop for lunch. When they arrived at this remote and lovely spot they tethered their ponies to the adjacent trees and sat on the river bank eating their sandwiches, chatting and laughing. What a lovely day! Lovely weather, lovely friends, lovely ponies. Perfect!

The group spent the next hour gobbling and scoffing, swapping sandwiches laughing and chattering about the ponies, extolling both the virtues and vices of these adored creatures. Louise listened and smiled.

After about an hour she checked her watch. It was time to be off. It would take them about two hours to get back. She noticed a dark threatening cloud gathering over the mountain, obscuring its peak.

"Right girls, pack up and saddle up. Time to go!!"

When the group was assembled she gave them a tack check and warned them to be careful crossing the bridge.

"Single file. Not too close together and WALK!"

What happened next was to plague each and every one of them for the rest of their lives.

Emily and her pony, Dandy, were in the middle of the bridge behind Sharon and her young horse, Hetty. Suddenly, without warning, Hetty shied and backed violently into Dandy knocking him sideways into the flimsy fence. There was a harsh splintering crack as the fence gave way and horse and rider fell backwards into the river. A loud splash and a piercing terror-stricken scream rent the air. For a few moments chaos reigned as the startled ponies leapt and tugged at their reins reacting to the powerful flight instinct. Then, typically, they stood stock still, tense and snorting, nostrils flared, staring at the river.

Louise was the first to react. Just as Dandy was struggling to right himself she handed her reins to Beccy, dashed to the river and waded out to rescue Emily who was still submerged. She plunged her arms into the water and dragged out the limp, unconscious form. She staggered with some difficulty through the waist-deep water, laid Emily's inert body on its side and pressed hard on her stomach. A belch of water poured from Emily's mouth then Louise turned her onto her back and tried to ascertain whether there was pulse or any sign of breathing. A-B-C rang in her brain—Airway---Breathing---Circulation---Get help! She fumbled in her pocket for her mobile phone. Shit! It's wet through!

"Has anyone got a mobile?" Rachel whipped hers out of her pocket "Quick—dial Emergency! We need a helicopter immediately. There's no time for an ambulance even assuming one could get here!"

Confusion followed as the calm voice on the answering phone asked for an exact location. Jumbled directions were given as Louise tried to prioritise actions and control the rising panic which was preventing her from thinking clearly. Emily urgently needs CPR but also professional help. The map would give the precise location but digging out the map and finding a grid reference would take crucial time. But it had to be done. She took a deep breath, "Jo, find the map in my bag and get a grid reference for where we are now—quickly!" She snapped. Then to the rest, "Can anyone do CPR?"

"Me!" cried Carys, handing her pony over and kneeling beside Emily.

The younger girls, over the initial shock, found their voices and began converging upon where Emily lay, towing their ponies behind them, babbling and bombarding the harassed Louise with pointless questions,

"Will she be alright?"

"Is she badly hurt?"

"She won't die, will she?"

Again the stalwart Louise took control.

"Keep back! Tie your ponies to the trees and stay with them! Tessa, make sure that no-one comes near!"

She and Carys began mouth to mouth respiration and heart massage which they had previously only practised on dummies, both hoping and believing that if they could keep these vital functions working until professional help arrived then Emily could be saved. Meanwhile Jo had found the grid reference and been assured that the helicopter was on its way.

Louise, now able to foresee yet another impending danger, instructed Tessa to take the whole group back the way they had come, so that when the helicopter arrived the ponies would not panic and cause mayhem during the descent of this huge and noisy apparition.

So ponies and riders confused and shocked into silence, were led away by Tessa leaving Louise and Carys to care for Emily.

"Can I stay?" Jo's entreaties that as Emily's best friend she should be allowed to stay, were refused

"No!" retorted Louise. "We need you to lead Dandy back as he and Dinky know each other. Now all of you, please, leave now before the helicopter arrives!" Feeling desperate and frustrated Jo took Dandy and left with the others.

The ride back was sluggish and subdued. Hardly a word was spoken. Even the ponies seemed to sense that all was very far from well.

The news that evening was not good. Despite the sterling efforts of Louise and Carys, Emily was pronounced dead on arrival at hospital.

The news of Emily's death evoked different reactions from all who were near and dear to her. After the initial shock Jenny and Tom were very concerned about the dreadful effect upon Jean and Bob who were still grieving the loss of their only child, Emily's mother, Rachel. The uncertainty of their daughter's whereabouts or even her continued existence must be unbearable. She had been missing without trace for thirteen years. How had they been able to live with that? And now to lose Emily must be utterly devastating. However, when they had accepted and come to terms with their loss, they bore it with remarkable fortitude underpinned by their unshakeable faith.

"The Lord moves in mysterious ways", quoted Jean despairingly, her voice breaking with emotion then added with almost defiant piety, "We know now that Rachel must be with God and this is why He has taken Emily away from us. We must bear our grief and ask God to give us strength to endure it until we are all reunited again. It isn't going to be easy. We will miss her but we have to accept God's will".

Such stoicism was both envied and admired by all who knew them except Jo, who was angry and inconsolable.

"Why Emily. Poor, poor Emily. It's not fair! Why does she have to die when she has done nothing wrong and there are so many rotten and evil people in the world who deserve to die? Don't tell me about God. If there is a God and He is what He's made out to be, things like this wouldn't happen. That pontificating pratt of an R.E. teacher spouts about, 'what you put into life, you get out of'," this quoted in a peevish and smarmy tone. Then in a voice choked with anger and anguish she yelled, "What a load of rubbish! What has Emily ever done to deserve to be killed in such a horrible way?"

A torrent of sobbing ensued and all her parents could do was to try to commiserate. No amount of preaching or poetry spouting would be appropriate or acceptable. In fact these would have the opposite effect and seem as trite and stupid to her as the pontifications of the R.E. teacher. No place now for the philosophical renderings of Omar Khayyam--'The moving finger writes, etc.----'

Such utterances can seem helpful and thought-provoking in some instances to help people accept the present circumstances when the stark shock and pain have subsided, but not during the early stages when tortured emotions repel platitudes.

Jean and Bob decided that Emily should be buried in the family grave in the Yorkshire village where they had spent most of their lives and that the funeral service be held in the church where Rachel and Emily had been christened.

The village was in a fairly quiet rural area surrounded by moorland. It was a bleak but beautiful spot. The stone built church dated back to the eighteenth century but was nevertheless well maintained and typical of rural churches, it had a tower rather than a steeple with a single lonely bell which tolled sonorously as the congregation wound its sad way past the tombstones to the hard uncompromising pews. As Tom took his seat he mused the reason for the discomfort afforded by these wooden edifices, "Was it to discourage the congregation from sleeping during the sermons?" Typical Tom. Such a cynic!

It was a lovely service, full of comfort for the Longton family with the promise of reincarnation and reunion in paradise. Jenny and Tom were moved to see the reassuring hope and peace brought to Jean and Bob at this time of utter bereavement. Their mutual hugs were warm and sincere but Jo was sulky and peevish. She still refused to accept the outrageous unfairness of Emily being deprived of life and herself being deprived of her best friend and soul-mate. The sermons and service to her were pure fantasy-- verbal placebos dispensed like drugs to ease the pain of those naive enough to believe! She could not hide her agonised frustration even from Jean and Bob. How could they just accept the horror and loss of Emily with such equanimity? How could they let her 'go gently into that good night' when they should be 'raging against the dying of the light'?.

Bob and Jean decided to move back to their home town after the funeral. The cottage they had bought seemed no longer right for them. Jenny was devastated to lose Jean who had been her neighbour, friend and domestic mentor. Bob too had helped so much in so many practical ways with the renovations to the house and the building of the arena. Soon they would be gone leaving a void in all their lives which would be hard to fill. Lines from Andrew Lloyd Webber's song in the musical, 'Chess', kept flitting through Jenny's mind,

> *Nothing is so good it lasts eternally,*
> *Perfect situations must go wrong------*

So crushingly sad and heart-breaking for all of them but now they must look forwards to the future---take what comes-- be it triumph or disaster---- and muster the strength and wisdom to deal with whatever destiny had in store.

Chapter 11

Jo changed after Emily's death. Her usual bubbling exuberance had faded into subdued almost sulky moods. Her parents had to deal with this as best they could. Counselling and cuddling were both rejected. She didn't even want to ride 'Dinky' any more. When her mother suggested this as a kind of therapy, Jo's retort was "NO! I don't want to. It's not the same without 'Dandy'", then with a choke in her voice, "And Emily------"

She needed someone to talk to. Someone who would listen to her heart's outpourings and not interrupt or offer their commiserations or advice. She refused at first to talk to Matthew believing that he would drag her down the well-trodden route of 'God-Bashing'. How little she knew him! She had made the same assumptions that many people would make about a vicar---that it was his duty and mission in life to convert everyone into the Christian faith and to preach death and damnation to non-believers. Therefore her chosen 'confidant' became 'Georgie' and she spent hours in his box, grooming him and telling him about the past, the present and the bleak future without beloved Emily and especially how unfair life could be.

One day whilst she was opening up her heart to the receptive animal, Matthew appeared at the stable door. Unbeknown to Jo he had been eavesdropping.

"Dad's not in", she said, immediately adopting a defensive attitude.

"I know", he said, "I came up on the off-chance. I really need a walk—some fresh air on the mountain. I've got a bad bout of 'cabin-fever' and brain-apathy trying to compose something interesting and meaningful for the Sunday service. I need to blow all the cares and cobwebs away. Your mum's busy schooling Bella and I don't want to go by myself. Do you fancy a walk? I'm sure 'Lulu' would love it".

Lulu, who had been sleeping on the straw at the back of the box, suddenly sprang into life hearing her favourite word ---WALK! She barked at Jo and grabbed her arm, tugging it in her entreaty.

Jo reluctantly agreed and they were soon walking up the field alongside Bluebell Wood. It crossed her mind to tell Matthew about her parents' wish to be buried there when the time came but more death, however distant, was something she could not bear to think about. Instead when they did speak they spoke of inanities like the weather, the view, and Lulu's cavortions.

Eventually they reached the rock and the stone wall which was the usual resting place and picnic spot after toiling up the hill.

Matthew fished in his pocket and produced some chocolate which they shared.

Jo looked at him then said, "Why haven't you got your 'dog-collar' on?".

He laughed, "I'm like royalty. I only wear my badge of office when forced to by tradition". Seriously though, I find it so uncomfortable especially when exercising".

She felt emboldened by his casual good-humour so she told him how she had hated Emily's funeral and found the service so trite and hypocritical. He listened, sighed and shifted his position on the rock.

"I can understand that. But it's only hypocritical for those who don't believe but pretend they know better. It doesn't matter whether they believe or not. What does matter is that we all have a duty to help and comfort everyone in their anguish and distress ---how would they cope otherwise? Religious beliefs have helped and comforted millions in the past and hopefully will continue to do so in the future so you should not be too hard on those who perpetuate this".

"What is there for those like me who don't or can't believe then?"

"Well", he said gently, "For you there is just your inner strength which you have to summon and muster with all your might. It *is* a lot harder for you. There is no panacea. Some turn to alcohol or drugs but these cannot and do not help. In fact if dependence turns into addiction you are in a much worse state than before. Is this a fitting memory of those you are grieving for?" He paused, turned his gaze to Lulu who appeared to be listening intently almost knowingly. He stroked her long soft ears. Then he continued consolingly, "One poor woman who lost all her family in a car crash told me that she had coped by building an imaginary wall, brick by brick, and she never looked back or looked over it."

Another pause, then sadly, "I can't advise you on what you must do. In time you will find your own way".

Silence followed as Jo thought about what he had said. She looked down and ran her hands through Lulu's fur. She hoped he hadn't noticed the silent tears that had fallen forming momentary bright beads on the silky coat. She sniffed and took a hold of her emotions----strength----inner strength.

Matthew broke the silence. "Do you want to hear a poem that I love? This would be *my* sermon. I can hear Emily talking to you, comforting you. Learn it, believe it and think about it whenever you feel sad. He cleared his throat and said in a quiet voice full of meaning and emotion:

> *"Do not stand at my grave and weep,*
> *I am not there, I do not sleep,*
> *I am a thousand winds that blow,*
> *I am the diamond glints on snow,*
> *I am the sunlight on ripened grain,*
> *I am the gentle autumn rain,*
> *Caressing you to ease your pain..."*

He paused, and sighed deeply,
struggling with his emotions.

Jo was the first to break the subdued silence. "I like it", she said in a choking whisper, "And I think Emily would too." She turned to face him trying to straighten the contortions in her face. "Thanks, Matthew, that's perfect. You're just like dad. He always finds the right quotations at the the time." she swallowed and asked, "Who wrote it?"

"Well, he said light-heartedly. It's attributed to the prolific and ubiquitous 'Anon'. It could've been anybody's and everybody's grandma! Come on, lets make tracks back."

They walked in silence for a while each submerged in their own private thoughts. Jo thought of the scurrying beetle and Emily urging her to let it live. Emily had a reverence for life, all life, and this made it even crueller that she had been robbed of hers when there should have been so much left for her to fulfil.

Matthew was the first to speak

"You know," he began reflectively, "When we lose someone so close to us, it can be a comfort to have something more tangible than a photo to remember them by. Some living thing which to us incorporates their 'being', whose very existence is a lasting tribute to their memory."

She looked at him attentively.

He paused, then continued, "Such as planting a tree in memory of someone we love. So why not do that? Then whenever you want to talk to Emily or feel her presence you can go to her tree---*your* tree. You can watch it flourish and develop as you care for it. It will be something clear and definite which will comfort you and help to alleviate the sense of helplessness and loneliness that you must feel—that we all feel, when loved ones leave us."

Jo pondered upon this for a while then said, almost ecstatically,

"What a lovely idea---what a very lovely idea. Thank you Matthew. I shall do that." She felt an impetuous urge to hug him but repressed it and thought instead of the type of tree she would choose---a conker tree--? Yes! They'd had so much fun last autumn collecting conkers and competing against each other and all-comers in the school playground. She remembered the Aunty Bitch episode and the 'Brownie Points' they had earned with their attempt to foil the Health and Safety fiasco. She smiled in spite of herself.

This sense of purpose helped to squeeze out some anguish and her steps became lighter and less ponderous as they made their way back to the farm.

Three days later Tom, Jenny, Matthew and Jo selected a sheltered spot and planted a hardy young chestnut tree in memory of Emily.

Chapter 12

They decided to sell 'Dinky' but Jo wanted to have a last ride on her before the new owners took her away. She wanted to go alone to the spot where she had last seen Emily. She wanted to believe the poem that Matthew had read to her and to keep alive the memory of Emily in a positive way. That poem would *her* placebo.

When they arrived at the river she lay on the bank and stared into the water while the pony quietly grazed nearby. The river, flowing on calmly and peacefully had an air of enduring destiny. On its journey to the sea it would experience many changes in mood and substance but its destiny was always the same—the unfathomable ocean, the ultimate mother of all water on earth. Some rivers shrivelled and died en route but were then reborn when clouds, those water-burdened wombs burst, shedding the life-giving gift yielded gratuitously by the sea. It was like a never-ending cycle: birth—death--rebirth. Could human destiny be like this? Are the lives of those who die perpetuated in the infinite cosmos? She stared at her wavering fragmented reflection for a long time and thought deeply of her friend.

The image staring back at her began to slowly change form matching her thoughts and it became Emily's face she saw swaying and shivering in the ripples. Moods and memories from Kingsley's 'Water Babies' flowed through her mind. How they had loved that story! And how happy and carefree their mood singing 'Hi Cockolorum' as they danced along!

"Oh Emily, Emily!" she sobbed, "I'll never let you go. You'll live in my memory for ever. You'll hold my hand whenever I'm afraid and we'll share all the good times and bad times together."

She was awakened from this trance-like reverie by 'Dinky' who began to paw and suck the water, shattering Emily's image which shook and shivered in the ripples and then shrank back into oblivion.

The following weekend 'Dinky' left for her new home. It was heart-rending for all of them to see her go. She had been an important part of their lives for the past ten years but they knew it was the best thing for her. She would have another little girl to spoil and adore her and Jo would have more time to devote to 'Georgie' and to learn to ride the talented 'Bella'.

The first few days of the new term at school were very hard for Jo. Well-meaning teachers and pupils commiserated and quizzed about the accident and her responses were unforthcoming almost to the point of rudeness. She became particularly aggravated by the RE teacher, Mr. Parry, nick-named 'Piggy' because when he cleared his throat or coughed he snorted like a pig. It was her first lesson with him since the tragic loss of Emily and as she passed him in his classroom he confronted her, snorted, and took her hand, no doubt about to spout platitudes. She instantly recoiled, wrested her hand away and hurried to her seat. Undeterred by this slight he then began to instruct the whole class on how they must deal with the loss of loved ones. This sermon was delivered in a deliberately sonorous voice which rose and fell and was accompanied by expansive arm gestures as he strode around the classroom apparently relishing his own performance before his captive audience. Jo felt her temper and resentment rising until it reached breaking point. She leapt from her chair and fled, slamming the door behind her.

"Bugger the school, bugger the teachers-- especially bloody Piggy!"

When she got home she went straight to her room and said nothing to her parents about the incident. They had become used to her moods and ascribed them to the trauma of losing her best friend and the onset of puberty. She had become more self-assured, more argumentative, more defiant and yet there was still an under-lying vulnerability which with the right approach could be tapped into.

The following day, she feigned a severe headache as she felt she could not face school. She did the same the next day too, which made her parents feel that there was something wrong although they did not tackle her directly about this. However at the dinner table that evening she asked if she could be withdrawn from RE classes.

"I hate the teacher and he hates me and I think RE, especially for an atheist, is a waste of time."

"Isn't that like saying chemistry and physics are a waste of time for non-scientists? You can make that argument for any subject you like or don't like", responded Tom, "Furthermore, religion is an absolutely crucial part of the world's history and has been since time immemorial. I assume you will be taught about other religions –how they arose and their contributions, good and bad to the societies they serve."

"Not by him. He's too thick. He's just a bible-bashing pratt!"

"I can see you don't like him", laughed Tom. "It's probably just a clash of personalities. Leave it with me and I'll see what I can do. Will your, ahem, headache be alright for Monday—will you be able to face them all again by then?"

She hugged him impulsively and ran outside to talk to 'Georgie' and tuck him up for the night.

Monday morning Jo was summoned to appear before the headmaster. His nick-name was 'King Leer' because he seldom smiled and and his emotions seemed hidden beneath a perpetual disapproving sneer. She knocked nervously on his door. The electronic light bade her enter so she sidled in and stood before him wondering what his reaction would be to her bunking out of school. He regarded her for some time before he spoke sucking in and releasing his cheeks silently. She stared back at him in an attempt at defiance but felt herself crumpling under the fierce unwavering leer directed at her. Eventually he spoke in a calm yet measured tone.

"I know you are going through a difficult time but that does not excuse you from bad behaviour. I think you should apologise to Mr. Parry for your outburst and you must never leave the school premises again without express permission. We are legally and morally responsible for you during normal school hours."

She began to fidget and was about to protest when he added sternly, "If you have a problem in school whether it be with a member of staff or another pupil, you must not take the law into your own hands. You must come to me or the Deputy, or the Head of Year. Do I make myself clear?"

"Er, yes sir," she stammered, "But Mr. Parry hates me and I want to drop RE."

"Absolutely no chance! If younger pupils were allowed to pick and choose their subjects as the whim took them there would be chaos."

She stood her ground, "RE is different—many pupils with different religious beliefs, Muslims and Jews for example, are allowed to drop it---at least in England."

"Well this not England and you are neither a Muslim nor a Jew. And to say that Mr. Parry hates you is silly and unfair to him. He, like any other teacher, is intolerant of bad behaviour and should not have to put up with it. Now go to your next lesson. You can apologise to Mr. Parry at lunchtime. If you do not do this today then I will have no alternative but to suspend you until I have spoken to your parents and this matter has been resolved."

She left his room shaking with emotion, "Pompous old pratt—that's what they all are, pompous old pratts!" and she ran to the toilets for a good old weep.

How could she apologise to Piggy without losing face? If she didn't then there would be even more trouble and she didn't want her parents to be involved. If it did come to that then this 'storm in a teacup' would develop into a full-blown tempest. She decided to swallow her pride and to say 'Sorry' haughtily, looking down her nose at him, making it obvious that it was not a sincere apology. How would he react to *that* she wondered.

She sought him out at lunchtime and peering through the window into his classroom, found him apparently engrossed in something on his desk.

"Probably perving over some porny mag.", she thought bitterly.

He signalled her to enter and she faced him and cleared her throat.

"The headmaster has sent me to apologise, so I'm sorry if I was rude last Wednesday." This delivered in a monotone.

Such an ungracious apology obviously insincere and said with a sneer on that pubertical face already spawning spots was his assessment of this charade. However, he was not in the mood for further confrontation with this difficult girl.

"Go away," he said sighing rather than shouting, "And try to behave yourself in future." Wearily he went back to his marking.

"Who'd be a teacher if it weren't for the holidays-------?" he sighed to himself.

That evening Matthew came to the farm for dinner and to play chess with Tom. Once the stage was set for the match the atmosphere in the lounge was solid with tension and concentration. They were great rivals and very competitive in this strategic game so the rest of the family stayed clear. Billy was in bed, Jenny was either out schooling Bella or busy in the kitchen whilst Jo stayed in her room doing homework. However on this occasion she asked them if she could stay and watch the game. Tom had taught her the rudiments and she had played matches with him in which he had analysed and instructed her every move. Eventually when she graduated to playing independently, he had given her an advantage by sacrificing his queen and sometimes his rooks too at the start of the game. In spite of these advantages she had never beaten him.

She found it intriguing watching and studying each individual move and wondered at the motives and possible outcomes. She was as concentrated as the players who seemed unaware of her presence.

It was 10pm when Jenny opened the door and announced with a mixture of relief and surprise, "Oh there you are! I've looked everywhere. Time for bed! School tomorrow."

"Please mum, can't I wait to see who'll win?"

"No! You can find out tomorrow. These games can last all night."

She got up reluctantly and Matthew and Tom grinned at her, bade her 'Goodnight' then continued their game.

Next morning Tom and Jenny discussed Jo's fascination in the development of the game.

"She sat like statue for a good two hours. She never spoke a word the whole time," remarked Tom.

"Seems out of character for a fidgety girl who more often than not has too much to say," reflected Jenny.

"Yes, both Matthew and I were surprised. He suggested that we play as a threesome next time. She and I against him. It would be good for her to broaden her horizons. At the moment horses seem to be her only interest".

"Good idea. She does need something else and Chess is brilliant. I wish I'd learned to play when was young."

"So do I," he laughed, then added facetiously, "You're far too jumpy though and I doubt you could sit still for longer than ten minutes. I think you should stick to 'Draughts'!"

"Cheeky Devil!" She poured out his tea then went to check Billy.

Jo seemed disinclined to make close friends at school. She and Emily had been so self-contained that they had frozen out any attempts to join them both in and out of school. Also, neither of them could speak Welsh fluently and it was perfectly natural for the majority to speak their native language. This fact had alienated the two friends from their contemporaries and made them feel like outsiders. So Jo, now bereft and alone, attended school, took part in lessons and left as soon as she could at the end of the day. Extra-curricular activities were comprised solely of team games and were organised in the main for those who represented the school in their chosen sports. Jo's life was centred around horses so she had neither time nor inclination for further commitments. This was a pity because team games can engender cooperation and closeness between all team members as they strive together to achieve a common aim—victory over any rival teams. Maybe in this environment she could have experienced a different challenge and maybe found a new friend who would help her to get over her bitter sense of loss. But it was not to be.

Every day when she arrived home from school she would change into her riding clothes, brush Georgie until he shone and then take him into the arena for backing and schooling under the watchful eye of Jenny.

This process of educating young horses to accept a rider on their backs requires time, patience and empathy. Jenny disliked the term 'breaking'. For to her it implied domination and subjugation. She preferred to think of it as engendering trust between the animal and its trainer. Georgie was a spirited horse but he responded well to love and kindness tempered with firmness when his boisterous antics over-stepped the mark. He was barely three years old yet Jenny and Jo were riding him in the arena and around the farm. He was already bigger than his mother and had inherited her elevated paces. Jo adored him and was already planning their future together.

"Look at him, mum! He's so beautiful and he moves so well. We'll soon be beating you and Bella in dressage competitions."

This was said jokingly as Jenny and Bella had been winning all the local events and were steadily moving up the ladder in more advanced competitions further afield. This travelling to prestigious events had been made possible by Tom finally agreeing to buy a trailer and a towing vehicle. Jenny's burning ambition and cherished dream remained steadfast--to qualify for the National Championships at Olympia. Wasn't that what every serious competitor wanted? Could she achieve it? Was it just a tenuous dream? No, it had to be more than that. She remembered the last words her father had spoken to her before he left on that final adventure: "Follow your dreams-----" This was her inspiration and fuelled her confidence and self-belief.

Jenny smiled indulgently at her daughter, "Well go for it love, if its what you want and you think you can do it. This challenge will keep us both on our toes!"

That same evening Matthew came for dinner and Chess and Jo was invited to play with them partnering Tom. It was not a serious match. Both men regarded it as an educational exercise. It was fascinating for her trying to foresee the outcomes and strategy behind every move. Sometimes they would encourage her by praising a certain move and explaining why. At other times they would shake their heads and discuss, suggesting possible reasons for a poor prognosis.

She loved sharing this time with two intellectual giants and they were happy to share their knowledge and experience. It was heartening to have a young person who preferred to exercise her brain rather than choose the ubiquitous effortless and addictive television.

"It's such a pity that more children don't have the opportunity to learn Chess these days." observed Matthew.

Tom nodded his assent then added, "I was lucky enough to attend a Grammar school and we had a thriving Chess club. We even had competitions against other clubs. I loved it. It seems to be dying out now, more's the pity."

"That's given me an idea actually, Tom!", Matthew responded excitedly "I could go to the local school and ask the headmaster if he would be happy for me to start a Chess club after school—for teachers and pupils. I hope he will agree. It would help the students to see *me* in a different light too. Maybe some of them would even be inspired attend church! It could even be thrown open to parents and ex-pupils. So many of them are out of work it could give them an added dimension. What do you think?"

"Well, it's certainly worth a try, but don't hold your breath. Not many teachers are willing to give up time after school these days. They are so bogged down with paperwork. You never know though. Some may be interested and even if it starts in a small way then it could develop into something worthwhile. Go for it, and good luck!"

Matthew decided he would make an appointment to see the headmaster tomorrow.

Not surprisingly the headmaster enthused about the idea and in a subsequent staff meeting volunteers were co-opted to organise the school's first Chess Club. Matthew undertook to teach and coach the members. The formation of this club provided a new diversion for Jo and a different outlet for her competitive nature. More importantly it gave her the opportunity to compete and cooperate with a wider range of fellow pupils. Jenny and Tom were very pleased and supportive as they believed that the best antidote to her pain and depression would be to fill her life with as many new interests and activities as possible.

Chapter 13

Jo was readjusting to life at school, Tom was settling well into life at university, Jenny was dividing her time between domesticity and dressage training. Billy, a lively and happy child, was ready to attend play-school. Jenny enrolled him for three days a week. She was a little concerned at first as Welsh was the sole language and she thought that this might alienate him especially as his life hitherto had been almost totally centred around the immediate family. However, he soon settled in and delighted them by singing and chanting nursery rhymes in Welsh. Billy in his turn, was equally delighted to teach them Welsh vocabulary. They realised that it would not be long before he became fluent. Jo on the other hand was struggling to learn what was to her an alien language and one in which she was greatly disadvantaged with her peers. Tom and Jenny wished that she had been exposed to the language at an early age when children are programmed to absorb language as a crucial method of communication. Also they both felt an inner guilt at not making an effort to learn Welsh themselves but their lives were so full in other ways that to prioritise leaning Welsh would mean sacrificing something else which at the moment they were not ready to do.

Jenny met other mothers at play-school but found it hard to form close friendships as none them were 'horsey' and they all seemed to have formed their own close-knit groups. Also Jenny was always in a hurry to return home to continue the rigorous training programme she had devised for Bella. Her burning ambition to compete in the National Championships was stronger than ever as week by week, competition by competition, she and Bella climbed further up the ladder of success. Sometimes when things were not going right or when the strict regime seemed too much, her father's words would ring again in her ears, 'Follow your dreams----!' Follow your dreams at whatever the cost? It seemed that her parents had paid dearly for following their dreams, but it didn't always have to end like that.

Jo too was making good progress with 'Georgie' and looking forward to the New Year when he would be four years old and able to compete. He was a talented and spirited animal and could cope easily with the basic moves required for the preliminary tests. At the moment she was going with her mother and watching her compete in qualifying competitions at Advanced Medium level where some of the moves were quite complex and had to be executed perfectly in order to obtain good enough marks to qualify for the National Championships or to move up to the next level. To Jo, there was no-one better than her mother and she truly believed that Jenny was capable of gaining a place on the British Team. Whenever she enthused about this, Jenny would laugh and say, "One step at a time," and then add, "What I'm doing now is breaking us financially. If only I could get a sponsor! Almost all British Team members are either very rich or have sponsors and usually both! No, at the moment I am happy to be doing what I'm doing and my only dream is to qualify for the National Championships and compete at Olympia. What a brilliant Christmas present that would be!"

Jenny had been to Olympia as a spectator but how much more exciting to be there as a competitor!

"It won't be this year though." she added, "Maybe next year if things go according to plan."

This was Jenny's dream---at least for the present--- and luckily for her it was supported by Tom who had every faith that it was and would be achievable.

The year struggled its way through Autumn with its usual blow and bluster, littering leaves and dead branches everywhere. The birds flocked ever closer to the house in expectation of the nuts, seeds and crumbs so generously bestowed daily by the family. The sun slunk slowly to the southern hemisphere and the days became colder and shorter. Jenny missing Jean, had miserable moments as she remembered nostalgically the days spent together in the cosy kitchen cooking, chatting and laughing, never imagining what lay ahead. She shuddered as she thought about the cruel blows fate had dealt this kind and happy couple and marvelled at the comfort and solace afforded to them by their unshakeable faith. Again she found herself thinking about *her* parents. What had happened to them? Was it possible that they were still alive, perhaps detained as prisoners in some far-off land? Or had they been shipwrecked onto some desert island? She believed that if this were the case they were both well able to survive by hunting and foraging for food and building a shelter. This would be a real-life shipwreck and survival without the eight gramophone records, The Bible, the Complete Works of Shakespeare, a chosen book and some cherished luxury. She surmised that her father's chosen luxury would have been complete set of tools so he could build another boat, another 'Vagabonde'. They would make it alone. Her father she knew would try to build a boat from whatever was available and set sail again! What an amazing self-sufficient couple they were. Selfish—yes, but to achieve what they achieved required selfishness. Their own dreams and ambitions took precedence over all else.

Jenny's daydreams imagining them still alive, still enduring all hardships and overcoming all dangers were pure make-believe inspired by wishful thinking. Dream on, Jenny! It was sixteen years since they had left. Sixteen years! She could hardly believe it. They must be dead! No news is good news? Should she ever give up hope? Mike and Danielle were survivors, indestructible. Or so it always seemed.

She tried to banish these morbid thoughts by bashing the wooden spoon round and round in the mixing bowl as she stirred the Christmas pudding. Christmas cake next. Too early for mince pies unless she froze them. She felt an unquenchable need for hard physical exercise, the best antidote to depression. So as soon as the pudding and cake were mixed she donned her Wellingtons and jacket and set about chopping wood. As soon as she started, Bob sprang to mind. He had always done this whilst she and Jean were baking. Poor Bob! Emily was the apple of his eye—the embodiment of Rachel, his lost and longed-for daughter-------! She shuddered, experiencing their anguish and pain. Then she took hold of her emotions. Steeping herself in morbidity would *not* do. It would *not* do!

"Stop it! Stop it!" she choked. "Now keep calm. Nothing can change or alter the past. Think philosophy---*The moving finger writes* ---Aagh, sod the bloody moving finger! Stick it up your arse!"

This obscene untypical outburst made her laugh at herself, another good antidote to morbidity, so she continued her exertions: lift and swing, chop, chop; lift and swing, chop, chop; feeling immense satisfaction as the blocks of wood splintered and yielded to her strength. She worked solidly for a good half hour until her arms ached and her breath came in gasps. She felt much better afterwards. She had driven out her demons—at least for the time being.

She returned indoors carrying a basket of newly chopped logs, struggling against the power of the wind. She fed the hungry log fire and felt soothed as she thought of the homely welcome it would give to her returning family. She couldn't hate the winter. Well, not all the time, as there was something so warm, safe and comforting in the bosom of the family sitting by a crackling fire glowing in the hearth whilst the weather did its worst outside. And Christmas was coming. Who cared whether it was a Pagan or a Christian celebration? It was a special time for families and friends to get together and celebrate their loves and their lives.

As Christmas drew near, life became more hectic Tom took Billy and went to spend a few days with his sister Julie, who adamantly refused all invitations to visit Bryn Celyn. Jenny and Jo decorated the Christmas tree and swathed the beams and window sills with bright berried holly, Jenny dreaming and imagining Jean, laughing and helping by her side. Jo remembering Emily—their jokes, their dancing and their making fun of carols—Shepherds washing their socks, seated round a tub when the angel of the Lord came down and gave them all a scrub!

Good King Wenceslas being hit on the snout by a snowball----! That lovely smile, infectious giggle and those beautiful blue eyes------ So cruelly poignant that this season of joy should be marred by sadness.

Next morning the postman arrived with a cheery smile and a bundle of Christmas cards, some from barely remembered long-lost friends. Jenny, as was her custom, sat before the fire with a glass of sherry and read each one noting that many had been chosen with her particular interests in mind and noting too those that had been bought to support a particular charity. She was over-joyed to open one with the latest news from Liz and Brian in New Zealand. She immediately rang Tom.

"Fantastic news! Jan has had a baby boy—Graham. They're over the moon!."

Jenny felt guilty about the lack of correspondence between them. They had once been so close and now it seemed as if the old cliché, 'out of sight, out of mind', described the whole relationship because neither party contacted the other, except at Christmas.

On Christmas Eve the family made their usual pilgrimage to the little church for the Christmas Service and all of them felt acutely the loss of Emily and the absence of the only real friends, apart from Matthew, they had made in the four years they had lived in the area.

On Christmas day the weather was wet, wild and windy so they took their usual 'work up an appetite' walk on the beach instead of on the hills. The sea, whipped up by the wind, tossed its white horses high into the air and smashed them against the rocks and the sea wall showering spume everywhere. Even Lulu was discomfited and kept close to them.

Again Jenny found herself thinking about her parents and wondering if they had met their demise in such a storm pitting themselves and their tiny boat against the tempestuous might of the sea and its powerful ally, the wind, and at last, losing the fight.

The walk was bracing and gave them all a good appetite for dinner. However, there was not the same jollity and carefree joviality of previous years. How could there be?

New Years Eve too had a shadow shrouding over it as the old year gave way to the new. How could any of them have foreseen what destiny had in store for them as they had laughed and sang 'Auld Lang Syne' to the dying year and whooped and celebrated the coming of the New Year full of hopes and aspirations. Fate, that pursuer of destiny, had betrayed them. They closed their eyes, linked hands and sang the traditional 'Auld Lang Syne' again this year but slowly, poignantly, and devoutly to honour the memory of Emily.

However, as fireworks began to explode and sparkle in the sky to welcome and celebrate the birth of the New Year, hope sprang anew in all of them. They had surely experienced more than their fair share of tragedy. Would this be the year when dreams were fulfilled? Yes, yes, yes, please!

Chapter 14

After Twelfth Night the fripperies and foibles of Christmas were consigned to their customary hibernation and life returned to its normal routine.

Jo felt she had little to look forward to as she dragged herself to school. It was unbearable without Emily.

However, at the first meeting of the Chess Club in that spring term, a new member was enrolled. She was a remarkably pretty girl, tall and slim with lustrous yet expressionless dark brown eyes complementing rich dark brown hair which she wore tied tightly back away from her face highlighting her features which were perfectly symmetrical and set into pale unblemished skin. She had high cheek bones and full lips which seemed to have a permanent pout. Her expression however, was deadpan as Matthew introduced her to the group. She neither smiled nor scowled and even her large brown eyes remained cold.

"This is Kate Johnson," said Matthew. "This is her first week in school and we are very happy to welcome her into our Chess Club."

Curious looks from the members but no other response.

As usual, Matthew spent some time talking tactics then the boards were set up and partners chosen. As she had no particular friends, Jo usually waited to see who else was left. She always hoped she would be the odd one out so she could partner Matthew which the others naturally construed as favouritism.

However, this week, Matthew partnered her with Kate who won the toss and opted to play the white pieces. Jo too could be deadpan and silent, so not a word was spoken between them as the game progressed. They were very evenly matched so when the two hours allocated to the club had elapsed, neither had the advantage in position or possession of pieces. Matthew smiled as he took a picture of the board.

"Well, well! Quite a needle-match. Very interesting and exciting for next time."

Kate got up and left without a word.

"What a strange girl," remarked Jo to Matthew. "If she smiled her face would crack!"

"Don't be too hard on her", he replied, "She's probably very shy and it is her first week in a strange school and she knows no Welsh at all which will make her feel alienated at first. Make an effort to get to know her tomorrow. You may find you have much in common and could become good friends."

Jo doubted it but decided she'd give it a go for Matthew's sake and besides, Kate was a good chess player. Better than any of the others she'd played against.

At break-time the next day Jo sought out Kate Johnson only to discover that she had been given permission to stay in the library, ostensibly to learn Welsh.

"That sounds like a good scam", she thought, "I wonder if I could do the same."

Permission was duly granted so at lunch-time Jo took her Welsh books into the library and greeted Kate with a cheery smile. A flicker of recognition flashed across Kate's face then her attention returned to the book in front of her.

Jo tried again, "Good match yesterday. How long have you been playing chess?"

Kate stared at her then sighed, "Not long." and again returned her attention to her book.

Jo refused to be discomfited by Kate's dismissive attitude. She sensed that there was acute vulnerability beneath this defensive veneer. She tried again.

"I'm not very good at Welsh either but in this area you have to learn to speak it if you want to get anywhere."

Kate replied with an edge of bitterness in her voice, "I don't want to get anywhere here. I just want to get away!"

"I feel like that sometimes too, especially after I lost my best friend."

There was a catch in her voice as she said this which did not go unnoticed.

Jo swallowed hard and continued, "She was my one and only friend. We didn't fit in very well as we both lived out of the village and no-one else liked us or what we did."

This last statement intrigued Kate as it seemed to imply nonconformity and rebellion.

"What did you do?"

"Nothing really," came the non-committal reply. "It's because we were different and we had each other. There was no room for anyone else."

There was venom in Kate's voice as she responded, "Well I had no choice and no '*best friend*' to lose. I was dragged and dumped here and I hate it!" With this Kate lowered her head and again concentrated her gaze on the book before her.

It seemed like another gesture of dismissal but Jo refused to be put off.

"Are you going to Chess club this week?"

"I'll have to. There's no-one in the house until six on Wednesdays."

"Oh good! We can carry on with our game. You're a good player. I thought you were going to win last week. I've been swotting up on 'end games' to try to beat you."

To her immense surprise Kate actually grinned.

"So have I." she rejoined and from that moment a bond, albeit fragile, was formed between them.

It was recognised by the teachers that Jo and Kate could be good for each other so permission was granted for them to stay in the library at least at lunch-times, as otherwise their paths would not cross as Kate was a year below Jo.

Gradually they began to get know each other better but Kate's past remained a mystery. It was obvious that she had experienced family problems as she was living with foster parents who were kind and understanding and trying their best to integrate her into their own family life. This was not easy as she remained sulky and hard-bitten and refused to confide in anyone, even Matthew who knew when to leave well-alone. Jo stopped trying to pry into her past for each time she did Kate retreated deeper into her shell and Jo could almost feel the angry thorns of her resistance. As long as their relationship was kept on a superficial level they got along fine.

Kate won the chess match. She had the ability to shut out everything and concentrate entirely upon one thing at a time. Jo, who was also good at focussing her mind found herself so intrigued by her opponent's total absorption that she was unable to counteract the moves. In some ways she was pleased that Kate had won. This victory might build a positive block in Kate's shattered self-esteem.

Their friendship grew and one weekend Jo persuaded Kate to visit Bryn Celyn. Kate bonded immediately with Lulu and the horses. It was as if the hard shell which kept her inner secrets intact crumbled away as she caressed the happy and responsive animals. She joined in with the essential chores and relished the hard work and exercise. She refused to sit on the horses but enjoyed watching Jenny and Jo putting 'Bella' and 'Georgie' through their paces in the arena. This became the pattern of their weekends. Sometimes on Saturdays they would go for long walks with Matthew and Tom with Lulu leaping and bounding along. The dog's infectious 'joie de vivre' would lift everyone's spirits. Kate would laugh and play with the dog but she would not get involved in any discourse with the two men. When they tried to involve her in any conversation she would revert to her monosyllabic responses. What had she suffered to have such a deep mistrust, almost a dislike, of her fellows? It was as if she had a congenital condition like a strange form of autism but the symptoms were not as clear cut and there was nothing in her notes to suggest this. Sometimes she and Jo were as normal happy friends together and the hard unyielding shell had become more of a facade but one which prevented Jo from discovering anything about her past or her innermost secrets. Another strange thing was that her foster parents would not allow her to have a sleep-over at Bryn Celyn and insisted that she return to the house by 10pm.

The daffodils began to sprout early that spring in deference to a mild winter and were in full bloom by St. David's day. Jo and Kate encouraged by Jenny, gathered armfuls to take to take to school. The response they received for their thoughtfulness was a mixture of warmth and surprise.

"That should earn us a few Brownie points", smiled Jo to herself as she graciously accepted the almost gushing thanks from her Form teacher.

It is a tribute to the strong sense of their national identity that the Welsh revere and celebrate their adopted saint. It seems right and natural to them but can seem a little strange to incomers and outsiders like Jo and Kate.

"When's St. George's day?" asked Kate.

"God knows!" said Jo and they both laughed.

March came in like a lamb and every living thing at Bryn Celyn seemed to leap incautiously back to life. The bluebells burst forth, the buds on the trees were swollen with promise but the grass sprouted tentatively, half expecting a late frost to chill and kill the tender shoots. The weather teased and caressed nature's offspring until the end of the month. Then at the dawning of British Summertime it unleashed its forces. March went out like a lion! Hailstones as big as peas fell clattering to the ground covering it instantly in a cold white carpet. The trees shivered and shook and the older ones creaked and groaned as their limbs were torn away. Birds in their blast be-ruffled plumage reacted angrily, squawking and quarrelling as they hastily attempted to repair and rebuild their nests. The horses charged around the field then resolutely and resignedly turned their backs to the whipping wind.

"Welcome British summer!", muttered Jo grimly as she struggled across the yard, head bent to protect her face from the pelting hailstones.

She stood at the gate and gave a shrill whistle. The horses turned instantly and galloped enthusiastically to the comfort of their stables. She thought again of Emily and her delight when she eventually mastered the technique of the loud and piercing whistle. "Oh, Emily--." She sighed, then shuddered at the memory of her loss and slunk indoors

April, mild and drizzly, melted into May. The trees, recovering from winter, regaled themselves in bright blossoms. Hibernating insects emerged from crevices and cracks, hurrying and scurrying, buzzing and biting, all renewing the routine of their daily lives. And the days were longer and warmer. So much to look forward to.

Jo and Kate remained close friends but still Kate's past remained a mystery and although Jo was curious she no longer tried to press or pry. Instead, in calm and quiet moments before she fell asleep she wove all kinds of stories appertaining to Kate's family history: perhaps she had been beaten. Or maybe she was illegitimate and never knew her real parents. Could they be crazy and in an asylum? Or in prison for some heinous crime? Anyway whatever it was Kate was most unwilling to divulge or give even the tiniest clue. This made it even more intriguing—fascinating in fact, and frustrating!

Jenny and 'Bella' were going from strength to strength in their dressage training and were winning classes further afield where the standard was much higher and the competition fierce.

More often than not Tom would drive her to the venues towing the trailer. He was proud of her success and to see her so happy and fulfilled gave him pleasure and satisfaction. Whenever they went away Jo and Kate remained at the farm looking after Billy. When the weather was fine they would picnic in Bluebell Wood revelling in the peace and solitude taking it in turns to read to Billy and in giddier moments climbing the trees and playing 'Hide and Seek'. These were lovely relaxing times and when Billy was engrossed in his own pursuits building Lego or crayoning his books, Jo and Kate would talk about their dreams, discuss their likes and dislikes. Their discourse always centred around the present or the future. Kate confessed that she did not like her present foster parents. She could give no convincing reason for this. She admitted that her feelings did not amount to actual dislike—she was more or less neutral towards them. She did not want to get close to them nor encourage them to get close to her. They were stuck with each other—for the present at least.

One Sunday evening towards the end of the summer holidays, they were reading a bedtime story to Billy when they heard the trailer pulling into the yard and a welcoming neigh from 'Georgie' as 'Bella' clattered down the ramp.

They quickly tucked in the sleepy child and ran downstairs.

"How did it go. Mum?", cried Jo. She knew it was the last qualifier of the season and if unsuccessful Jenny would have to wait until next year to fulfil her dream.

Jenny, exultant, jumped up and down on the spot before running to hug her daughter. "We did it! We did it! We're through! Olympia here we come! Magnificent Meribel!

The shouts and shrieks of the two girls as they all danced around the yard sent 'Lulu' frantic and 'Georgie' pricked his ears and stopped chewing wondering what was coming next!

"We've got a special treat we've been saving for this occasion," announced Tom. "Follow me!"

The bottle of Champagne was opened with a loud pop. Glasses were raised and toasts drank to Jenny and the talented 'Bella'. The hours, days, weeks, months and even years they had spent working together striving for this goal had come to fruition, and Yes! —a toast to Tom too, for without his loyalty and support this achievement would not have been possible!

Jenny closed her eyes and her parents' faces swam before her.

"Thanks, both of you", she whispered fervently, "For giving me the strength of your example to follow my dreams."

Chapter 15

Summer shrivelled into autumn and the customary routines began anew. Tom, now lecturing at Uni, had new students fresh from school. Some were full of hopes and aspirations anxious to absorb whatever they could. They sat before him in the large lecture room, notebooks at the ready, alert and attentive. Others would saunter in late and slouch at the back. Still fairly new from teaching and being used to all his students ready and waiting, he could not tolerate this 'laissez-faire' attitude so he laid down the rules from the start. This made him unpopular at first with the over-confident and cocky brigade and he found the first few weeks of the autumn term quite difficult. However when the day was done and he arrived home greeted by the warmth and welcome of Bryn Celyn he relaxed and his problems, real and perceived, melted away.

Jo was much happier at school now that she had found a friend. Kate could not replace Emily. They were so different. Emily had been as an open book wearing her heart on her sleeve and sharing her innermost secrets. Kate would still retreat into her shell of secrecy if she felt pressured. She was a strange anomaly of light-hearted enthusiasm and deep depression. Jo had learned to accept these variations in her character and knew when to leave well-alone.

The best therapy when Kate relapsed into these dark moods was to leave her alone with Lulu. It was as if the animal could sense and share the pain of her deep dark secrets and soothe them away. She would snuggle close to Kate on the sofa and the rest of the family would close the door and leave them alone.

Billy had now graduated from Play-school to the local Primary school where he spent three mornings each week. He never made a fuss when Jenny left him. He scarcely seemed to notice her going as he ran across the yard to be shepherded indoors by the waiting teacher. What a confident and happy child he was turning out to be.

Jenny would return home from shopping and teaching riding and use this time to continue training 'Bella' for her debut at Olympia. She found these training sessions so exciting and satisfying as the lovely mare responded and improved.

"Please God keep her fit and strong and don't let anything go wrong", was her fervent and frequent prayer.

The date for Olympia was December 18th which luckily coincided with Tom's Christmas holidays and meant that he could tow the trailer down to London.

They proposed to leave early in the morning and return the same evening after the competition. A punishing schedule but one they both preferred because they did not want to leave Jo and Billy alone overnight.

Jo could not go with them as they needed her to stay at home to look after Billy and the animals.

Preparations for Olympia and Christmas were taking place. Jo was very disappointed that Kate would not be around to share them. Her foster parents had booked a holiday in Spain for two weeks. They were leaving on the same day as Olympia.

On December 17th Jenny spent the whole day preparing for Olympia. All the equipment was packed in the car, the trailer was clean and ready and 'Bella' 's mane and tail were plaited and her velvety coat brushed until she shone. It was so exciting and nerve-racking. Here at last, the culmination of a dream she had nurtured for years even from the first time she had seen 'Bella' as a baby at Beechwood. She had enclosed a letter with her Christmas card and told Liz and Brian of her success with 'Bella'. She knew that they would be proud and delighted. 'Bella' had been conceived and born at Beechwood out of Liz's favourite mare by a local dressage stallion. It was with deep nostalgia that she thought of Beechwood and could not, dare not, revisit the area now. Not now that it had been destroyed to make way for a Supermarket!

It was pitch black as they drove out of the yard at 5am. The rest of the household was fast asleep, not even a wicker from 'Georgie' nor a bark from Lulu wished them 'Bon Voyage'.

Throughout the cloudy murky day Jo found it hard to concentrate. What are they doing now? Have they arrived safely? Dusk slunk in at 4pm and Jo shivered as she contemplated the long nights and the damp and dreary days ahead. She gave hay and food to 'Georgie' and cheered up as he whickered a welcome. She patted him and assured him that 'Bella' and Jenny would be home soon. Wouldn't it be wonderful if they were placed at Olympia! 'Dream on----!'

As she walked back to the house she paused to watch the wintry sun sliding into the sea which seemed to be slowly swallowing him, consigning the the earth to darkness and the dead of night.

That evening Jo and Billy were sitting together before a cosy fire. Lulu was curled up contentedly on the rug twitching and snorting quietly in response to her doggy dreams. The Christmas tree resplendent in its trimmings winked its lights from the corner of the room whilst the garlands hanging from the beams swayed and twinkled above them and the blood-red holly berries fell singly and silently from the grasp of the protective prickly leaves. Jo was reading Billy one of their favourite Christmas stories. Suddenly the phone rang causing them all to jump in surprise.

It was Jenny breathless with excitement, "Jo, Jo darling—we won! I can't believe it! She was foot perfect. What a sweetheart! I can't wait to tell you all about it! We'll be home around midnight. It was-----" Burr, click. Out of signal.

Jo gasping in excitement grabbed Billy and began to dance around the room, "They've won! "They've won! Fantastic! Yippee! This is beyond our wildest dreams! The best Christmas present ever! Good old mum! Good old Bella! We're gong to have the best Christmas ever! Whoopee!" and she bounced up and down with the chortling child singing an old much-loved ditty, which had become part of their Christmas preamble:

*"Christmas is coming,
The geese are getting fat,
Please put a penny in the old man's hat,
If you haven't got a penny
A hae'penny will do,
If you haven't got a hae'penny
God Bless you!"*

Billy joined in the singing and they whirled around the room accompanied by Lulu jumping on and off the furniture and adding her doggy descant.

Their happiness was delirious and lasted until Jo began to feel dizzy.

"Time for bed, Billy. Mummy and daddy will be back when you wake up tomorrow morning." and she carried him up the stairs and tenderly tucked him up, gently kissing the already half-closed eyes.

She couldn't go to bed. She wanted to be ready to greet them when they arrived so she refuelled the fire and settled down in front of it with her book. The comforting crackle of the glowing logs and the soft winking of the fairy lights relaxed her into a peaceful slumber.

She was awakened at about 3am by banging on the door and Lulu barking frantically. She shivered and stared at the dying embers of the fire. It took her several seconds to gather her wits and her immediate thoughts were that her parents had arrived. Confusion! Why would they hammer on the door like that? Still in a half dream-like state she stumbled across the room, grabbed the door handle and tried to wrench it open. Lulu backed off and growled,

Destiny Obscure

hackles rising. It can't be mum and dad. They have a key! Who the devil is it?

"Hello, hello", demanded a stern voice, Open up, please. It's the police!"

Jumbled thoughts rushed round inside her head.

"Police? What for? What's happened?"

Then a woman's voice, much quieter and calmer, "Jo. Let us in please. There's been an accident. We need to talk to you".

She grabbed the snarling yapping Lulu and pulled open the door.

The outside light lit up two uniformed figures shrouded in swirling mist with fine drizzle clinging to their clothes. It was a sight that would haunt her for the rest of her life.

"What's happened?, she gasped, "Where are they?"

Cold fear and dread grasped at her heart.

"There was an accident on the motorway. I'm afraid, er", a momentary pause,

"Nothing could be done to save them."

This dreadful speech was delivered in a sighing monotone by the policewoman who approached Jo and stretched out her arms in a gesture of comfort and support.

Jo threw back her head and screamed, "No--No---not dead! They can't be! Wake me up----I'm dreaming! You're not real. Get away! Leave me alone!" and she charged at them, arms and fists flailing.

It took a lot of strength to restrain her but at last rage and fury gave way to helpless grief. Her whole being was convulsed with great heaving sobs which totally possessed her and all she could say in her anguish was, "No, no! Please no! Mum, dad, say it's not true. Come back! Oh please don't leave me!"

But it was true, and they had left her, for ever-------

The police remained with her until Matthew arrived closely followed by the doctor. She was in a state of total shock and disbelief and her moods alternated between hysteria and deep sobbing anguish. Matthew managed to hold her close and attempted to comfort her but all she could say was, "Why? Please Matthew wake me up and tell me that it's not true! Bella too---poor, poor Bella! What happened? Please wake me up Matthew and tell me it's not true!"

She repeated this cry over and over again, her body convulsed with violent uncontrollable tremors. At last the doctor was able to persuade her to accept a drink which she gulped between choking sobs. The drug had the desired effect and she gradually became calmer until she shuddered into sleep. Matthew laid her gently on the sofa, covered her with a blanket and stayed by her side, holding her hand which was limp and lifeless now.

"Poor, poor girl! First Emily and now this. How will she cope. God give her strength and help me to find the wisdom to guide and help her through it".

He closed his eyes and prayed fervently.

She lay on the sofa in a drug-induced sleep until morning. Matthew was there when she awoke. Her eyes were swollen and bloodshot, her face red and crumpled. She blinked and shivered and it took her several minutes to regain consciousness. Realisation of the tragedy slowly dawned upon her and she curled up into a sitting position and buried her face in her hands. Hysteria, dampened down

Destiny Obscure

by drugs gave way to helplessness, hopelessness, emptiness and futile acceptance.

"It's true, isn't it Matthew. Mum and Dad and 'Bella'."

This was said in a whining whisper with infinite sadness and surrender. She realised that, as with Emily, she could do nothing to turn back time. She had to deal with it herself, alone. This cruel and dreadful pain. This blinding shock. There would always be another void in her life which would eventually be encased in a deep emotional scar. At the moment it was a gaping agonising wound. She turned to Matthew. There was anguish in her pleading, "Help me please! What am I going to do? I can't live without them."

He held her shaking body close, "You have to. For Billy's sake, for their sakes and for everyone's sake. You've had a very rough deal but you must try to think positively, even more-so now."

Jo breathed deeply in an effort to control her raging emotions which were threatening to take over again. Then she spoke with a catch in her voice in a peevish tone which was almost matter-of-fact, "Mum had this dream---this burning desire. This ambition to prove herself in her chosen sport. She said she'd dreamt about it for years. We all encouraged her. Nobody expected that it would end in tragedy." Then she sobbed and choked again, "Poor, poor mum!"

"Yes," said Matthew, his voice full of sadness and sympathy as he attempted to soothe and comfort her, "Jenny had a dream and she fulfilled it. It takes a special person to put effort and determination into achieving goals. Think of all the famous mountaineers and explorers who followed their dreams. Many ended in tragedy even before the dream had been realised. Accidents, illness and death are everyday occurrences. We can try to prevent them but ultimately our lives are in the hands of fate. Fate is the hidden power which controls destiny".

"Not God then?"

"No, certainly not God. God is here to comfort and help us find the strength to cope. It's our belief which gives strength and if we don't believe in God, then we have to rely on our own inner strength. One or the other and usually both are needed to help us to defeat despair." She buried her head in his chest and breathed deeply, trying to control the wracking sobs. "It isn't true, I'll wake up soon. I'll wake up soon."

Suddenly they heard Billy crying from upstairs, "Mummy, mummy, I want to get up now!"

Jo felt a gush of anguish and anxiety as she heard this plaintive cry. How could she explain to a four-year-old that his parents were dead?

She turned to Matthew for help.

"Act as normally as you can. He'll see that you're upset, but he won't realise the extent. Explain that they've gone away---that they'll be back—sometime. Use Heaven if you like---he'll associate something nice with that. Oh dear! This will not be easy." Matthew stumbled uncharacteristically over these words and in some strange way his discomfiture gave Jo strength. Ultimately it was up to her to help her little brother cope with this traumatic and for him, incomprehensible, situation. Matthew retreated to the kitchen to make them both a cup of tea and Jo ran upstairs to her little brother. With immense effort she suppressed her pain and agony forcing them deep down inside her and taking a deep breath she entered the bedroom and took her little brother into her arms.

She brought him down and dressed him and told him in as steady a voice as she could muster that mummy and daddy had gone away for a while. He was puzzled but not tearful. He looked at her grief-stricken face, "Why Jo-Jo crying?"

"Oh, it's because they've taken 'Bella' too and I wanted to ride her. Now, Billy-Boy, what shall we do today?"

Matthew knew that this strength and reserve that Jo had marshalled would not last. Her pent-up emotions needed to be released and she needed some solitude.

"Hey Billy! How would you like to build some Lego with your uncle Mattie?" and they retreated into the lounge.

When they had gone Jo, once again gave vent to her feelings, this time with 'Georgie'. She sobbed into his silky mane, "At least I still have you! We're both orphans now but we have each other." She said this, not wanting to believe it, still hoping that she would be shaken awake and normality would return.

The gelding paused briefly in his pulling down the hay to rub his head against her. "Would he miss his mother?", she mused, "Or would he, a bit like Billy, miss her for a while and then accept the situation? And would she herself do the same? She doubted that she could ever accept it. Life had treated her so cruelly. There was no future for her. Just a bleak nothingness—a meaningless void."

For the next few days Jo was immersed totally in grief and disbelief that life could be so intensely cruel and unjust. Her moods alternated between hysterical anguish and deep soporific depression the latter induced by medication supplied by the doctor. Matthew stayed at the house and was a tower of strength until Julie arrived two days after the accident. She was devastated by the loss of her brother but true to her character blamed everything on Jenny.

"I knew this move to Wales would end in disaster! I had a premonition that it would! He didn't want to come here either! I begged him to stand firm, assert himself and refuse but she had some kind of hold on him. She bewitched him. He was never the same after she got her claws into him! Oh, Tom—if only you had listened to me!"

This discourse was delivered in a blend of sobbing anger, frustration and grief. Matthew listened quietly but said nothing except to add his condolences.

As Julie was the only adult next of kin she had the overall responsibility for dealing with the necessary practicalities which she wanted to discharge as soon as possible so she could be rid of this stressful situation. Typically, every decision had to be hers and she paid scant regard to the feelings and emotions of Jo whom she had never liked. She was no part of Tom. She was the illegitimate offspring of the hated Jenny.

Bryn Celyn would have to be sold and any residue left after settling the mortgage would have to be used to pay off other outstanding debts which, according to Julie were considerable.

"The horse will have to go too", she said firmly. "There is no way that it can kept near where we live, and the dog too. I can't have a dog in my house!"

Jo was aghast, "What! You mean both Georgie and Lulu have to go! You can't—they're all I've got left!"

She began to scream at Julie, "You are such a bitch! You can't do this! I hate you!"

"Don't you dare talk to me like that you little madam! I'll show you! You aren't coming to live with me! I'll have you put into a home for bad girls!"

"I'd rather go to hell than live anywhere near you!" Jo yelled and began to shake uncontrollably.

Matthew tried to mediate, "Calm down, both of you." He turned to Jo and said gently, "Jo love, Julie's right. She can't keep or be responsible for Lulu or Georgie".

"What! You too! Siding with her!" Jo face him incredulously.

"Listen, love," he responded gently, "I have an idea. I'll keep Lulu until such a time as when you can have her back. And why don't we ask the local riding school to take Georgie on loan for a while. I know you like Louise and she will take good care of him and I promise to keep an eye on him too".

"Wait a minute!" shrieked Julie, "That horse must be worth several thousand pounds and believe me the money will be needed to pay off all the debts. They didn't have any insurance at all, not even life insurance and the funeral arrangements will cost a fortune!"

"If there isn't enough money left after the sale of the house, I will buy the horse", said Matthew quietly and firmly, "So let's not have any more of this futile arguing. I will buy him and he can stay at the riding school until Jo can decide what she wants to do with him. We are all in a state of shock and grief. Quarrelling like this and all this tension is no good for us or the present situation and certainly not for the memory of Tom and Jenny. So, let's control our emotions and make rational decisions".

So that was that, for the time being at least.

The next bone of contention arose when Julie announced that she wanted to make arrangements for the cremation and whether the bodies after post-mortem should be brought back to Wales or to her home in Lancashire.

Jo pleaded with Matthew to insist that they were brought back to Bryn Celyn and buried in Bluebell wood which they had chosen as their ultimate resting place.

Julie was furious, she was determined that they must be cremated and their ashes scattered on the family grave where their parents were buried.

Jo beside herself with frustration, recounted to Matthew the day when she and Jenny had sat in Bluebell Wood and Jenny had told her that it was their dearest wish that they should be buried together under the birch tree where they had had known such nuptial bliss and where Billy had been conceived—the ultimate fruit of their relationship.

Matthew was moved by this and promised that he would do his best to ensure that this final wish was honoured.

Julie fought against it insisting that as they had not previously registered their intentions with the local authority it would be illegal.

Matthew, deeply affected by the loss of his friends and peeved at Julie's intransigence and insensibility, visited the local authority offices.

He convinced them that he had been testimony to this last request. Much discussion ensued about 'proper procedures' but his arguments were lucid and convincing. At last because of his respected position in society the inevitable 'red tape' was ignored and permission was granted.

All he had to do now was to convince Julie that this was the best thing to do. Used to having her own way, Julie was unwilling to give in but Matthew promised to take care of all the necessary funeral arrangements. He would provide biodegradable coffins, organise the digging of the graves and personally administer the last rites. It was what they wanted, both of them. If it didn't happen he would have broken his word to Tom, his best friend. No-one should ever break their word. That was a fundamental part of his Christian teaching. Surely Julie could not be responsible for encouraging him do just that! Thus he urged, argued and pleaded, appealing to her better nature, which if she possessed, she kept hidden. Also, he asserted that the cost would be minimal compared to a formal funeral which could amount to several thousand pounds. Eventually, with a bad grace she gave in and agreed

The bodies could not be released until post-mortems had been carried out and this could not be done until after the Christmas recess so the suggested date for the funeral was January 6th twelfth night.

Julie went home before Christmas and Billy was happy to go with her. He sensed that there was something wrong at Bryn Celyn and he had spent many happy times being indulged by Julie when he had stayed there with Tom. Also he had an inkling that maybe his parents would reappear there—at least this is what he had been led to believe.

Jo could not bear to spend Christmas at Bryn Celyn and so she stayed at the vicarage where Matthew and his mother did their best to salve her wounds. She was excused attendance at the Christmas Eve Carol Service. She did not want to be the centre of attention for the congregation, well-meaning as it would be. She crept into bed in the high ceilinged bedroom followed by a downhearted Lulu and they cuddled and shivered until sleep, nature's soft nurse, overcame them.

It was the most miserable and meaningless Christmas of Jo's life.

Georgie was taken to the local riding school where Louise was pleased to accept him on loan. So that was that! What else was there left for her to worry about. Nothing except herself. What would she do? Where should she go?

On the morning of New Year's Eve Matthew suggested that they go for a walk on the mountain. Jo concurred. They walked in silence through the farmyard and up the field until they reached Bluebell Wood.

"I'd like to plant a tree for them—like we did for Emily but I can't decide which sort. What do you think----something different to all the other trees in the wood. Something meaningful."

Matthew considered for several minutes then suggested thoughtfully," How about a Ginkgo Biloba?"

"A what?"

"Gingko Biloba. It's a unique tree, native to China. In fact it's their national tree. It's been around for millions of years, a living link to dinosaurs and botanically, the only link between ferns and pine trees. It's long-lived too. Some in Chinese monasteries are believed to be over a thousand years old! And it's a very tough tree—almost indestructible. You've heard of Hiroshima?"

"Oh, yes. When the allies dropped atomic bombs which obliterated a huge area killing and destroying human, animal and plant life and radio-active fall-out caused cancers for years afterwards."

"Yes", he relied sombrely, "A particularly chilling part of recent history," He paused, then continued, "Well, out of the charred remains when all other species had been destroyed, Gingko Bilobas survived and grew again. Pretty amazing! It is meaningful for you too because it known as the memory tree. It's nuts and leaves are said to be good for memory retention".

"What does it look like and how big does it grow?"

"It grows very slowly at first and doesn't reach full maturity until about thirty years. After that it grows more quickly and can grow to thirty metres. The leaves are shiny green, fan-shaped and with a split in the middle, hence biloba, two lobes, very distinctive, and they turn yellow in autumn. I think it would be a perfect tree to plant for your parents".

"How come you know so much about it?"

"We planted one in Cornwall in memory of my father. That one must be reacing maturity now. Thinking about it makes me feel guilty. I haven't been back there for ages and I think mother would like to revisit her old haunts".

They walked on in silence each preoccupied with their own thoughts, then Jo said suddenly, "I'll plant a Gingko. We'll get one tomorrow".

Matthew smiled and said, "And I'll talk to mum about a trip to Cornwall".

Jo looked at Matthew and realised how much she had come to depend on him. He was a mentor and a very good and reliable friend. She owed him so much.

She was the next to speak, "Thank you for persuading Julie to allow mum and dad to be buried here. It's what they wanted and I promised mum I would see to it." Her voice broke, "I didn't expect it would be so soon though. Will the people who buy it allow us to come and visit?"

"Well, the exact spot has to be marked on the deeds and we can specify that family be allowed access, even if that access has to be limited. We mustn't mention that to Julie though because she'll think it will lower the value of the property. She may know already. She's probably making enquiries right now." He grimaced as he said this.

Jo's voice shook with anger tinged by despair, "I hate her and she hates me. Will I have to go and live with her? I don't want to. I'm not going to. I'd rather be fostered than that."

Matthew thought for a moment then stooped to pick up the stick which Lulu had dropped at his feet.

"Whatever is decided, you've only got to put up with it for two years. As soon as you reach sixteen you can please yourself." And he threw the stick as far as he could for the distracted dog.

"Thank you for taking on Lulu too. I know she'll be happy with you."

"I've always wanted a dog," confided Matthew. "My mother was always dead against it but she's changed her mind now after having Lulu for a few days and when you're in a position to have her back, she'll be waiting for you."

"Georgie too is settled, thanks to you. Louise has promised to take good care of him until I can have him back. Two years isn't such a long time. Really Matthew, if it wasn't for you, I wouldn't want to live any more." Again the catch in her voice and the tightly clenched hands. He resisted the temptation to hug her feeling that this would trigger a torrent of sobbing emotion. Instead, he stared at the surrounding stark rocks and pondered upon how much she had matured over the last year and reflected on how tragedy can affect different people in different ways. Some crumble and are unable to cope often turning to religion for comfort; others rely on drugs: some seek blame and revenge. Thankfully there those who discover strength within themselves and are, in time, able to use this to build moral fibre. This moral fibre not only helps them to deal with adversity but it also enables them to empathise with and to help others. This is what he hoped would happen to Jo. He placed his hands on her shoulders and turned her towards him, "Come on now, you're doing fine. You still have Billy too. What would he do without you?"

Jo felt unable to answer this question. Billy would be with Julie and she knew he would settle there. After all, Julie had brought up Tom. Billy would be a Tom substitute. She, knew, however, that there was no way that she could live with Julie even though this was the generally accepted solution. What was the alternative for her? A foster home like Kate? Misery enveloped her again.

They trudged on in silence as the grey clouds glowered above them and the chill wind became stronger. The much-loved familiar environment seemed stark and hostile and the large rocks which had littered the hillside for centuries seemed menacing and ready to upheave and hurl themselves upon the unsuspecting village.

She was not enjoying this walk. She had believed that it would be therapeutic and soothing to her soul to relive some of the carefree and joyful times she had shared with her parents. They had all felt that they belonged here and were part of nature's changing moods and scenes. Today she felt like an intrusive stranger lost in a threatening and alien environment.

Matthew shaed her misery and suggested that they return to the farm.

The farmyard and house also had a bleak and uninviting aura and she had no wish to enter. To look upon it caused a stab of pain in her heart.

They made their way slowly down the lane towards the church and the adjacent vicarage.

Jo felt weary and defenceless. All the anguish and anger which had possessed her drained away. She felt empty and incapable. A bleak and uncertain future loomed ahead.

Chapter 16

On January 2nd Kate arrived at the vicarage feeling awkward and discomfited. She and Jo stared at each other, at first feeling like strangers. Kate shuffled uncomfortably on the doorstep then mumbled, "Er, sorry to hear about your parents."

Her natural reticence prevented her from rushing to hug her friend and Jo would not have reacted well to this either so they both stood rooted to the spot for several moments until Matthew appeared.

"Hello Kate, welcome back! Did you have a good holiday?" without waiting for a reply he continued, "I hope you're feeling fit. I have a strenuous job for you today."

He had organised a couple of men from the village to help him and Jo to prepare the burial site in Bluebell Wood. He explained to Kate what they would be doing and she stifled her surprise and readily agreed to help.

Jo had insisted on playing her part, weird and traumatic though it seemed to the less pragmatic. Thus, armed with pick-axes and spades they made their way to Bluebell Wood.

Jo indicated the exact spot and they all set about tearing up the resisting turf. Dozens of bluebell bulbs were unearthed and Jo looked anxiously at Matthew. He read her mind and said, "Steady on guys, we have to preserve the bulbs as we'll be be replacing them all soon!" They complied and carried on digging, panting from their exertions and tossing the unearthed bulbs to the side. It was hard physical work and for Jo it was mental masochism to be digging her parent's grave but she knew she was toiling to fulfil their last wishes. It would have been so much easier to succumb to Julie, to let her take over and have her way with this as with everything else. Jo gritted her teeth and took strength from reliving the closeness she had felt to her mother that afternoon in Bluebell Wood when she had made the promise that this cherished spot would be the eternal resting place for her and Tom. Had she failed to keep this promise she would have regretted it for the rest of her life. The men who came to help were surprised and intrigued to see a girl digging her own parents grave! It seemed weirdly bizarre to them and they paused from time to time from their labours to regard the small strong body totally absorbed in the dreadful task. They looked at Kate too and wondered why she should involve herself. Kate became aware of the older one leaning on his spade contemplatively so she broke the silence, "Is this what you do for a living? I mean, is this your job, grave-digging?" This was said derisively, almost belligerently.

He pushed his cap further back on his head and stared thoughtfully at this strange rude girl before answering wearily, "Not all the time, now. Only if I'm asked. There's not much call for it these days. Most of the churchyards are full and most people are cremated anyway. Not that I

Destiny Obscure

agree with that, but if everyone was buried, we'd soon run out of space."

"Yes," rejoined his companion, "You're lucky. You've got the choice and you don't have to pay for it either. Plots cost a fortune these days."

Aghast at his bluntness, Jo paused to stare at him. Is this the sum total of their sentiment? Pure pragmatism? She came to the conclusion that for many people, finer feelings were a rarity and easily outflanked by financial and conventional considerations. Then she asked herself if it was finer feelings that were compelling her to do this arduous task. Or was it sheer cussedness? Both—-or neither? She truly felt that she was doing it for love and duty and consoled herself with the thought that her parents would approve and be proud of her.

The hole grew deeper and soon the ground surface was above her head. Her arms ached with the effort of throwing out the heavy damp soil but she did not weaken. Zombi-like she dug and threw—mentally and physically aware of nothing but the burning in her limbs and the hard physical toil. She was not unaware though of the outraged hurry and scurry of the myriads of insects whose eternal sanctuary was being disrupted and destroyed. She apologised mentally to them as she remembered Emily's reverence for all living creatures. So wickedly cruel that she should be deprived of her own life so young, so full of potential. She closed her eyes, drew a deep breath and summoned all that inner strength that Matthew had urged her to draw upon and then with tightly clenched teeth she continued with renewed vigour.

Eventually the job was finished and Matthew hauled her out. It was then that she became acutely conscious of her burning limbs and blistered hands and the thick cloying clods of earth sticking to her boots.

The toil and effort had focused Jo's mind and the stark reality did not hit her until the job was done and a black gaping hole lay beneath them ---a void soon to be filled by the bodies of Tom and Jenny.

She began to shake and was surprised and embarrassed to feel the sudden warm grasp of Kate's hand. She withdrew her own hand quickly and choked down the surge of emotion threatening to overwhelm her.

She was strong! She did not want sympathy or people assuming that she could not and was not coping. Again the physical exercise had denuded her of the energy to react emotionally. She would let rip with her suppressed feelings when she was alone. She would bawl, beat her breast, tear her hair, give vent to all her bottled-up emotions. She would do it as an intensely private act. No-one could interfere or judge her or try to salve her pain with platitudes, however well-meant. This would be her way of dealing with the dreadful adversities fate had forced upon her. Stand alone to be strong.

One more task remained which she and Matthew would undertake together. The planting of the Ginko Biloba. This would be done after the burial.

The next few days were taken up with the legal formalities surrounding the accident. Once these were completed the bodies of Tom and Jenny were delivered to Bryn Celyn where they lay in their biodegradable coffins.

Julie arrived the day before with dismal Desmond, the Doormat, tagging along beside her. She was appalled at the sight of the coffins. To think that this is how he should end up---a paupers funeral in a paper bag! After all she had done and sacrificed for him—the best years of her life ensuring him an Oxford education. All that to be dragged down by that back-street bitch and culminate in this! She wept bitterly, for herself and her shattered dreams. He could have and should have done so much more with his life after all the opportunities she had set out before him. This was not what she had destined for him. Cruel, cruel fate had intervened once more and *she* felt like the victim.

The cause of the accident according to the police had been Tom, falling asleep at the wheel. No trace of alcohol or drugs had been found in either of the bodies. The car and trailer had veered in front of a 17 ton lorry. Luckily no other vehicle had been involved. Tom's utter worn-out exhaustion as Julie saw it, gave her yet another reason to blame Jenny. Her thoughts ran on bitterly in tune with the smarting tears running slowly down her crumpled careworn face. Why did Jenny make him drive? She was probably asleep herself, selfish cow, when it happened. Poor Tom. That bitch had completely taken over his life and was instrumental in causing his death. Poor, poor Tom. At least in Billy she would have a part of him to care for as she'd done for him after their parents died. Strange how history often repeats itself---their parents too had been killed in a terrible car accident. She wiped the tears away fiercely with a crumpled paper tissue as she remembered the shame and blame of her parent's accident. At least Tom hadn't been drunk and nobody else had been hurt or injured!

The funeral went ahead on January 6th as planned. The only people in attendance were Julie and dismal Desmond, Jo, Kate, Matthew, a sad and subdued Lulu and the two men who had helped prepare the grave. By common concurrence, Billy had been left at the vicarage with Megan. It was a sombre scene on a dismal day. It seemed fittingly ironic that they should be laid to rest on Twelfth Night, the day when a celebrated festival finishes and frivolous trappings are taken down. This was no celebration of Epiphany, no thought of the Magi celebrating the birth of the baby Jesus as was the custom in many other Christian countries. This was the end of the mortal lives of Tom and Jenny. Their celebrated lives were being consigned to hibernation, purgatory, thence to be re-awakened on Judgement Day. Jo wished she could believe it.

Following a brief but poignant sermon delivered by Matthew in which he avoided alluding to stereotypical religion, Tom and Jenny were laid to rest, albeit prematurely, in that hallowed place that had always been so special to them.

He ended with an extract from Keats', 'Ode to a Nightingale', which he knew they had loved and which would be meaningful,

> *I cannot see what flowers are at my feet,*
> *Nor what soft incense hangs upon the boughs,*
> *But, in embalmed darkness, guess each sweet*
> *Wherewith the seasonable month endows*
> *The grass, the thicket, and the fruit-tree wild;*
> *White hawthorn, and the pastoral eglantine;*
> *Fast-fading violets covered up in leaves;*
> *And mid-May's eldest child*
> *The coming musk-rose, full of dewy wine,*
> *The murmurous haunt of flies on summer eves.*

There was complete silence. It was such a fitting tribute.

That night Jo crept to bed in the vicarage bedroom and shivered between the starched sheets with a tightly curled-up Lulu at her feet. The faithful sensitive animal knew that there was something tragically wrong and her way of dealing with it was to retreat into herself and shut out everything else. Jo, feeling utterly alone and devoid of comfort wished she were not here, that this was not reality but an awful dream from which she would soon be awakened and back in the real world—if only---! She tossed and turned until at last she lapsed into a troubled sleep. She was on a strange featureless beach. The restless body of the sea was dark, deep and swollen with pent-up power. The white-tipped waves crawled across the sand eerily but somehow beguiling and beckoning. There was no retreat and the crawling waves were silent, soundless.

Her parents were walking ahead of her slowly yet purposefully towards the summoning sea. Jo yelled to them to wait for her, but there was no reaction. She tried to run to catch them up but could make no progress. They were moving further and further away inexorably, oblivious to everything except their mission.

"Mum, dad, please wait!" she felt desperate now but still no response. She redoubled her efforts to run after them but the distance between them remained the same. She watched helplessly, panic- stricken as they walked steadily side by side, deeper and deeper--ankles, knees, hips shoulders into the quietly waiting sea. She screamed and struggled desperately to follow. The last she saw of them was their heads disappearing, engulfed, devoured.

"No! No! Oh please no!" Suddenly she was released from the powerful magnetic grip of the sand and she charged heedlessly towards the crawling foam. Just as she arrived at the water's edge a monstrous wave loomed up in front of her barring her way, smashing her down, engulfing her, smothering her. She struggled violently, gripped by uncontrollable hysteria. She could neither escape nor breathe. Gasping, choking, terror-stricken, she became vaguely aware of a bright light, restraining hands and calm comforting voices.

"It's alright. You've had a bad dream. You're safe now." Matthew and his mother were there wiping the sweat from her face, holding her hand. She was ghastly white and seemed strangely detached from reality.

"Don't leave me! Oh please don't leave me!" she begged.

They held her close and took turns to stay with her throughout the rest of the night. Lulu shrank away and slunk downstairs and curled up even more tightly in the darkest corner under the stairs.

The following morning when she recounted the dream to Matthew he interpreted it in a way which gave her little comfort but made sense to her. He said that it was telling her that it was futile to try to follow her parents. She must accept that they are untouchable and that it would be self-destructive to attempt to join them. The monstrous wave was testimony to that. It was a warning for her not to meddle in a situation that was irreversible. She accepted this interpretation but shuddered as she tried to come to terms with the implication. Matthew maintained that she could and should gain comfort from the fact that they walked willingly and peacefully towards their destiny and that they were together for eternity. Nothing could harm or hurt them now.

After the traumatic dream Jo, still in a state of detachment and disbelief, wandered through the ensuing days with no idea of the future. It was as if she were completely under the influence and control of all those around her and atypically, she appeared to accept and concur. However, this apparent subjugation was a ploy to distract those who had total control over her immediate destiny from even imagining her real intentions. She had decided that she must escape from the constraints and decisions about her life that authority had the power to impose upon her. She convinced herself that she needed to start a new life far away from here. In other words, she planned to 'run away'. She felt that if she stayed in this area which now held so many traumatic and tragic memories she would shrivel into deep depression and even become suicidal. She had to get away. She needn't do it alone. Kate she knew would be complicit. They could embark upon this adventure together. It just needed planning—careful planning. It was the only way out.

Kate had returned unwillingly to school. Jo had not. She had the perfect excuse that for the moment she was not strong enough emotionally.

On Saturday the two girls went for a walk with Lulu.

"Let's kill your dream," urged Kate. "Let's go to the beach. What was it Hamlet said 'er, lets -'take up arms against a sea of troubles and by opposing, end them!"

Jo agreed. Her inner strength was turning into defiance.

It was a miserable day, dull and drizzly but they didn't care. They were together and about to plan their daring and unlawful adventure. Lulu, frivolous and oblivious was now in her element. The beach was Lulu's very favourite place and she leapt in and out of the sea chasing seagulls and shaking the life out of huge strands of smelly seaweed. She raised the spirits of the girls as they laughed at her antics.

"I envy dogs", said Jo. "They experience physical and mental pain and loss but after a short time they get over it and continue with their lives as usual."

"She's not been through what you've been through and some dogs carry the scars that bad owners impose upon them for ever. But I know what you mean. Look at her now—she's more like a puppy than an eight-year-old!"

They laughed and walked on until they reached a sheltered spot where they sat leaning their backs against the rocks.

"Are you sure you want to do this?" asked Jo earnestly.

"'Course I am. I've wanted to do it for years but not had anybody to do it with."

"Well, it needs careful planning. They're bound to alert the police and be looking everywhere for us and we mustn't be caught or we'll end up in some bloody juvenile prison where they'll lock us up to make sure we can't do it again."

This prospect made them both shudder but did not weaken their resolve.

"I've thought a lot about it and decided that we should avoid London. Everybody seems to go there and that's where they'll concentrate their search. Also, I don't think I could stand living there. Too many people—bad buggers too!

I think we should go somewhere like the Scottish Highlands. We'll be more anonymous there and they'll never think of looking for us up there either."

"I've never been to Scotland, have you?"

"No, but my mother used to talk about it a lot. She used to go up there with her mum and dad, camping and walking. They were a bit crazy my grandparents. They could never settle anywhere for long. They were always off on one adventure or another. Poor mum used to be palmed off on kindly neighbours while they went off adventuring. That's how she got into horses. She lived at the local riding school when they were away. Granddad spent years building his own yacht. Then when mum left school they sold the house, and planned another trip—sailing round the world! Mum didn't want to go so she went to university instead and met my dad, my real dad, Joe—I'm called after him. He was crazy too and got killed on his motor bike before I was born. Mum was only nineteen—pregnant, single, no house, no money, nothing. She went back to the riding school, to Liz and Brian who were like parents to her. She worked and lived there with me until she met Tom. They got married and came to live in Wales. There you are—a potted history of my life".

"Wow, that's quite a story! What happened to your grandparents"

"Well, nobody knows for sure but it's assumed that they were lost at sea. Mum never knew my real dad- Joe's- parents. He was brought up in care, a bit like you I suppose. Tom's parents died in a road accident too. Weird!" She paused then went on, "That's how come he was brought up by Julie. Now it's your turn to spill the beans about your family."

Kate stiffened and seized a handful of sand which she squeezed until her knuckles went white.

"I can't. It's too horrible. I'm too ashamed".

Jo turned to face her friend but resisted the temptation to make physical contact

"Don't be ashamed—whatever it is I will still be your friend and stand by you. Please trust me. This secrecy is the only thing that stands between us now. I just feel that you can't or don't trust me. Please trust me. I will understand and support you however bad it is. Whatever it is won't weaken our friendship. In fact it will strengthen it as this mystery surrounding you and the fact that you don't trust me enough to share it is a rift between us."

Kate flung the sand away and thrust her hands deeply into the dry coarse grains as far as she could then withdrew them and hugged her knees close to her chest burying her head in the space between.

There was a long silence as Kate struggled to take control of her emotions. Jo remained patient, waiting, listening.

Kate began in a voice strained and tight, forced from a constricted throat, "When I was a little girl my father used to play with me. He called it tickling." She choked before continuing, "He told me it was our special secret, our precious time together and I wasn't to tell anyone or we couldn't play any more. I liked it and didn't want it to stop so I didn't tell anybody. It got worse and became more than tickling but I still liked it and didn't want him to stop." Her whole body convulsed with emotion and gasping sobs retched from her lungs and throat. "I can't remember just how old I was before I realised that it was wrong, very wrong and even dirty and disgusting in the eyes of other people. I didn't care at first. I liked it and looked forward to him coming into my bedroom—how disgusting is that! How horribly disgusting is that! I was always *going* to tell him the next time. Tell him that it was wrong. But I never did---I *liked* it. I never wanted him to stop. Sometimes he would tease me and ask me if I wanted him to stop. *'Say please'* he would ask and I would beg him *not* to stop! How horrible is that! I'm so ashamed of myself. So, so ashamed! I felt so dirty and disgusting after it and promised myself that it was the last time but it was a like a drug—a wicked horrid habit that I loved and couldn't resist." The sobs became loud anguished cries and her convulsions more violent as her body rocked back and forth and tears and nasal slime covered her face which was contorted with pain. "I had no friends—no-one I could trust. I was too ashamed. I felt tainted. I had nobody close to me except *him!*" She wailed, gasping and coughing, her face covered in mucous which she was unable to wipe away as her hands were covered in sand.

Jo whipped off her silky scarf and handed it to her friend who accepted it gratefully and buried her face in its warm soft comfort.

"What about your mother? Couldn't you tell her?"

"No, my mother was a naïve stupid cow and I know she would have blamed me---just like she did in the end. There was no-one I could trust except my Auntie Beth but she was away a lot of the time and I was never alone with her. She loved me and I was even scared to tell her as I thought that even she would be ashamed of me." Kate rocked back and forth, her whole body taut with powerful feelings of guilt and shame.

Jo remained perfectly still and quiet allowing Kate to give full vent to her overwhelming emotions. Eventually the release of these pent-up feelings enabled Kate to continue in a calmer, more measured way but the sobs and chokes could not be completely suppressed. She sat up straighter and more stiffly and continued between residual sobs, "I got pregnant. I was only twelve. He told me what to do. I was to tell my mother that I'd been a naughty girl with a man on a building site near school. I didn't know him and they'd gone now so there was no chance of catching him. I said this to her and she was very angry with me and told the police. They kept on and on questioning me. They knew it was a lie. In the end I told them the truth. My mother went berserk and said she would kill my father but she said it was my fault for not telling her."

She paused and rubbed the coarse sand hard between her hands as if this punishing pain was partial absolution. She battled with her emotions then added, "Anyway, I had an abortion". She paused again and dug her hands deeper into the rough sand. Her face was screwed up tightly and it took a great deal of effort before she could continue. When she did so her tone was strangely matter-of-fact. "The nurses were very kind. They felt sorry for me but I felt guilty and ashamed because I was to blame. I hated myself! I could have told him to stop or told my mother but I didn't want to tell her because I was ashamed and it was all my fault and I knew that it would ruin everybody's lives--- my two younger brothers, my grandparents, everybody. I was so ashamed—I felt so dirty that I couldn't tell anyone—at first not even my auntie Beth who was the only adult I really liked and trusted. I didn't want her to know how weak and stupid I was. Anyway, when it all came out she was somewhere abroad. She and my mother never got on. Another pause, then, "If only I'd told him to *stop! Made him stop!*" These last words were screamed out as she re-lived the past. More silence followed apart from residual snivels and gasping intakes of breath.

Jo, shocked and upset by these revelations sat still and said nothing.

Kate continued, "All their lives are ruined anyway now and it's all my fault. My father got sent to prison for five years and my mother could no longer bear to be near me so I was taken into care. I spent nearly two years in a home and then they found the foster parents for me and that's how I came to be here. Nobody in my family knows or cares about me now except Aunty Beth and I haven't seen or heard from her for ages. She and my mother had a massive row. I hate my mother and I never want to see or hear anything about her ever again!" A touch of defiance, even rage, in these final words.

At last all the guilt and shame which had been bottled up inside her was now released and the hard impenetrable shell she had built around herself had disintegrated and melted away. Now Jo dared to hug her. The slim body, still shaking with emotion, felt so helpless and vulnerable to Jo as she held her close. For a long time neither of them spoke and the convulsive sobs and sniffles diminished then disappeared and the only sound on that lonely beach was the ceaseless ebb and flow of the tide, powerful yet poignant and into Jo's conscious mind crept the lines from Matthew Arnold's poem, Dover Beach,

> *Begin, and cease, and then again begin*
> *With tremulous cadence slow, and bring*
> *The eternal note of sadness in------*
> *The turbid ebb and flow of human misery----*

She shivered and felt herself being overcome again by her *own* misery. This would not do! She must be strong for herself and for Kate especially now she had been allowed to penetrate Kate's darkest secrets, so she held her friend even closer and said in a firm but gentle voice,

"Don't ever think you are remotely guilty for any of this. You were an innocent child taken advantage of. The law and everyone recognises this, which is why your father was punished. He intimidated and blackmailed you and gave you this guilt complex and for you that's a normal reaction. This is why other people who've endured what you've been through don't tell anyone until years after. They feel guilty and ashamed too, as if somehow it's their own fault. They only find courage to tell when it becomes known that other vulnerable children have been taken advantage of. They realise then that they are innocent victims. So you see it wasn't your fault. You are certainly not to blame. Please, Kate, believe that". She paused, then with heart-felt emotion, "Come on now---try to put it all behind you and look forward instead to our big adventure!"

She hugged the still quivering body more tightly then the realisation of the whole purpose of their visit to the beach flashed into her mind and she released Kate, sat up straight, rubbed her hands together and with the air of a sergeant issuing orders to his troops, she began, "OK, let's get down to details. "The first thing is for us both to join the YHA that way we'll have somewhere to stay at first and we can use the hostels as a base and maybe look around and find jobs in the area. I think if we join before we go then the wardens won't scrutinise us at all and no-one will think of looking for us in a Youth Hostel especially if we go somewhere remote. We'll be far away from the police and the media and they'll stick our names on a list of 'Missing Persons' and after a month or so other newer and more exciting things will occupy their time and interest and 'Hey Presto', we'll be forgotten and free!"

Kate, still emotionally abject, listened but said nothing.

Jo, warming to her subject continued, "I'll have the membership cards for both of us, under false names, sent to the vicarage and I'll make sure that I'm around when they're delivered so Matthew won't suspect anything. You must pack a rucksack in secret and hide it. Just take what ever clothes you think you'll need, say a couple of spare sets, a large poly bag for dirty washing et cetera. We'll make a list. If you haven't got a sleeping bag I can lend you one, and bring however much money you can scrounge. I reckon we can have everything organised in less than a couple of weeks".

All this was said with mounting excitement and Jo, in a sudden rush of wild frenzy noticed Lulu still leaping in and out of the sea snapping at the waves, and had a crazy urge to join her.

She seized Kate and dragged her to her feet.

"Come on!" she yelled, whipping off her shoes, and outer clothing, "Let's wash all the dirt and crap away from us, inside and outside. Nothing better than the sea for that!" and she bounded through the shingly sand towards the crashing waves. Momentarily taken aback, Kate paused, then with a wild shriek, she too tore off her outer garments, charged after her friend and launched herself into the sea.

It was bitterly cold and the waves were wild and strong and hurled themselves at the heedless girls who shrieked and screamed and thrashed about. Lulu barked frenzied encouragement from the safety of the shore. Jo and Kate accepted the challenge thrown at them by the wild, uncaring sea, overcame the physical pain and acute discomfort and felt strong and elated. They were champions, conquerors! The potentially destructive emotions which had plagued them both were washed away, annihilated---at least for the present.

Chapter 17

There was a lot to sort out at Bryn Celyn. Matthew decided that the sooner things were done the better it would be. Jo dreaded returning to Bryn Celyn, the place which had until recently been a welcoming refuge full of warmth and love. Now, even as they approached, it looked dreary, dull and lifeless. The drizzling rain trickled tears of misery down the windows and the creak of the heavy door as they entered was like a whine of pain and surrender to abandonment and neglect.

The ghosts of her parents were everywhere and deep dark nostalgia possessed her. She was pale and detached as she wandered wearily from room to room collecting personal belongings which she thought would be useful or even crucial to her in the immediate future. She selected sleeping bags and large rucksacks which she succeeded in secreting in a copious suitcase hoping that no-one would notice and question her need for such items.

Matthew too felt deep pangs of pain and regret but he hid his innermost feelings and concentrated on the tasks in hand.

The house needed to be cleared and put on the market. Matthew and Julie cooperated in this respect. Matthew organised a local Estate Agent to value and sell the house. Furniture which could not be sold would be dispersed amongst various charities. Julie took charge of all Tom's personal effects but showed scant interest in Jenny's. Matthew took care of these as he believed that ultimately Jo would like them. Jo did not want to participate in this clearing away of her parents' lives so she was content to leave this to the adults. She knew that Matthew would do his best for her. From the bedroom he took the picture of 'Vagabonde' believing that one day Jo would treasure it as her mother had and value it as the only tangible link to her maternal grandparents.

They had pretty well finished when Julie arrived slamming the car door and striding up to the house leaving Dismal Desmond alone in the passenger seat. Lulu ran to greet her but Julie pushed her away roughly snarling, "Get down you dirty dog!" Lulu retreated, and slunk back to Jo, her tail between her legs.

Jo had little to say to Julie. There was a great gulf between them but she did venture to enquire about Billy. Julie assured her that he was well mentally and physically and that he still sometimes asked when he would see his parents and Jo again.

"I told him that you would be coming quite soon to live with us. I think that's what the authorities will decide. I know we have had our differences but should they decide that it's the best option for you, then we will both have to make an effort to try to get on better. I know Billy would love you to be with us so we'll just have wait and see".

This was delivered in a toneless matter-of-fact way and Jo's only reaction was a heavy sigh which Julie took to be resignation.

Julie then went from room to room with Matthew and decided that the furniture was of no real value and that he could dispose of it as he thought fit.

At last, Julie took leave of them, her car tyres blowing up the dust and scattering stones as the car screeched its way through the farmyard. It was to Jo a defiant 'up yours' departure. Jo, glad to see the back of her, stuck out her tongue, a childish rebellious reaction. She was sorely tempted to stick two fingers up too but did not want to shock or upset Matthew.

It was now nearly two weeks since the funeral and time for definite decisions to be made regarding Jo's future. Matthew was in a cleft stick. The authorities wanted a decision to be made and a conclusion reached. That would be their job done and the file on Jo Weston, orphan, could be filed away and forgotten. He knew that Jo trusted him. She had no-one else. Ultimately she would follow his guidance. Accordingly, on Wednesday evening after he returned from the school Chess Club, they sat down together by a glowing fire in the large vicarage lounge. To Jo it felt formal and austere. It didn't have the emotional comfort and cosiness that had embodied Bryn Celyn. The sombre picture of Christ on the cross dominated the wall above the hearth. For the first time in her life Jo felt an empathy with this image of suffering and forbearance. Matthew was the first to speak, "We missed you at Chess Club, especially Kate. She has no competition now you're not there. She ended up playing against the computer. We'll have to get her here one night"

"Yes, that would be nice," said Jo, flatly. She knew the purpose of this evening's talk and did not relish deceiving Matthew into believing that she would do whatever he thought best but she knew that this was what she must do.

"Well Jo", he hesitated" Er, we have to decide what you want to do. Julie has the ultimate power over the next couple of years as she's your nearest relative".

"She's not a blood relative, thank God, and she hates me."

"I don't think she does hate you. I think she wants a truce now. At least that's the impression I got from her last week. And just think, you'll be with Billy. He would love that. Also, you'll have new start in a new school with new friends".

Jo grimaced, so he continued, "If you really want to, you can stay here. I know mum's a bit grumpy at times but her heart's in the right place and you'd be with Kate."

Jo sighed deeply, "Thanks, Matthew. You've always been so good to me and so has your mum. It's just that as long as I am here I can never forget what happened to us." she choked, then continued, "I have to get away so I can build that high mental wall you told me about. Every time I try, I can't find any rocks, just sand which runs through my fingers. No substance. No good. I have to get away". She stared at him and wrung her hands.

"So you'll agree to go to Julie?"

"I don't have a choice do I? And like you said, it's only for two years".

He relaxed and rubbed his hands together in the manner of someone for whom a problem has just been solved.

"Good girl. I'll drive you up there if you like. How about next week?"

This was not what she wanted to hear. This did not fit in at all with her plans.

She hesitated, then said in a cool and measured tone, "Thank you, Matthew, but that is not a good idea because if you did come with me it would be much harder to let go of my past. I would want you to stay and wouldn't be able to bear watching you drive away. No, just take me to the station and the train will take me away from here to a new start and it will be easier to look forwards instead of backwards".

At that moment Matthew's mother came in with tea and cake for them.

Jo thought she looked older tonight. Was it the added stress she had suffered recently on her account? Poor old thing. She must be in her eighties. Matthew she judged to be in his mid-forties. Was she his real mother or was he adopted too?

When she had left the room Jo looked at Matthew and enquired, "When are you going to take your mother to Cornwall to visit your father's grave? Remember you said you were going to when we got the Ginkgo tree?".

"Ah yes, I must organise that."

She went on,"You know all about my family and background but I nothing about you. Was your dad Welsh too?"

"No, he was Cornish, but the Cornish and Welsh have a great affiliation and strong historical ties. They are both Celtic in origin and shared the original Brythonic language. They feel themselves to be the true Ancient Britons dating back to before the Roman conquest. Anyway, mum is ethnic Welsh, born in Aberystwyth. They met on holiday at Land's

End in Cornwall. Dad was a vicar and mum a teacher. They got married. Mum was in her mid-thirties and dad in his early fifties. I was born five years later, an only child, when mum was pushing forty. I followed in dad's footsteps and went to Oxford to study theology and religion. When dad died mum hankered to come back to Wales. I landed this job seven years ago and we are both quite settled here now. Neither of my parents has any brothers or sisters so I haven't any family ties. So that's it. My uneventful life story!".

"Better to have an uneventful life story than one full of tragic events". She said mournfully.

He sensed the onset of self-pity in her voice and demeanour so he rapidly changed the subject. "When should we tell Julie that you've agreed to stay with her? And is there anything you want to do before you leave?"

"Well, I should like to see Georgie again and see how Louise is getting on with him and er, to say goodbye to Kate. It's Wednesday today, do you think we could organise everything for next Sunday?"

He agreed. So that was it. She shivered in excitement. She and Kate would make their final plans this week.

Part of her plan was to write a letter to Matthew explaining that they were running away and begging him not to worry about them. In it she would apologise for deceiving him and explain that if they did encounter any serious problems or mishaps she would contact him. She would end with, "Remember, dearest Matthew, 'no news is good news' and I'll definitely contact you on my sixteenth birthday—now less than two years away!"

It ran thus:

Dear Matthew,

Please forgive me for my deception. By the time you read this Kate and I will be far away embarking on a new life which we feel is the only way to help us to forget the tragedies which we have both experienced over the past couple of years. You have been a rock for us so please do not feel that you have failed us in any way. Rest assured that we will contact you if we encounter any serious problems. Our destination must remain a secret. This will make things easier for you when the authorities contact you. We are sorry for the stress this will cause. Remember, dearest Matthew, that 'no news is good news' and I will contact you on my sixteenth birthday, now less than two years away!

Much love,
Jo and Kate xxxx

The letter was placed in the box containing his chess set.

Chapter 18

They had laid their plans so carefully. On Sunday Matthew drove Jo and her huge heavy suitcase to the local railway station. At the next station Kate was waiting on the platform with an enormous rucksack. The girls made eye contact but stayed apart. When the train arrived at Manchester Jo removed her rucksack from the suitcase and deposited the latter under a bench in the in the waiting room. They boarded the train to Carlisle as strangers, each occupying separate compartments. So far so good. They had another train to catch in Carlisle and planned to continue the journey from there mingling with the crowd but staying apart believing that in this way they would not be noticed. However, this next train was delayed and arrived at the small rural station two hours late. This was the first setback. It was dark and raining and they had missed the last bus which would take them close to their destination, an isolated Youth Hostel overlooking a lovely loch.

"Damn! What the hell do we do now? How far is it and what time does it close?" demanded Kate.

Destiny Obscure

"It's only five miles away. We could walk that in less than a couple of hours", replied Jo consulting the map. "Its eight o'clock now. We could be there before ten. Otherwise we could thumb it".

"Let's do that then. It's chucking it down and this sac is heavy!"

They donned their waterproofs and followed the quiet country lane which wound its way through the desolate and deserted countryside with huge pine forests on either side. They were both tired and beginning to despair of ever getting a lift when they heard a car approaching. Jo immediately flashed her torch and waved her arms excitedly. It was a large white van which stopped alongside them and the driver, a swarthy middle-aged man, wound down the nearside window.

"Where are you going?" he demanded.

"To the Loch-side Youth Hostel. Do you know it?"

"Sure", he said, jumping out of the van. "Give me you bags!"

He was a big man, bearded and brawny and he seized Kate's bag before she had put it down. He then seized Kate. "Get in!" he roared and proceeded to haul the resisting girl towards the van. His intentions became starkly obvious. He released the bag to open the passenger door of the van and attempted to force Kate inside. She screamed and tried to struggle free.

Jo, standing behind, momentarily frozen with shock, was suddenly galvanised into action. She kicked him from behind between his legs as hard as she could. He let out a roar of anger and jerked forward in agony. Unfortunately for Kate, his head struck her face a glancing blow and she fell to the ground with a shriek. The man, whose groaning had changed to growling, spun round to face Jo. Another kick, also on target, increased his pain and he staggered towards her, bent low and cursing. She kicked him again and again, this time aiming at his lowered head. He fell to the ground, groaning loudly, his face pouring with blood. Jo hauled the whimpering Kate to her feet and grabbing both rucksacks, shrieked urgently, "Come on! Let's get out of here!"

They plunged in panic-stricken haste through the tulgy wood struggling through thick undergrowth which grabbed and tripped them but still they kept on running until at last, breathless and exhausted they stopped and listened for noises of their pursuer. Nothing. Just the spattering of rain and the rustling of branches. It was miserable, cold and dark. The trunks of the pine trees were choked with moss and long, thick grey-green strands hung eerily from their branches. Kate began to wail, "I don't like it here. I can't go any further. My head hurts so much where he head-butted me. I think my nose is broken. I'm frightened. I want to go home".

Jo ignored her and looked around. "Which way out?", she wondered. "This a dismal place. It reminds me of where the Vampires live in 'Twilight'!" She shuddered then turned to Kate whose wails had changed to despairing moans.

She took Kate's hands and said gently but firmly, "Come on, Kate. Pull yourself together. Giving in will get us nowhere. We're not that far from the hostel now but I don't think it would be wise to try to get there tonight. We'll never find our way out of here in the dark. I suggest we find a place to camp and then set off at first light."

"What! Camp here in this horrible place! We haven't even got a tent. I'm cold, tired and hungry. I wish I'd never come here. I didn't know it was going to be like this. I want to go home."

She began to choke and moan and kept repeating her wish to go home.

Jo felt like giving her a good shake and began to wish she hadn't brought her. The last thing she needed was someone who would collapse at the first hurdle.

However she realised that she was the strong one and she must take charge and try to give strength and comfort to her companion.

She forced a cheery tone in her voice, "Hey, it really isn't the end of the world although I agree—it would be easy to think so in this god-forsaken place!

My crazy grandparents would have thought it was ace—another character-building challenge. I guarantee we will laugh about this in a couple of weeks and our self-esteem will rocket. And what a tale to tell *our* grandchildren!"

She threw her rucksack to the ground and began to rummage in the side pockets.

"Hey-up! There is a God after all----look what I've found!" and she produced a bar of chocolate, a packet of raisins and a bottle of water.

"Right!" she said looking round, "This is our pad for the night. Let's make ourselves comfortable. It looks fairly flat and there should be some shelter under this tree and", she added with a grin, referring to the hanging moss, "Those pretty curtains will help keep the wind off. Come on now Kate, cheer up! Let's have a snack then decide where best to put our sleeping bags".

Kate still snivelling, sat on her rucksack and accepted some food. Then she said,"I'm sorry for being such a wimp, Jo. You're so brave."

"Don't be daft. You were the one that low-life grabbed---not me! All I had to do was boot him in the balls. I enjoyed that. Sorry he head-butted you though. How's your nose now?"

Kate sniffed, "Well it's a bit sore but I don't think it's broken. This chocolate's good. Is there any more?"

"Yep! Let's eat the lot. We've earned it. We can replenish supplies tomorrow at the hostel."

The rain began to ease so they unpacked their sleeping bags and put them inside the bin bags they had brought. They then crawled into their sleeping bags, fully clothed apart from their boots. Jo said nothing to Kate but she clutched her camping knife, at the ready, just in case---!

They lay in silence for a while watching the clouds gradually dispersing and the moon and stars coming into view.

"Matthew said that Scotland is one of the best places in the whole of the UK to see the stars." murmured Jo.

"Matthew is so clever." Kate replied. "Brilliant at chess too. I've been playing against him quite a lot recently and he always concedes his rooks or his queen at the start and even then I can't ever beat him. When we're getting into the end game he'll sometimes swap pieces and take over mine and he still manages to win!"

"I know. I used to wonder why he chose theology at Uni instead of rocket science, or brain surgery."

They both giggled.

"He told me his life-story last week. Well, just the bare bones. He's led a very sheltered life, or so it seems. He went into the church because it was expected of him. His father was a preacher."

They both thought for a while then Kate said, "I wonder if he's ever had a girl friend. I mean he's a good-looking guy and a lovely person."

Silence again whilst they both considered this.

"I wonder," Jo ventured, "If he's gay."

"Could be, I suppose. It does seem strange that he hasn't got a partner, male or female."

"Perhaps he's sexless." Jo suggested. "Maybe he hasn't any sex hormones, male or female. I've heard that there are people like this. I think it's very rare though. His mother didn't have him until she was turned forty. Maybe that could have something to do with it."

"I doubt it. I know a few people born to older parents and they seem perfectly normal."

"Whatever 'perfectly normal' is." responded Jo with a touch of irony.

"If he is gay, he wouldn't want to show it. His mother would be so upset and ashamed. She's very old-fashioned and he wouldn't hurt her for the world."

"I know." Kate replied. "And what does it matter anyway. I like him just as he is. He helped me settle into school far better than any of the teachers did. He's just the sort of person that you trust instinctively and you know that he'll never let you down and will always be there for you."

"True," sighed Jo. "I feel awful deceiving him like I did—even lying to him. Poor Matthew. He'll get it in the neck from the school, the authorities, that bitch Julie- even though he's not to blame in the slightest. Also, he will be so worried about us. He'll feel that in some way he could have done more to help and protect us. I did say in my note that no news is good news. Maybe that will help a bit. Anyway, Are you cold?"

"Course I bloody am! Aren't you?"

"A bit. Try sticking your head into your sleeping bag and breathing warm air into it. I've heard that helps." advised Jo.

Kate was not convinced

"Now I've got a better one for you. Pee into the empty water bottle and use that as a hot water bottle. Just be careful it doesn't burst."

They both laughed, "Good idea." said Jo. "Baggy me first!"

"I think whoever pees in it should have it first", responded Kate, "And anyway, it was my idea."

They laughed again, the previous trials and tribulations fading and forgotten, at least for now. The rain ceased and the clouds responsible for it drifted away revealing the magnificence of the starlit sky beaming down upon them.

Neither of them felt sleepy, nor did they want to induce sleep by giving way to exhaustion. To stay awake meant they could stay alert and aware of any impending dangers, real or imagined. So instead, they both looked up at the sky and marvelled at its immensity and the brightness of the stars.

Jo was the first to speak, "Look at the moon. I love it when it's crescent-shaped. It's waxing now. See!" She took her right hand out of her sleeping bag and made a crescent shape with her thumb and first finger. "If you can hold it, make its shape that is, in your right hand, then it's approaching full moon, in other words, waxing. If you can do it with your left hand then it's waning, getting smaller. I'm glad it isn't a full moon. There are lots of legends and beliefs associated with full moons, some good, some bad."

"I know. My aunty Beth is an astrologist."

"Wow! Does she interpret dreams and horoscopes?"

"Oh yes!" said Kate, adding proudly, "She's a professional. She writes horoscopes for magazines and newspapers and she has a few private clients too. She used to take us kids outside on starry nights and tell us stories and legends. We loved it. It was so fascinating."

"Can you remember any of them?", asked Jo eagerly.

"I'll try. Let's start with the moon," Kate began cautiously, "Did you know that the 'Man in the Moon' was a poor beggar who was caught collecting firewood on Sunday and his punishment was to spend eternity collecting sticks on the moon. Not such a bad punishment compared to some in Greek mythology! Oh, and the full moon is said to make some people crazy. That's where the word 'lunatic' comes from. This belief was once so common even amongst the the educated classes that patients in some mental hospitals were chained up and beaten during Full Moon. Poor things! And if you committed a crime during Full Moon your sentence could be lessened because it was believed that it wasn't entirely your fault. So some criminals and murderers deliberately planned their crimes when the moon was full and this, of course, strengthened the belief. How naïve of the authorities! Apparently there were more murders during a Full Moon than at any other time." she paused as they both reflected on this then she continued, "Dogs, especially hounds, howl at a Full Moon and vampires and werewolves stalk their prey—shuddery stuff, but there are some nice things too. "Er, if you make a wish and keep your fingers crossed until you see a shooting star your wish will come true. I suppose that's a bit like wishing on a star. And if you have silver in your pocket and you turn it over your riches will increase. I can't remember anything else about the moon except that because it controls tides it influences water in our bodies too and as the highest tides are at full moon this is why it sends people and animals crazy."

"Wow- that's fascinating! Do you feel different at full moon?" asked Jo, then added, "I don't but it could be because I've never really thought about it. Next time I see a full moon I will and maybe something will happen to me."

"It will if you want it to---if you convince yourself. Aunty Beth said that it is impossible to convince some people about the truth in their horoscopes. They tell her it's fanciful rubbish whereas others, even amongst the well-educated, believe it and come back time after time to ask her advice about what they should do in certain situations."

"Was she always right?"

"Well she must have been right a lot of the time or they wouldn't have kept coming back.

Jo thought about this then said, "What's a 'Blue Moon'?"

"Oh, that's when two full moons occur in the same month. I don't know why it's called a 'blue moon' The colour is the same as any other moon. It only happens once in two to three years. That's where the expression 'once in a Blue Moon' comes from. I don't know any legends about it but maybe there were twice as many horrible happenings--murders, werewolves, vampires, Ugh!"

"Can you do horoscopes?"

"No. My mother thought it was rubbish. She calls her sister 'Batty Beth', so I never got into it but I do know a bit about the star signs. What's yours?"

"Capricorn, the goat. Supposed to be naughty and capricious, I think!"

Kate smiled, "That's probably a modern interpretation. Actually, Capricorn is the God Pan in disguise. He was attacked by a giant and in order to escape he turned himself into a goat. He has the form, half man, half goat. Capricorns are said to be hard-working and ambitious, independent, brave and bossy—and moody—capricious, in fact!"

"That's me!" laughed Jo, "What's your sign?"

Kate paused before she answered, "It's quite weird and on the surface seems inappropriate." She hesitated again, shuddered slightly, then answered in a measured tone, "It's Virgo, the virgin. Aunty Beth who was the only one in the family to stand by me during the hell I went through, said it was significant. She said that what happened to me was written in the stars. She hesitated again then continued, "According to legend all the Greek Gods lived on Earth and Zeus, the supreme God, told Prometheus, a Titan, to make the first woman out of clay.

Jo interrupted, "So she's the Greek equivalent of Eve then except that Eve was made out of Adam's rib?"

"Yes, that's right." she concurred, then continued, "Lots of other Gods and Goddesses gave her attributes like beauty, grace, courage, and so on and she was called 'Pandora' which means 'gifted'. Anyway, Zeus entrusted her with a box as a test of her obedience and forbade her ever to open it. She was tormented by curiosity and one day she decided to open the lid just to have a peep. As soon as she did, all the plagues, evils and nastinesses escaped to torment mankind. Because of this, most of the Gods, to escape all these evils, decided to retreat back to heaven. The last one to leave was Astraea, Goddess of Justice. When she left Earth she became Virgo, the only female star sign. She judges evil and innocence by balancing all the facts and she grants forgiveness to all those who are wrongly accused or," she hesitated and her voice broke, "who are taken advantage of and robbed of their innocence. This is what Beth said had happened to me."

Silence for while as Kate recovered her composure, then Jo said, "Funny how women are always blamed for all the evils on Earth. Eve couldn't resist temptation either and she, according to Christian belief, was goaded by Satan to eat the forbidden fruit and because she did and disobeyed God, peace and innocence were lost for ever and God banished her and Adam from the garden of Eden. So silly and unfair! I wonder if Matthew believes it."

"I doubt it, and aunty Beth said that there lots of legends blaming women for evil, yet Satan, the epitome of all all evil is male!"

They both considered this then Jo said, "I'd like to meet your Auntie Beth. She sounds like a very interesting person."

"She is, and she's very warm-hearted and kind too. If you don't believe in Astrology, she doesn't take offence or try to ram it down your throat. She just tries to help anyone who needs help whatever trouble they are in. She just talks to them and tells them stories, fascinating stories. She's a bit like Matthew. Her mission in life seems to be bringing comfort and hope to those who need it. Oh, and I forgot—the last thing in Pandora's box was 'Hope' and this is what helps to sustain us in hard times."

"There you are!" laughed Jo, "That's what's sustaining us now. The hope for better fortunes tomorrow." Then she asked, "Is Beth married?"

"She was. She got married very young to her childhood sweetheart then he died of cancer. He was only thirty-three. They had no children. As far as I know she hasn't had another serious relationship since."

"Pity we can't introduce her to Matthew. They're 'chalk and cheese' in their beliefs but they seem to have similar missions in life."

"I don't think they are 'chalk and cheese', observed Kate, "They both have open minds. They'd probably respect each other's beliefs and have endless conversations and discussions. Also she's a good chess player too. It was her who taught me. Everyone thinks of chess as being a game for educated intellectuals but if you think about it, it involves imagination fired by fantasy. I think she and Matthew would get on very well."

"I doubt Matthew's mother would approve." said Jo then she startled suddenly at a rustling noise, "What the hell was that!"

Kate heard it too and they both sat bolt upright in their sleeping bags and stared around at the trees and the undergrowth. They saw nothing but the heavy curtain of moss suspended from a nearby tree swaying gently.

"This is so eerie. Thank God there isn't a Full Moon or I would die of fright! What do you think caused that noise?" demanded Kate.

"Probably some harmless little animal going about his nocturnal business." assured Jo, "But this area is certainly creepy. It reminds me of the rainforest in 'Twilight'. Have you read it?"

"Ages ago." replied Kate. "But you're right. It is creepy here and it does look a lot like the forest where the vampires hang out in 'Twilight'. It's set near Seattle in Washington isn't it, the rainiest part of America? And this must be the rainiest part of the UK." Then added sarcastically, "If you don't count North Wales!" Jo agreed and they both laughed ruefully and snuggled deeper into their sleeping bags

It was still pitch black apart from the silent sky which glittered with myriads of stars, beckoningly beautiful.

"No wonder so many stories and legends have been written about the sky and why it's thought of as heaven. I wish my mum and dad and Emily could be up there. I wish Matthew could be here to give me hope. It's easy and trite to say you don't believe in anything which can't be proven beyond doubt and yet it's hypocritical to pretend you do believe." This was said by Jo with a deep sigh of infinite sadness and Kate sensing that that her friend would lapse into one of her moods of deep depression and self-pity changed the subject at once.

"Hey, I thought I saw the moss curtain move a minute ago and guess who emerged? Only briefly, but he was there." Without waiting for Jo to reply she continued in a triumphant tone, "Edward Cullen, the brave and beautiful Vampire. He could help us to get out of here. If he comes back I'll ask him."

Still no response from Jo so she continued excitedly, "Perhaps the next thing to appear will be Jacob, the friendly Werewolf. He would help us too. If they both come, I bag Eddie!"

Jo said nothing. She was still feeling sick inside. She understood why Kate was trying to distract her. Something simple and childish was needed. Her eventual response was to repeat a ditty which sprang into her mind no doubt inspired by Kate's reminiscing about vampires and werewolves,

> *"From ghoulies and ghosties and long-leggity beasties and things which go bump in the night, May the good Lord protect us."*

"Ha ha!" laughed Kate, "I've heard that one too."

"Who hasn't." responded Jo, then added wearily, "I wish morning would come. This has got be the longest night ever."

Then she remembered that other night. December 18th. Barely a month ago. That was the longest and worst night of her life. Would this running away, this attempt at escapism help her to forget? Would it not have been better to stay with Matthew, martial moral courage, face facts, rather than taking the easy way out? The cowards way out? This way she was causing hurt and worry to all those who knew her and cared about her. And worse—she had persuaded Kate to come with her. Poor Kate, who was already mentally scarred and emotionally wounded. And she had been terrified earlier by that dirty old man who had tried to abduct her. Nothing so far had gone according to plan. Poor Kate. No doubt too that she would be blamed for all this. And where will it all end? If they were caught and forced to return, things would be much worse for both of them. What would happen then? They would be separated. Kate would be put back into care, and she, Jo, may also be taken into care. Everything would be worse, much worse. By running away she had taken the coward's way out. It had seemed so easy, so obvious, so exciting. She had thought of nothing but herself. It was as if she had been the only one to be hurt and deeply affected by the loss of her parents and Emily. The disconsolate feeling of cold dread returned and she squirmed in her sleeping bag. She felt desperate and useless-- a shuddering mass of failure and self-pity.

Kate was the next to speak, "One hell of a long night!" she agreed, then added, "Are you OK?" Jo's back was to her and she saw that she was trembling and shaking.

"Yes, I'm OK." Jo lied, "I'm just so cold and I'm moving to try to warm my muscles up."

"Good idea." responded Kate, then added, "I'm afraid to go to sleep in case I die of exposure. Can people die of exposure in their sleep?"

"That's how they all die." answered Jo glumly, "After a while the heat drains from the body's outer shell in order to keep the vital organs alive and so you don't feel the cold any longer. You just drift into a peaceful never-ending sleep. It's supposed to be a painless way to die." There it was again. A reference to death. Another stark reminder. Would it always be like this? She hoped and prayed that her parents hadn't suffered. That their deaths although violent had been sudden, not protracted and that there had been no time for pain or fear. And poor 'Bella' too. And Emily------!

Kate responded at once to Jo's advice about hypothermia and started half shouting and half singing, "Well in that case, pleasant or not, I'm not ready to give in to it yet so I shall keep moving and make sure I don't fall asleep. 'Twist and shout and shake it all about!'" she sang even louder and began to gyrate.

Jo, somewhat comforted to see her companion in fairly high spirits and making the best of a bad situation, joined in the gyrations and gradually the gloom departed and slunk back into her subconscious.

Thus this long night passed in chatter, singing, staring at the clear awesome sky in that cold and creepy forest. At last, at long last, the vestiges of dreary darkness glimmered into the promise of dawn and a new day.

Chapter 19

The rigours of that cold night left the girls feeling physically and mentally exhausted and as they struggled out of their sleeping bags and repacked their rucksacks they felt the pressure of a new challenge. How were they going to find their way out of the dense sameness of this featureless forest? Their bodies ached and were very cold and stiff. They were hungry too and what bit of food and drink they had packed had all gone. Both were enveloped in despair and felt that this whole 'running away thing' had been a terrible mistake and the most tempting thing to do would be to lie down again in this closed-in forest and sleep, sleep, give-in and give-up. Jo recognised that they were both suffering from the early onset of hypothermia and they needed warmth and sustenance. Vigorous exercise was not a good idea. They had to conserve their energy in order to stave off this potentially fatal condition. They would have to plod on and hope that the rising sun would give some warmth until they arrived at their destination, the Loch-side Youth hostel. Jo took out the map and compass and found the spot on the road where they had been before their encounter with that dirty old man and

Destiny Obscure

their panic-stricken flight into the forest. She orientated the map and compass and calculated the direction to the hostel. This positive action motivated her. "Come on," she urged Kate. "Its not that far. We must just keep going!"

Their rucksacks were heavy and the route through the resisting shrubs and unyielding branches was tough and tiring. They both began to feel dizzy and the temptation to lie down and sleep was overwhelming but somehow through sheer cussedness and determination they made it at last to the edge of the forest and incredibly, there in front of them was the loch and beside it the Youth Hostel! It snuggled between the forest and the loch, a place of sanctuary and comfort. They both remembered Hansel and Gretel and how they had felt when they saw their haven. But somehow at that moment, they forgot about the witch! It would surely be an angel who greeted them.

The warden, middle-aged and matronly, was working in the garden. She saw them approaching and hailed them, "Hello, Joan and Kathleen? I was expecting you last night!" She had a soft endearing Scottish accent, more acquired than indigenous.

"We missed the bus and got lost in the forest," gasped Jo.

"You mean you spent the night there?" she sounded aghast, "You poor things! Come in and get warm and have something to eat."

They followed her into the cosy kitchen-diner and gratefully sipped the proffered warm sweet tea whilst she plied them with hot buttered toast and questions which they were too tired to answer except in monosyllables. Realising their utter exhaustion she said, "What you two need is sleep. Come on, follow me! We can do the formalities later."

She bustled along a corridor and indicated a small bedroom with four bunk-beds. "Choose whichever you want. The hostel's empty this week. I kept the heater on in here for you."

They undressed mechanically, still feeling stiff and chilled, donned their pyjamas and snuggled down under the heavy blankets. All their recent trials faded as they sank into rapturous oblivion.

The warden, Fay, was a kindly middle-aged woman married once and deserted after only four years which for her had been deliriously happy. Her husband had suddenly decided that monogamy was not for him and so he left her, not for one particular woman but to give himself the freedom to play the field and seduce any woman he fancied. He decided he did not want to make a commitment to anyone. He told her he still loved her and always would but he was bored with her now and that desertion was better than deceit. Fay had been devastated. She was hurt and humiliated and needed to start a new life. As a girl she had stayed in many Youth Hostels and felt that to escape to the countryside was the tonic she needed so she became a youth hostel warden. This was twenty years ago and during this time she had been shuttled around the whole of the UK, finally settling here in the faraway North of Scotland. She loved Loch-side and the remoteness and was never lonely. She was a self-sufficient woman confident in her own company but not a recluse. The hostel was popular in summer and at holiday times with walkers, climbers and cyclists and she looked forward to welcoming them. In the busiest seasons she usually took on an assistant or two to help with the increased workload which included cleaning, cooking and gardening. At the moment though, it was just the occasional one or two during the week and a few more at weekends. This gave her time to pursue her own passions which included landscape painting and gardening. The walls of the hostel were hung with her work which portrayed landscapes from all the places where she had worked as a warden. However, there weren't many local ones to be seen. She had sold most of these to visitors who had begged to buy them as permanent and precious souvenirs of their holiday in this tranquil and beautiful area. So once the girls were settled, she took out her easel and sitting beside the window overlooking the loch she began to paint the scene before her. The distant mountains glittered with snow and the loch had a purplish hue and she soon became utterly engrossed in her work.

Jo and Kate slept until four o'clock in the afternoon and caught the last rays of the winter sun fading over the loch. They showered and felt refreshed as they made their way into the dining room. Fay looked up and greeted them, "Did you have a good sleep? You must feel better now, and hungry, no doubt."

The girls approached shyly and looked at the painting on her easel, "Is that the view from the window?" ventured Jo.

"Yes, it's going to be. I've painted it so many times that you'd think I could do it from memory but it changes subtly every day, even in similar weather conditions. This is why I always take photos before I begin so even though it's going dark now I can still carry on if I'm in the mood."

"Please don't let us stop you!" begged Jo.

"You're not, don't worry. I've had enough now and anyway I'm starving. I didn't have any lunch and neither did you so you must be starving too, especially as I suspect you didn't have dinner last night." she looked at them quizzically then added, "I expected you for dinner and made a beef stew. It's in the freezer but I can thaw it and pop it in the Aga. It should be ready in about half -an-hour. We'll eat in here, by the fire."

"Do you cook meals for all the hostellers?" asked Jo.

Fay laughed, "Not during peak periods. Meals have to be booked in advance and I do have help. The 'self-cookers' kitchen as it's called is in the small annexe. It's very self-contained-- ten gas rings, three microwaves, a large water heater, kettles, pans, crockery, cutlery—everything you need and a dining area adjacent. It gets quite busy in the summer when visitors need more flexibility about mealtimes."

"How many does the hostel hold?"

"Thirty in total, and there are facilities for camping too but most people prefer to camp at the farm site just outside the village."

As Fay withdrew to the pantry, Kate said, "Please don't pinch me to wake me up. This has got to be heaven."

They looked around at their surroundings. Alongside the wall at one end of the room a shiny black Aga stove breathed warmth into the room and set into another wall an open fire crackled and glowed, fed from time to time from a huge basket of logs lying alongside the slate hearth. A sofa and various easy chairs completed this picture of warmth and comfort.

In the middle of the room stood a large pine table with bench seats on either side suggesting and inviting conviviality at communal meal times.

The walls were hung with paintings depicting scenes from some of Britain's most beautiful countryside. They walked around the room studying each picture in turn, then Jo said in surprise, "That looks like Snowdon!"

"It is Snowdon." laughed Fay as she came in carrying a steaming tray of food. "Do you know that area?"

"Er, a bit. I've er, been there on holiday." The lie did not come easily.

"Well I was a warden at Snowdon Ranger Youth hostel for a couple of years. "Do you know it?"

"Not really." Jo felt the need to change the subject, "Mm. This looks delicious. Thank you so much."

They all tucked in to the tasty stew and nobody spoke until the edges were off their appetites then Fay said, "What brought you up here at this time of year. You must have had something in mind."

Now was the time to tell their carefully rehearsed story.

"Well," began Jo, alias Joan, "We just got fed up of slaving in a city. The rain, the pollution, the traffic, the never-ending noise. It just got through to us in the end and we both decided to try somewhere else."

"From one extreme to the other then." remarked Fay.

"I suppose you could say that." said Jo with a nervous laugh.

"What did you both do? Job-wise, I mean."

"Oh, er, I worked in a supermarket, at the checkout and Kathleen was a waitress."

"Did you not think of going to university?"

"We thought about it, yeah, but the tuition fees put us off."

"There aren't any tuition fees in Scotland," asserted Fay.

Another awkward silence broken at last by Kate, alias Kathleen, in another effort to change the subject, "This stew is really delicious." she enthused. "Will you give me the recipe?"

Fay was no fool and she suspected that the girls were keeping something from her. They looked so young. Much younger than the 'over eighteen' they had stated on their membership cards. However, she decided to keep her counsel for the moment and wait until they were off-guard. She was a good judge of character and they both seemed such nice girls and vulnerable. Whatever it was that had driven them up here, whatever trouble they were in she would give it time to surface then see if she could help them.

After dinner, they relaxed in front of the open fire sipping tea and chatting.

"This is such a lovely, homely hostel," said Jo. "I love this room with the Aga and the open fire. It's so cosy and welcoming."

"Yes, everyone who comes here feels the same. It is rather special. I love it too." agreed Fay, "But I think the open fire will be bricked up soon."

"What! Why, what do you mean?" shock and surprise from Jo.

"Well, apparently it does not comply with the current 'Health and Safety' regulations. I have been told that it is a fire risk, thereby dangerous and so it will have to be removed and replaced by an electric or gas appliance. Well, we have no gas here and it would be too problematical to install a gas tank so at the moment no final decision has been made as to what we can substitute for it. It's ridiculous! We have so much wood around here which means we can heat the hostel for nothing and it is a very reliable source of heat. Sometimes we have power cuts but we can still cook and keep warm. There's a back boiler behind that fire which means that we can heat the water and a few radiators too. Did you notice that your dorm was warm enough this morning?" Her frustration became apparent in her voice, "This hostel has been here and burning wood on open fires for the past seventy-odd years and there has never been a fire nor a recorded case of anyone being burnt or injured yet some bright spark, no doubt on an inflated salary, has to come up with ways of exterminating all risks, however slight or unlikely." She paused, then added, "What it means ultimately is that no-one will ever have to even think about protecting himself and behaving responsibly. 'Nanny State' will do that for all of us. Alas, we are entrenched in the culture of blame and whatever happens has to be someone else's fault. There will always be accidents and irresponsible people who cause them but everyone should be taught to be responsible for their own actions. The risks we take are up to us and we must do what we can to reduce them. We must educate, not legislate. Another pause, then she continued in a lighter vein, "However, it will be a while yet before the legislation reaches here so let's make the most of it whilst we can!" so saying, she seized another log from the hearth and fed the glowing fire which responded by crackling happily and sending up a shower of bright sparks which no doubt contributed to the assumption of danger.

She took a deep breath and seemed satisfied to have unburdened herself of something she felt strongly about.

They were quite surprised by this outburst and show of rebellion but they found themselves agreeing with most of what she said and they construed that in her position she must feel vulnerable to blame and retribution.

Absorbing the warmth from the fire and able at last to relax, the girls felt embraced by an inner peace and security in this soothing and remote sanctuary under the guardianship of Fay. They had known her for less than a day but they trusted her intuitively. They felt warm and safe. Such a contrast to the rigours and fears of the previous night when each of them had felt that the decision to run away had been a bad mistake. They were here. They were safe, at least for the time being, but what next?

"What are your plans for tomorrow?" demanded Fay as she gathered up the dinner plates.

"Well I guess we'll explore the area, weather permitting, answered Jo.

"The weather is set fair for the next few days according to the forecast so you could walk or cycle to the village if you fancy that. There's not a lot going on there at the moment except plans for encouraging more tourism. Anyway, I'm off to bed now. If you want breakfast, will eight-thirty suit you?"

"Perfect. Thank you." responded Jo.

"Goodnight then, and sleep well."

Fay retired to her own quarters and the girls sat before the warm fire and discussed their next move. Originally they had planned to look for jobs near to the hostel but they hadn't realised just how remote it was. The nearest village was at least five miles away and they had no transport and very little money left. Maybe they would have to seek out a town and hope that the publicity in connection with their disappearance would be of no significance there. They were both very tired and long-term plans could not be made until they were more familiar with the region. So tomorrow they would check out the local village and see if there was anything on offer there. Meanwhile they were more than happy to make the hostel their base.

They placed the guard in front of the fire, turned out the lights and made their way to the dormitory and were soon snuggling down into the creaky bunk beds. Kate fell asleep almost immediately but Jo was tormented with doubts and fears and memories. Gruesome images were conjured up by her fertile imagination. Emily, disappearing into the dark depths of the river, struggling to surface, to survive. What must it be like to drown? Choking pain and terror? Poor, poor Emily to be robbed of her life at such a young age. Kind and loving Emily, revering the rights of all living things---even insects! She thought again of the time when Emily had prevented her from squashing the scurrying beetle. Poor, poor Emily! And her own parents-- Did they suffer? Matthew said they died instantly. How does he know that? He would say that to try to comfort her ---- 'Died instantly'! Yes, it is comforting to believe that their suffering was not prolonged. Is this the only comfort there is for those who have lost their loved ones forever? Mobilising inner strength is no comfort. It crushes and drains away emotions and forces you to accept the inevitable! Mental agony is prolonged and punishing. It is a form of torture that will subside for a while and then resurface. She gulped and prayed inwardly, "Matthew, where are you? I need you now to counsel me. Please help me to stop torturing myself!"

But Matthew was not there. No-one was there and she could not rid her mind of these desperate images. "Am I going mad? Will this anguish ever end? I ran away to escape all this but I know now that there is no escape. Time may help to salve the wounds but the scars will be with me forever!" Every nerve and muscle in her body was taut as she tossed and turned throughout the night in desperation. The old iron bed rattled and creaked a dismal accompaniment to her anguish and the opening lines of the sad and poignant Beatle's song, 'Yesterday', echoed in all the nooks and crannies of the small characterless dormitory. Meanwhile, Kate slept on, oblivious to her companion's torment.

The next morning Jo admitted to Kate, without going into detail, that she had suffered a restless night. Fay too, noticed that Jo looked pale and tired and asked her if she was feeling unwell and if she needed anything. Jo shrugged off Fay's concern and assured her that she was fine and fresh air and exercise would make her feel better.

The weather was bright and cold and the two girls borrowed bikes from Fay and set off to explore the area. Jo's black memories of the night before faded with every powerful push on the pedals and every breath of the crisp morning air. They both felt happy, light-hearted and optimistic as they rattled and bumped along the unmade road.

The village consisted of a main street lined on either side with small cottages with a Post Office-cum-general store, a couple of craft shops selling souvenirs and postcards, a DIY store a cycle hire and repair shop, and a cafe. At one end of this quaint and narrow street stood a pub, whilst at the other almost directly facing as if in direct opposition, was the church. This was an attractive granite building dominated by a sturdy tower which housed a large bell. Below the bell and facing the main street a large clock set into the granite blocks chimed every quarter with a sombre note more like

Destiny Obscure

a nudge than a stark reminder of passing time. It added character to the village.

Leaning their bikes against the wall they went into the cafe and ordered tea and toasted teacakes. The cafe was warm and welcoming and amidst the clatter of cups and plates there was a hubbub of laughter and conversation. It was as if everyone knew each other and the girls were soon engaged in conversation with the waitress and other customers who recognised them as strangers and chatted to them amiably about where they were staying, what they were doing and their opinion of the area. It was all very pleasant and affable and made them both feel that they would be happy to be part of this community. If only they could find jobs and avert suspicion from the truth that they were runaways, hunted by the police!

Back on their bikes, they explored the surrounding area. I was very rural and largely unspoilt although they could see various building projects in operation. These were the beginnings of the tourist attractions mentioned by Fay. The local camp-site was being enlarged and modernised to include spaces and facilities for caravans. Progress was being made too in establishing a new garden centre. Tennis courts and a Sports Centre with a swimming pool were also well under way. All these projects were bringing work into the area for the local residents who had been jobless for so long and hopefully would help to reduce the number of young people who were leaving the area to find jobs elsewhere. Another spin-off would be that an increase in the population would mean building more houses providing even more employment. All very well--- but where would it all end? Would the natural unspoilt beauty be sacrificed under the banner of development as happens in so many rural areas?

They made their way back to the village and decided to have lunch in the pub. It would be a good test to see if the landlord would suspect they were under-age and refuse to serve them. All went well. He was used to strangers and barely gave them a second glance as he took their order. The pub was quite busy and there was much loud laughter and greetings as the pub began to fill with diners, mostly local workmen by the look of them, joking and guffawing together enjoying their lunch and each other's company In contrast to the cafe the presence of the girls was scarcely noticed as they tucked into steak and ale pie and drank shandy in the cosy lounge with its black- leaded grate fire.

There was a darts board in the adjacent tap-room and they decided to have a go. Amid shrieks and laughter they muddled their way through a game of 'Round the Board' then one wild shot from Kate rebounded and narrowly missed a young man sitting nearby.

"Very sorry!" gasped Kate, "I'm not very good at this game."

"I can see that!" he laughed, "No harm done, but how much longer are you going to be?"

"Oh, sorry. We didn't realise you were waiting. We're only messing about. We've finished now."

"Thanks a lot. I'm James and this is my mate, Stuart. Watch us and wonder at our skill!" This was said teasingly and they all laughed.

They watched admiringly for a while noting the concentration, the stooped forward posture, the follow-through arm and the accuracy. "Fancy a lesson some time?", joked Stuart, "It'll cost you a pint!"

The girls laughed and left the pub with a half-promise to return for lessons in the 'art of darts' at a later date.

It had been a good day but the weather was closing in and it would be dark soon so they jumped on their bikes and began the return journey to the Youth Hostel. They had reached the bumpy track on the edge of the forest when a girl on a big bay horse appeared in front of them. The horse startled and shied when it saw the bikes and they stopped at once. The rider patted and reassured her mount and explained that he was a young horse and therefore still quite spooky.

They introduced themselves and exchanged pleasantries and the rider, Vicki, invited them to visit her livery yard. They gladly accepted the invitation then continued on their jolting journey. Both their minds were filled with images of Stuart and James. "Not bad-lookers, those two," observed Jo. "Nice and friendly too. I wouldn't mind taking them up on their offer to teach us how to play darts." Kate said nothing but renewed her efforts pushing down the pedals as the bike bounced up and down on the bumpy track.

When they arrived back at the hostel they recounted their experiences to Fay who was happy for them. She knew Vicki and guessed who some of the others were who they had chatted to.

"I'm so pleased you've met some of the locals. It isn't hard to make friends here but how long are you planning to stay?"

This question floored them. They hadn't yet made any plans—just vague hopes and possibilities. They really needed a mentor, like Matthew, but at the moment there was no-one It was too soon to rely on and trust Fay.

Chapter 20

On Wednesday morning Matthew received a phone call from the police asking if he had any idea as to the whereabouts of Kate. She had been reported missing since Monday evening. He was shocked. Surely she hadn't gone to Julie's with Jo! He called Julie immediately. She informed him that she knew nothing about either of them. Jo had phoned her last week to say that she had changed her mind about coming to live with her and had decided to stay at the vicarage instead. Julie had been relieved about this as Jo had always been a difficult and awkward child, just like her mother, and anyway she had her hands full with Billy. However, she was not in the least bit surprised that Jo had absconded. That was typical---and blah, blah, blah! Matthew put the phone down. He was shocked. It became clear to him that they must have run away together. But How? Where? He thought he knew, 'Why'!

Wheels were set in motion by the police to investigate the disappearance of the two under-age vulnerable teenagers and the rest of the day was spent creating dossiers of information about them. Matthew was in a daze. He was

Destiny Obscure

hurt and offended and felt that he had failed them both. The discovery later of Jo's letter in his chess set was of little comfort to him and he handed it over to the police.

He thought long and hard as to where they could possibly have headed. Very unlikely that they had sought out Jean and Bob, Emily's grandparents. Since Emily's death these two had cut themselves off almost entirely. They had declined the invitation to attend Tom and Jenny's funeral. They had written a letter of condolence and excused themselves on the grounds that it would be too traumatic for them to return to the area where they had suffered their latest tragedy. Matthew suspected that another reason could be their shock and disapproval of the humanist ceremony which was completely alien to their religious beliefs. So, who else did the girls know? It would have to be someone who would hide them away and not hand them over to the authorities. There was no-one he knew of. They must have gone somewhere where they were completely unknown and could achieve anonymity.

The most likely place seemed to be London. Wasn't this where most runaways went? Where they felt they could lose their identities mingling in the 'madding crowd'. What would they do there? Where would they stay? And would they be safe? This was the most haunting question and he shuddered to think about all the dangers two young and innocent teenagers would be confronted with. What could he do except pray and this he did with all the fervour and sincerity of his calling. But he was a practical man too and knew that prayers alone were not enough. He had come to know Jo pretty well and he tried to put himself in her position. Like her mother, she had an inborn dislike of crowds and cities so perhaps London would not be her choice. She had spoken to him a lot about the English Lake District and how her parents had planned to take their next family holiday there. However it would not be easy go unnoticed there. And the weather would be harsh at this time of year. And where would they stay? His thoughts turned to their last conversation. She had asked him lots of questions about Cornwall and he had painted a rosy picture of this beautiful county. Could she have decided to try her luck there? She had urged him too to take his mother back to Cornwall to pay their respects to his father's grave and take pictures of the gingko biloba tree. At last he decided that this is what he would do. With any luck, the runaways would be there too. Also he needed a break after all the extra pressures that he had been subjected to over the past few weeks. And he owed to his mother.

The phone rang. It was the local press asking him for an interview. It was the first of many over the next few days and some reporters actually called at the vicarage and took pictures—BAH! Others took pictures of Bryn Celyn and reports and distortions of the facts concerning the families, the tragedies and the latest disappearance of the two girls seemed to dominate the columns in some newspapers. Mercifully there was nothing about the sordid side of Kate's background and what she had suffered. Matthew remembered Jo's quote in her letter, 'no news is good news'. If this was all the local press had to fill their papers with then 'no news was bad news' for them!

This torment was too much. He had to get away.

The following Wednesday Matthew and his mother were on their way to Cornwall and a relief vicar took over the duties of the parish pending Matthew's return. He could hardly have begun his search in a place much further from reality.

Meanwhile a winter storm was unleashed around Loch Side. Snow and hail whipped up by the wind howled through the pine trees and battered against the windows and the the turbulent loch looked black and angry. In these harsh conditions the girls were obliged to stay indoors all day. They played chess together while Fay got on with her painting using the photograph she had taken on the day she began.

Conversation was sparse between them as each was absorbed in her task and time ticked by unnoticed until 'stale mate' was agreed between Jo and Kate and their thoughts turned to food. They asked Fay if they could make dinner as they could see that she was still absorbed in her painting. She readily agreed and they decided upon vegetable soup followed by cottage pie with baked bananas for dessert. Neither of them had a great deal of culinary experience so they consulted Fay's recipe books and followed the instructions carefully. The resulting meal was very good and Fay was impressed.

"Are you going to be here over the weekend?" she asked, "There's a group of walkers coming, eight of them, and I could do with help. My friend Ellen will be here too but we can always do with a bit of extra help."

"We've no definite plans yet. We'd love to stay and do whatever we can." enthused the youngsters

A group of walkers arrived together on Friday evening and the hostel absorbed the hustle and bustle of dinner, bed and breakfast for the next two days.

Jo and Kate enjoyed the involvement and they swept and scrubbed, chopped vegetables, laid and cleared tables and chatted to the hostellers.

"Look at them!" remarked Ellen, "You'd think they'd been doing this for years!"

"Yes." replied Fay thoughtfully, "They're a bit of an enigma. I haven't quite worked it out yet but so far so good. They haven't told me their plans though. Originally they just made a booking for a week. Mmm, I wonder." she paused, then continued her train of thought, "They can't stay here indefinitely. I've a strange feeling that they're running away from something. Whenever I ask them about their homes, their past, or what their plans are for the future, their answers are always evasive."

"Well, you need to just ask them how long they intend to stay here and take it from there. I know what you mean though. They do seem to be very nice girls but they do look very young for their age---if eighteen is indeed their age!"

Fay nodded thoughtfully and resolved to talk to them in the morning.

That night as they snuggled down in their beds they chatted about the weekend and how much they had enjoyed being involved in the running of the hostel.

"I wish we could stay here", sighed Kate, "I feel so safe and settled but I doubt it will be possible." She sighed deeply then continued earnestly," Jo, what are we going to do? Before we ran away, it was horrible and we were both unhappy but at least our lives were all set out and planned for us. Now I feel we are in limbo with no idea about what will happen now or in the future."

Jo responded calmly and deliberately, "We never know what will happen in the future. We can make plans and have hopes and dreams but destiny and fate change everything---sometimes in the wink of an eye. We couldn't have carried on as we were and it's no good harking back to the past and nurturing regrets. Regrets just grow and flourish and serve no positive purpose. They just taunt and torment. We have to accept the situation without 'ifs and buts' and make the best of it. Look-- we're young and strong we have each other and we're living in a beautiful place. Tomorrow we'll take a trip to the village-- maybe go and visit Vickie and her horses then call at the pub for lunch and see James and Matthew, the darts gurus! At least that way we can make friends and maybe get jobs. I'll do anything that's offered, cleaning, cafe work, mucking out. Everything will turn out fine if we make an effort and stay positive."

"You're right." sighed Kate, "Thank you for being so strong. Good night, sleep tight," then she continued with a silly rhyme,

> *'Mind the bugs don't bite,*
> *If they do, grab a shoe*
> *And bash 'em 'til*
> *They're black and blue!'*

She turned over with a girlish giggle and was soon sound asleep.

Little did she realise that her reciting of this ditty jerked Jo's memory back to her own childhood when Jenny would tuck her into bed laughing and repeating this same rhyme. Poor Jo. She was hit once more with the dreadful despair that she was struggling so hard to subdue. The horror that she had tried to run away from was again haunting her, possessing her. She tossed and turned in the narrow bed consumed again with the agonising pain of her loss. Kate's gentle rhythmic breathing made her long for the same escape. Please, please let me sleep! But she knew that whilst she was consumed by anguish and desperation, sleep, Nature's soft nurse, would not, could not rescue her. She remembered the tablets the doctor had given her and fumbled in her rucksack. She couldn't read the dosage in the dark but she longed so much for solace that she placed three in her palm and swallowed them whole. She lay back down in bed and waited for the release from mental agony that sleep would afford. Gradually she felt herself sinking into oblivion. The walls and ceiling of the dormitory seemed to grow and grow and as they receded they changed form. They became the grey sky and the bunks were transformed into large granite rocks. It was weirdly familiar. It was the mountain behind Bryn Celyn appearing slowly and gradually before her. All was shrouded in swirling mist. She shivered and looked around seeking some familiar landmark, some comforting companion. She could dimly discern two figures ahead and a horse walking beside them. She stared again. Could it be- -- was it---? "Mum, dad!" she screamed, "Bella!"

No response. Nothing! The apparitions continued walking slowly, purposefully, backs turned. She yelled again. Her voice came echoing back, ricochetting mockingly from the immense rocks. As her screams hit these boulders their rough surfaces were transformed into demonic images, monstrous faces which snarled and growled menacingly. Jo, gripped with fear and dread struggled through the mist towards the departing figures shouting, sobbing, screaming their names. She came almost within touching distance of them and reached out in desperation. Just then a roar like a thunder clap rent the air and the boulders were thrust up from the ground by a devilish force and began to roll, and tumble as they bounced down the hillside like a rampaging army bent on destruction. Bella neighed and reared in terror as she was mercilessly struck and crushed. At the same moment, Tom and Jenny turned round and faced Jo. Their faces were gaunt and grey with the pallor of death, their eyes, bulging and bloodshot. She appealed to them again in anguish, "Mum, dad, help me!" They showed no expression nor sign of recognition as they stared at her. Jo saw the snarling boulder behind them but could do nothing but scream, "NO! Watch out! Aagh! Seconds later Tom and Jenny too were dashed and buried under the debris. Jo wanted to join them, to be crushed as they had been and to be reunited with them in the void of oblivion. She spread her arms wide and stood in the path of the bouncing boulders. "Come on! Get me!" she screamed. "Crush me, kill me, *please*!" Ghost-like they passed straight through her. She felt nothing—nothing except the sickening horror of helplessness as she watched the crumbling avalanching mountainside consumed with murderous fervour, enveloping and destroying everything in its wake-- even Bryn Celyn, which succumbed to the power of this onslaught like a helpless stack of dominoes. Total annihilation of everything she had known and loved. She choked and screamed again, "No! No! No! Stop! Aagh! She tore at her hair and clawed her face in her anguish and terror. Then, something was shaking her, restraining her, and she was aware of Kate and Fay beside her, comforting and reassuring.

She was soaked in sweat, shaking and trembling violently. Fay wiped her face with a cold flannel and murmured, "There, there, come on now, it's all over. You've had a bad dream. Would you like a nice cup of tea?"

"Don't leave me!" begged Jo, "I'm sorry. It was a nightmare. A horrible nightmare."

"I know, I know," said Fay comfortingly, and wrapped a warm blanket round Jo's shoulders. "Go and make some tea, Kate. We could all do with it."

Kate went to make the tea whilst Fay held the trembling girl who, child-like, sucked her thumb and snuggled up to the comforting bosom. The sobbing spasms gradually subsided and before Kate returned, Jo had sunk into a deep yet snivelling sleep, safe and secure as a baby in the arms of Fay.

After breakfast the following morning Fay decided that she needed to find out more about the girls. Whilst Jo was taking a shower she sat down with Kate and began to question her. Kate had already told her that Jo had recently lost her parents in a tragic accident, hence the nightmare, and that they had decided to make a new start away from painful reminders.

Fay looked intently at Kate, "Understandable, but why did you leave *your* family and friends, Kate?"

"Because Jo is my best friend and anyway I was brought up by my grandmother." she lied.

"You told me you came here because you were fed up with living and working in a dirty city."

"Er, yes, that too. We were both so fed up with everything and the accident just brought things to a head."

"Well, what do you intend to do now and how much longer will you be staying here?"

At that moment Jo appeared somewhat refreshed by the shower but still looking pale and pinched. She apologised again for the trouble and upset she had caused and thanked Fay warmly for her kindness. Fay shrugged off the thanks and resumed her questioning.

"I was wondering how much longer you intend to stay in the hostel and if you have any plans for the immediate future."

"We've talked about it," answered Kate, "And we would both like to stay here for as long as we can but we do need to find jobs."

"Well, I can find work for you here during the weekends but I can't pay you. All I can offer is free board until the high season then the regular relief wardens come and are paid directly by the Youth Hostels organisation. However I may be able to put in a good word for you amongst my friends in the village. There could be someone who needs cleaners or chambermaids."

"We'll do anything!" responded Kate enthusiastically, "Problem is, where could we live?"

"Well," said Fay thoughtfully, "You could stay here a bit longer until something turns up." Then she added, "Can either of you drive?"

"No, er, not yet. That is, we haven't taken our driving tests yet. Ahem, no real need in a city. Good bus service, no parking."

Jo who had played no part in this discourse thought Kate was handling it very well.

"Fair enough," rejoined Fay, "Well if you did get jobs in the village and were forced to stay here then you could always cycle. Mind you, the weather's not always as mild as it's been this last couple of weeks. It's very unpredictable---like now---dreadful yesterday, milder today with the sun struggling to come through! The rain isn't a problem but sometimes we can have heavy snow which lasts for weeks. Still, no use meeting problems half-way. Well then, I'll make a few phone calls and I suggest you cycle to the village this morning, and maybe stop off at the riding school on your way and have a chat with Vickie."

They agreed enthusiastically and went to get their coats and boots. Before they left, Fay scrutinised Jo and said gently, "Are you sure you're feeling up to it?"

The look of concern on Fay's face touched Jo and she threw her arms around Fay and hugged her, "Thank you so much—for everything!" she said, her voice choking with emotion.

Fay, pleased and a little surprised at such a warm and impulsive gesture, watched them until they cycled out of sight then she sighed, got out her easel and began to paint.

When they arrived at the yard Vickie was brushing a large chestnut gelding and she welcomed them warmly.

"Hi! Fay told me to expect you. Can you both ride?"

"Not me," answered Kate, "But Jo is very good."

"Oh, do you have your own horse?" she asked turning to Jo.

"Not now. I used to, er, when I was younger."

"OK, right then," she rejoined in a business-like manner, "I'm always short of people to exercise the horses here---especially the trekkers who are the breadwinners, in other words, the ones that earn the money in the tourist season."

"Well, ventured Jo, "If you want some help, just let me know. We like it here and are looking for work."

"Have you got your riding gear with you?"

"No, but a helmet is all I need really."

"No problem. I have all sizes here for the tourists. Would you like to sit on Rufus here and try him out in the arena?"

"OK," responded Jo.

Twenty minutes later she was riding the big gelding in the sand arena under the critical eye of Vickie.

"You ride very well! He's not an easy horse. Er, would you be willing to come and work here?"

"I'd love to!" gasped Jo, hardly able to believe her luck.

They were given a guided tour of the yard and stables and met Vickie's parents, a couple in their fifties full of vim and vigour. They were both mucking out boxes and greeted the girls warmly.

"We have fourteen horses here," explained Vickie, "Ten are trekkers and they earn the money in the tourist season which keeps us afloat. Of the other four, two are young stock in training, potential competition horses, like Rufus, and the remaining two are my horses which I compete on a regular basis. If you work for me you'll be expected to help with all the chores and to exercise whichever horses need it. When can you start?"

"Er, whenever," replied Jo enthusiastically, "How about next Monday?"

"OK. Can you be here for 8am?"

So that was that. A stroke of luck! A job for Jo doing the only thing in which she felt competent and capable.

They left the stables and cycled to the village with Jo pedalling on air, feeling more confident and optimistic than she had felt for a long time. Kate, although happy for her friend, felt left out and began to wonder what she could do. She had no skills and no qualifications whatever. Her only accomplishment was her prowess in chess, and it was highly unlikely that she would earn a living as a mediocre chess player. She felt useless. She was an abused girl, in part guilty and responsible for her abuse which had ruined her family and put her father in prison!

This was her mood when they arrived in the village and entered the Drovers Arms. They ordered soup at the bar and sat down before the glowing fire. They were hailed by James and Stuart, the two darts players they had met on their previous visit.

"Och Aye! Have you come for your darts lesson? It'll cost you a pint if you have!" greeted Stuart.

"OK!" agreed Jo, "But it's payment by results. If we can't get round the board after ten minutes coaching, then no deal."

"No chance! laughed James. "More like if you can hit the board instead of the wall!"

"Well, wait until we've finished our lunch then we'll see." Jo rejoined jokingly.

Kate remained silent throughout this banter. The dismal and down-hearted mood which had affected her when they left the stables deepened when she saw the two young men. What would they think of her if they knew about her awful past? She squirmed with shame and embarrassment and withdrew into herself. What a sad pathetic person she was! It was all her fault. She could have stopped it at any time.

All she had to do was tell someone or even tell *him* to stop! But she didn't. She was a moral coward. Ashamed to admit it that she actually derived pleasure from it until it was over, then the shame, guilt, humiliation and revulsion kicked in---until the next time! She pushed the bowl of soup away and hurried to the toilet where she coughed and retched. When she returned to the others, she apologised and said she'd eaten something that didn't agree with her but that she was better now. Her face however, still portrayed her black mood which did not go unnoticed by Stuart so he tapped her on the shoulder, "Hey Happy! Come on! Give us a grin and you can borrow my darts."

She stood up reluctantly and accepted the proffered arrows. She knew it would be rude and that Jo would be upset if she refused to join in.

They teamed up—Stuart and Kate versus James and Jo and they spent a happy hour laughing and teasing in good-natured rivalry.

"You look a lot more cheerful now," remarked Stuart, What was the matter?"

Kate clenched her hands and looked away.

Jo answered for her, "Well, we are both looking for jobs here and I was offered a part-time job at the stables this morning and Kate was worried that she might not be so lucky."

"What sort of a job are you looking for?"

Again Jo answered for her, "Anything. Cafe work, shop assistant, cleaning. Whatever's available."

"There's tons of work in the tourist season, but that doesn't start 'til Easter," explained Stuart. "Anyway, leave it with me and I'll make some enquiries. Now cheer up and give us a grin. We'll get you a job somewhere, don't worry". Then he added with a swagger as he patted her on the back, "At least we can thrash these two at darts!"

"Yes," joked James, "A fluke. Hey, don't forget your glasses next time, Jo!"

"Cheeky devil!" laughed Jo. "See you soon!" and the two girls grabbed their bikes and were soon cycling vigorously back to the hostel, glad of the exercise as the gathering gloom and the colder air descended.

Chapter 21

There was a lovely welcoming fire and a delicious meal waiting for them when they arrived at Loch Side and Fay was pleased when Jo told her about her job at the stables and the fun they had with Stuart and James. She was relieved to see that Jo had lost the pale pinched look she'd had when she left the hostel that morning and was now cheerful and glowing with health. In comparison however, Kate had a haunted look about her and seemed out of sorts. Fay conjectured that perhaps she too had something to hide which had risen to the surface. Then she sighed as she realised that she was becoming emotionally involved with these two girls after knowing them for such a short time and she wondered why. There was a vulnerability about them which unleashed strong maternal instincts which hitherto she had not known she possessed.

"What's the matter, Kate?" she asked gently, "You're not your usual cheerful self tonight."

Kate shrugged and turned away, so Jo answered for her, "She's worried about not having a job, especially as I've been lucky. Stuart said there weren't many jobs to be had until the tourist season and I can't drag her to the stables every day."

This was only a half-truth and as is always the case when one disappointment lowers confidence and self-esteem, past troubles and shame resurface. Kate needed a boost to lift her out of this. She needed to be made to feel worthwhile.

Fay took Kate's hand, "Don't worry-- something will turn up, I'm sure, but when Jo goes the stables on Monday, I can find something for you to do here. You can help me to make cakes for the freezer and there's some spring cleaning to be done before February half-term. I can't pay you, but you can earn your keep. How's that?"

Kate forced a smile, "Thank you very much. You've been so good to us!"

"Well, you can't stay here for ever, but as long as there's room, you're welcome. "She became practical again, "Right, come and sit down now and eat this dinner I've made for us before it goes cold!"

During and after dinner they chatted about what there was to do in the area and which books, films and music they liked. Such normal everyday topics were just what they needed. Fay deliberately avoided asking them any more about their past lives as she realised that every time this subject was broached, they both became tense and evasive. The log fire glowed comfortably as they chatted and relaxed. As the dying embers began to fade, their eyelids began to droop. Fay smiled. It was lovely to see them both so natural and tired. "Time for bed, girls!" she quipped, It gets pretty chilly in here later." They stood up and stretched and rubbed their eyes. Fay hugged them both as she bade them 'Goodnight'.

As Jo drew the curtains in the dormitory she saw the moon looming large and full in the crisp bright sky and she thought of their cold and sleepless night in the the thick pine forest and the stories they had told. She shivered, drew the curtains tightly together and decided not to tell Kate that the moon was full---just in case!

She crawled into bed and asked Kate, "What date is it tomorrow?"

Kate thought for a moment and then said, "January 19th."

"Good Heavens! Is it really? It's my Birthday!" Jo announced, "I'll be fifteen tomorrow. Only another year then I'll be free!"

"Are we going to tell Fay? I'm sure she'll make a cake for you."

"I don't know. Perhaps not because she'll think it'll be my nineteenth and she's always commenting on how young we both look."

"You're right. We'll have a double celebration next year!"

With that comforting thought to look forward to they snuggled down into the creaky beds and were soon fast asleep.

During the night the wind rattled the windows and whooshed through the trees but they slept through it all.

The next day it was too windy to cycle to the village so after a short but bracing walk alongside the loch they returned to the hostel. Fay was engrossed in her painting. The girls asked her if they could do some cooking. She readily agreed so they prepared dinner and made a chocolate cake which Kate secretly insisted was to celebrate Jo's fifteenth birthday.

During dinner Fay mentioned that January 25th was Burn's night and that there would be a big party in the

Drovers to celebrate the life of Scotland's most celebrated poet. There would be readings from his well-loved poem, 'Tam O' Shanter', traditional Scottish food, Cock 'a Leekie soup, Haggis, Neeps and Tatties, and Clootie pudding, and, of course a march through the village with Bagpipes!

"Sounds like something not to be missed," enthused Jo, "Will you be there?"

"Oh yes," replied Fay, "I'm making the Clootie pudding."

"What's that?"

"It's a fruity dumpling wrapped in cloth and steamed. It's called 'Clooty' because it's cooked in cloth."

"Sounds different! Can we help you?"

"Of course. We'll make a practice one tomorrow!"

The following morning all the ingredients, suet, oats, flour sugar, spices, milk were assembled and Fay explained, "Clooty pudding recipes vary but the cooking method doesn't. As I said before, it's wrapped in cloth and boiled or steamed. In the old days it was cooked in a pan of water over an open fire because poor people didn't have ovens." Fascinated, they divided the mixture in two, grabbed a bowl each, then they stirred, mixed and squeezed. When the consistency was right, they formed it into firm balls and wrapped it in muslin.

"What now?" asked Kate.

"Well, put it in the steamer and leave it to cook for three hours, but--- don't forget to check the water level in the pan!"

Later, by the open fire, they ate the pudding smothered in custard and agreed that it was good. Different, but good.

The following day they cycled to the Drovers Arms and were pleased to see Stuart and James who greeted them cheerily.

Destiny Obscure

"Come for another darts lesson have you?"

"Of course!" came the light-hearted reply

There was a mutual attraction between them and they had already decided on the pairing, Jo and James, and Kate and Stuart and this was how they teamed up again for their darts game. They felt so happy and relaxed in each other's company and before they parted, James asked them if they were coming to Burn's night on Wednesday.

"Oh yes! We made a Clooty pudding yesterday with Fay."

"Did you like it?"

"Well, yes. It was different, but quite good."

"Do you like Haggis?"

"Don't know. Never had it. What is it?"

"Well, it's a small mammal exclusive to Scotland." replied Stuart in a matter-of-fact tone.

"Oh, what's it like?"

"It's a brown furry animal, bigger than a rabbit. About the size of a badger but it has one strange anatomical feature." He hesitated whilst James turned away, apparently in the grip of a coughing spasm. Stuart ignored his friend and continued, "This may sound far-fetched but, true to the theory of evolution, the haggis has developed over time a very useful mutation---a longer pair of legs on one side than the other." He hesitated, coughed, controlled himself, then carried on in as serious a tone as he could muster, "This marvellous mutation has allowed the haggis to run along the steep Scottish mountainsides without impediment, but of course, he can only do this in a clockwise direction if the longer legs are on the right. Naturally, if on the left, then his favoured direction is anti-clockwise."

The girls listened to this then burst out laughing, searching his face for signs of humour but he remained serious and impassive. "Come on! Pull the other one!" laughed Kate. Then they turned to James, "It's not true is it? He's teasing us!"

James too kept a straight face, "He's the biologist, not me," was all he would say.

"You Sassenachs know nothing of Scottish culture and traditions." admonished Stuart. "Ask any true Scot and he will verify it for you. Anyway, you two 'doubting Thomases', we'll see you on Burn's night!" and they parted with a cheery wave and a chuckle.

On Monday, Jo cycled to the stables leaving Kate at the hostel to help Fay as arranged. Vickie gave her a young lively thorougbred and they had an exhilarating gallop along the forest tracks and bridleways. She was in seventh heaven and she and Vickie laughed and chatted as if they'd known each other for years. The rest of the day was spent brushing and grooming and getting to know the horses, cleaning saddles and bridles then tidying and sweeping the yard. It was good to be around horses again and the searing pain of the recent past was thrust aside as she immersed herself in caring for them. Vickie and her parents were so kind and friendly that she felt a warm glow in their company. She hoped that they would be happy with her as the present situation suited her so well.

On Wednesday morning Kate helped Fay to make the Clooty puddings. Jo came home early from the stables. They were both very excited about going to the Drovers to celebrate Burn's night and seeing James and Stuart again.

They showered and spruced themselves up ready for the party wishing that they had something more feminine and suitable to wear.

"I know we're not Scottish," said Fay, "But I like to think of myself as Scottish by adoption so I will wear a tartan shawl and I have a couple of scarves for you to wear as a token of respect for the occasion. Here they are. I chose MacGregor because I like the colour and design and because I love Rob Roy. Have you read the book by Walter Scott?" They admitted they hadn't nor had they seen the film.

"Well, he is a folk hero amongst the Scots. In fact, Wordsworth wrote a poem about him and he likened him to Robin Hood, fighting for his beliefs and the common good. Wait a minute, I think I can remember some of it," she hesitated, closed her eyes, then recited a few lines,

> *'A famous man is Robin Hood,*
> *The English ballad-singer's joy,*
> *And Scotland has a thief as good,*
> *An outlaw of as daring mood,*
> *She has her brave ROB ROY!*

The girls applauded, "That's great—good old Wordsworth! I'll bet he spent a lot of time in Scotland living as he did in the Lake District he could pop up anytime."

"Maybe," answered Fay, "But it wasn't that easy in those days. Come on. Let's go! We mustn't be late." so they donned their tartan scarves, placed the Clooty puddings carefully in Fay's car and were soon bumping down the road to the village.

The 'Drovers' was brightly lit and bursting at the seams. Long tables had been set in the large lounge and every space was packed with revellers proudly wearing kilts of many colours and clans. As they entered, Fay and the girls were greeted with shouts of welcome and were soon immersed in a hubbub of conversation punctuated by tumults of laugher.

Stuart and James pushed their way through the crowds, "Och Aye! There you are! You look gorgeous! What'll you have to drink---Shandy as usual? OK!" They were ushered to the table and introduced to all those around who welcomed them with warm hand-shakes and wide smiles.

Soon, kilted waiters appeared bearing the first course, Cock-a-leekie soup. When this was cleared away, an expectant hush descended and then, with a great flourish, the sound of bagpipes filled and thrilled the air and the haggis was piped in to uproarious applause! Jo and Kate were overwhelmed and felt themselves so lucky to be part of this unique experience as they tucked into the meal chatting and laughing with all those around them. Already they felt they were part of this happy and convivial community. Kate asked the man sitting next to her if the haggis was truly a mammal exclusive to Scotland and was assured that it certainly was! Had she not seen the story in the 'Goodies' when they captured a haggis and then encountered a bagpipe spider? She laughed and decided that she loved these myths and would not question them further and never try to dispel them.

After dinner, various guests recited pieces from 'Tam o Shanter'. Jo and Kate clapped and applauded. They loved the story and the humour, particularly the part about Tam's brave horse, Meg, escaping through the water from the witches and sacrificing her tail which the cruel and determined felons grabbed and pulled off at the last minute!

Then followed 'A toast to the Lassies', a teasing and good-natured tribute to the fair sex, delivered by the jovial landlord amid much laughter and barracking. This was followed by a tongue in cheek 'Reply to the laddies' ably given by the landlords wife! These joking 'tributes' evoked much good-natured banter from the audience.

By this time, everyone, drinkers and abstainers alike were in joyous mood and it was time for a sing-song. All the voices joined together and sang, 'Comin' thru' the Rye', 'Charlie is me' Darling', and many more traditional Scottish songs, all accompanied by clapping and stamping. By now all inhibitions had fled. A space was cleared in the middle of the room and the dancing began. Jo and Kate were dragged to their feet by James and Stuart to join in the traditional folk dances—a true Scottish Ceilidh! Tunes were hammered out on the piano, accompanied by a flute, tin whistle and banjo. Jo and Kate had never had so much fun in all their lives.

At last, it was time to draw the party to a close and everyone returned to their seats. There was a hush as a young man took his place at the piano and sang Robbie Burns' beautiful and poignant love song, 'My love is like a Red, Red Rose'', in a soft tenor voice. There was complete silence. Stuart took Kate's hand gingerly and gently but she withdrew it and blushed.

As this wonderful evening drew to a close, everyone stood, joined hands and sang, 'Auld lang Syne'. Such was her mood that Jo had the strength to dispel the memories of the times this very traditional rhyme had been sung at

Bryn Celyn and to join in with optimism for the future without marring it with pessimistic memories of the past. Much hugging and hand-shaking followed and then, as if to revitalise everybody, the bagpipes blared out again leading a a procession of happy and inebriated followers dancing and laughing as they made their way home.

Chapter 22

Matthew and his mother Megan were sitting quietly at the graveside of David Newton, late father and husband. The grave looked neat and well-cared for thanks to the clergy and congregation who still remembered him. The simple epitaph on the slate slab comforted and subdued them as they read it:

'Faith builds a bridge across the gulf of death'

It summed up his life's work and reinforced his own unshakeable beliefs.

The ginkgo biloba tree had grown quite a lot in height but bereft of its leaves it looked skeletal. Megan shivered. "The tree looks bare and miserable. Maybe we should replace it with something more colourful."

Matthew took his mother's hand, "These trees have been in existence for twenty-seven million years. They will never become extinct. For me, they symbolise eternity. Life handed down from one generation to another facing, overcoming and surviving adversity."

Megan moved closer to him and spoke in a soft tremulous tone." Matthew, you are and always will be the most precious thing in my life". She paused, "But the one thing I have always longed for is a grandchild so that *we* can hand *our* lives down to future generations, ensuring *our* immortality. I don't want to make you feel bad about this. I understand that your life has been full of devotion to others, just like your father. He was older than you are you now when we met so there's still time for you to meet someone and fall in love but don't leave it too long or it will be too late for me."

This was said with a catch in her voice and such heartfelt emotion that Matthew's initial reaction was surprise twinged with guilt and remorse. He hadn't considered his mother's feelings in this respect. He had thought tentatively about settling down with a partner at some stage in his life but it had never been a priority. His future seemed limitless with endless tomorrows but what happens when tomorrow never comes? It will never come again for Tom, Jenny and Emily. He shuddered and put his arm around his mother.

"I'm sorry mum. I've not given it much thought really. Like you said, I've been happy and fulfilled doing what I'm doing and you look after me so well I've never felt the need for anyone else. My congregation are my family and I'm never lonely. Besides, I haven't met anyone who I'd want to share my life with---not yet anyway!"

"You're just like your father, so unselfish. Putting everyone else first!"

"Until he met you," he said light-heatedly, giving her a squeeze. "Perhaps my 'Megan' will come soon and sweep me off my feet."

"You're a bit old to be 'swept off your feet!"

"Nonsense, mum! Don't be ageist! You're never too old!"

Megan shivered, "It's getting chilly now and it looks like rain. Shall we make tracks back?"

She seemed so sad and frail that he had to do something to cheer her up. He linked his arm through hers, "I know what we need! How about a Cornish cream tea in 'Betty's?"

"Good idea!" Then she looked again at the grave, kissed her fingers, touched the name on the slate tombstone and whispered, "Bye, my darling. We'll be together again soon."

Arm-in-arm they left the churchyard and were soon indulging themselves in a delicious cream tea amid the warmth and welcome of Betty's teashop.

When they returned home from Cornwall, Matthew, instead of feeling refreshed as one should after a break, felt strangely depressed. His mother was disappointed in him. She longed for a heir, a part of her and David, a testament to their unity and love and it looked as though it would not be possible. He had been so selfish in not even considering this. His shoulders slumped and he had a tight feeling in his gut. He thought of his life hitherto. He had been contented enough doing what he was doing, living from day to uneventful day but then he had met the Westons and his life had taken on a new meaning. They had become an extended family and now they had gone, for ever, and he had failed even to help Jo! What had become of her and Kate? Life would never be the same here without them and he could not summon up his former enthusiasm for his vocation. He was just a failure. How could he go on trying to help and counsel his parishioners when he had failed miserably in his own life? His mother was unsettled too and had instructed him that she wanted to buried with her husband in Cornwall. The logistics of conforming with that request made the burial of Tom and Jenny in Bluebell wood seem simplicity itself! He felt helpless and inadequate. His hitherto fulfilling vocation of counselling and helping his congregation deal with their routine problems of illness and bereavement; organising Weddings, Christenings and Funerals; preparing texts for Religious festivals, Sunday Sermons, together with supervising the never-ending chores for the necessary maintenance of the church and churchyard, seemed all too much for him. On top of all this was his mother's heartfelt request for a grandchild and the never-ending torment of the guilt and worry he felt about the disappearance of Jo and Kate. What was he to do? He had to face his problems, real and perceived, in the same way as he had counselled Jo to do. Face facts, summon your inner strength and get on with it! However, advice is so much easier than execution.

His former enthusiasm for the Wednesday Chess Club was declining too. He felt guilty and ashamed of his listless attitude towards the keen youthful membership who looked up to him for inspiration. It was becoming a chore and being there intensified his feeling of inadequacy. He had let Jo and Kate down. If they had really trusted him they would have taken him into their confidence and he would have found a way of comforting and guiding them thereby preventing their madcap escape. Wasn't this what his vocation was meant to do? And his mother? He'd let her down too by not providing her with what she wanted more than anything—a grandchild to love and cherish-- a tangible link to the future ensuring that hers and David's genes could live on for ever, or at least for the next generation. Matthew felt he had been insensitive and selfish not to realise this. Why was he so beset with these problems that he was turning them over and over in his mind-unable to think of anything else. Was he going mad? He had to overcome this sense of failure and inadequacy. So many people needed him to give them hope and strength. How could he do this when he himself felt so utterly bereft? *He* was the one who needed help and guidance now! Who could he turn to? There was only one person, one place ----. So he made his way, with quickening steps but shoulders hunched, to the tiny church. Not a soul was in sight. All was quiet and deserted. The graves stood still, waiting, some well-tended with fresh flowers laid by loved ones. Others dejected and neglected, rampaged by weeds. There was a parallel here with humanity---how poignant, how sad! He opened the heavy door and entered. The winter sun streamed through the stained glass windows casting coloured shadows which shivered over the altar and pews. He felt a strange power and presence presiding over him as he knelt down to pray. Abject and empty, he pressed his hands together and bowing his head, he prayed fervently, totally absorbed in communion with his God. At length it was as if comforting arms embraced him, soothing and gentle, stroking away his pain and stiffness; massaging away his shattered self-esteem. Gradually he felt able to cleanse himself of all the negative and hurtful feelings which had built up inside him and he began to replace them with strength and resolve. When he left the church he had a spring in his step and hope in his heart.

Several days later he received a phone call. "Hello, is that Matthew Newton, vicar of St. Davids?

"Yes. Who is speaking?"

"Beth Moore, Kate's aunty. I believe she knew and trusted you and that you were close to her friend Jo's family."

Matthew, momentarily startled, hesitated before replying.

"Well, er, yes! We were close friends. Have you any idea where they are?"

"No, I've been abroad for the past year and only just heard the news. Pretty worrying business. I've come to find out more and to see if I can help. Could we meet somewhere?"

"Er, yes, er when?"

"This afternoon if you like. If you have the time that is."

"Yes, yes, er, of course, er very well then. Say 2 o'clock in Wendy's Cafe? It's on the main street. Half-way down."

"OK. I'll find it. See you there at two. Bye!"

Matthew was intrigued. Kate had never spoken to him about her relatives except to mention that she had been taught to play chess by an aunt. This surely must be her!

He arrived early and scanned the diners. Some greeted him, somewhat surprised to see him there. However, they were all in company so he sat down at an empty table facing the door and was about to order when a woman entered. She was in her mid-thirties, slim and casually dressed. She too scanned the customers then her eyes alighted on Matthew and both knew instinctively that this was the person they had come to meet.

Matthew stepped forward and introduced himself. They shook hands warmly and Matthew ordered tea for two.

"How did you find me?" he asked.

"I found out from the foster family, Mr. and Mrs. Evans. They are very upset too and feel that they have failed although they admitted that Kate kept very much to herself and they were never able to win her confidence or get close to her."

Matthew sighed, "I felt I was gradually gaining her trust but mostly on a superficial level. Then this happened---no doubt planned and orchestrated by Jo."

"Probably," agreed Beth, "Kate was always easily led. That was her downfall."

Neither of them wanted to enlarge upon this so Matthew began to recount the whole history of the Weston family and how Kate and Jo had become friends, originally through their mutual interest in chess. As he talked, Beth listened intently and her blue-green eyes never left his face. He found this steadfast look disconcerting. It was as if she were seeing right through him and could recognise fact from fiction. He found it difficult to return her gaze so he paused intermittently and stared at the scuffs on the wooden table whilst he collected his thoughts. When he had finished, she sighed, her eyes softened and she shook her head and murmured, "Poor kid."

Now it was her turn. She asked if he knew why Kate had been taken into care. He replied that he knew that she had suffered sexual abuse from her father but that he had never spoken to her nor Jo about this.

"It went on for years. I had no idea. I didn't see them that often. Kate was always an introverted child, no wonder, and when I spoke to my sister about Kate's lack of friends, she would get angry with me. We never got on, my sister and I. She's seven years older than me and ignored me when I was growing up. However I was very fond of Kate. I was very surprised and pleased that she enjoyed chess and took to it so easily. I also loved reading to her and telling her myths and legends." she paused, "I'm an astrologer." she waited to see what effect this revelation would have upon Matthew, a theologian, but he remained impassive so she continued, "That's how I make my living. Some people think it's a bit corny and fanciful." she paused again, checking his face to see his reaction. Again he betrayed nothing but interest. "And my sister told Kate and her brothers to take no notice of me. She calls me, 'Batty Beth'!" She smiled and again those green eyes this time held his gaze. She continued, "I am just so sorry and ashamed that I didn't know what was going on." she shook her head in disbelief then continued, her voice strained with emotion. "I was abroad when she had the abortion. Poor, poor kid! She held her head in her hands in an effort to control herself then she continued bitterly, "My stupid pathetic sister blamed Kate for not telling anybody. She accused her of ruining the family and destroying all their lives."

Silence between them again. They were each enclosed in a shell of pain and privacy, oblivious to the spattering rain on the window, the shuffling and muttering, the clatter of cups and the ring and bang of the door as wet passers-by sought sanctuary in the cafe.

They agreed that both Jo and Kate had suffered cruel blows from life and had felt that the only only way they could cope was to run away and start a new life. But where? And how could two young girls cope alone in any environment? And what were they doing for money? Both Matthew and Beth knew that they had to find them and take care of them. Give them help and support, love and security.

They were in the cafe for more than an hour recounting the problem of the runaways. Eventually Matthew suggested that they go for a walk and discuss the best ways of ascertaining the most likely destinations and whereabouts of the two unhappy girls. The wild March weather was not conducive to walking outdoors as the wind and rain battered through the village street and angry clouds shrouded the normally beckoning hillsides. Beth shrugged off his concerns on her behalf and they walked in silence, shoulder to shoulder, heads down, conversation impossible but each immersed in thought. There was more shelter from the trees when they reached the park yet neither spoke. Beth's thoughts were concentrated on Kate and she was convinced that it was the influence of Jo which had induced her to run away. Kate was not an adventurous type and was easily led. Jo must be the ring-leader. Therefore she would have to learn a lot more about Jo's character before she could begin to guess their possible destinations. For his part, Matthew was studying Beth. She was comely and attractive but not at all glamorous. She gave the impression of being independent, intelligent and trustworthy. There was a warmth about her which seemed to embrace him. And those eyes--those incredible eyes! He wanted to get to know her better. He felt sure they could be good friends—soul mates, perhaps.

Beth broke into his thoughts "It'll be dark soon. We should think of going back."

Matthew looked at her. She was drenched and beginning to shiver."

He resisted the temptation to enfold her in his arms—to comfort and protect her. This was stupid! He'd only met her a couple of hours ago and already she had ignited his masculine urges—to cherish, to protect. She had said she was an astrologist. Was this related to witchcraft? Had she already cast a spell on him?

She broke into his thoughts, "I need to book in at a local hotel. Can you recommend one?"

Reality took over. "No, no, certainly not! Of course you must stay at the vicarage with us, er,—my mother and I. We have plenty of room. Where's your car?"

She tried to protest but she too had warmed to her companion and trusted him intuitively.

Megan welcomed Beth warmly, "Do come in. Good heavens you're soaked! You must have a hot bath. You'll catch your death of cold!"

Soaking and relaxing in the large iron bath Beth closed her mind to everything except Kate and her adventurous strong-minded friend. She needed photographs of Jo and a complete history of her life and her character. Tomorrow, this is what she and Matthew would do. Only by knowing the girl responsible for their absconding could she begin to guess where they had gone.

Megan had cooked a lovely meal for them all with wine and and had even produced candles whose flickering lights softened the austerity of the high-ceilinged oak-panelled room and they sat at the large wooden table eating and talking, totally at ease. Before the meal was finished they all felt as if they had had known each other for a long time.

Beth was the first to retire and Matthew and his mother sat before the fire in the lounge sipping the rest of the wine and chatting in a way that they had not done for years. They pondered on the plan to recover the girls and what part

Beth could play in it. Then Megan began asking questions about Beth.

"Did you say she was an astrologer? Rather an unusual profession. Does she earn any money at it?"

"Apparently so. She writes horoscopes in newspapers and magazines and she writes mythological stories for children."

"You mean 'Harry Potter' fashion?"

"No, not exactly. She rewrites authentic myths in ways that that children can understand, leaving out or watering down the more grisly bits."

"That's a pity. Children usually love the grisly bits best. So she's an astrologer who writes children's books! Mmm, is she clairvoyant too?"

Matthew began to get exasperated. He was tired and he thought he sensed his mother's cynical disapproval.

"Look, mum, I've only just met her! She doesn't seem like a crank to me."

"I never suggested that she *is* a crank but I have never met an astrologer before. Does she see herself as some kind of psychic?"

"I don't know. I don't think so." He thought about Beth's failure in not realising what was happening to Kate."

"Well," mused Megan, "If she writes horoscopes and tells fortunes maybe she's just super-intuitive. There's a parallel between clairvoyance and intuition. If she has regular clients she must be doing something right. Does she read palms too?" This was said tongue in cheek

"Come on, mum! You're being ridiculous. She's an astrologer not a bloody gypsy—and no, before you ask, she hasn't got a crystal ball either!"

Megan giggled then said mischievously, "That's a pity—it would be so much fun if she did have one! I used to love the witch in 'Somewhere over the Rainbow', cackling into her crystal ball!" She twirled the glass of wine, watching the way the reflected light from the candles ignited images in the blood-red liquid. "This is my crystal ball," she teased.

She was enjoying winding him up and she sensed his annoyance. She also sensed that there was an attraction between him and Beth, so she continued on a more serious note.

"In *her* way, she helps people to cope with their lives just as you do. She can give them hope and a helping hand. There are so many similarities between religion and astrology. In fact, religion is a refinement of astrology. Your father and I had many arguments and discussions about it."

Matthew looked at her in surprise. He never imagined that his mother had ever questioned the teachings of the gospel.

"Well," she began, her tongue unleashed as she warmed to her subject "It all started with the worship of the sun. A good start, as all life on earth is dependent upon the sun. Horus, the Egyptian God, was born of a virgin, as was Krishna of India and Dionysus of Greece and many more. Virgin birth signifies divine impregnation, so *all* were sons of God. They were all born on the 25th December. Also, they were all crucified and rose again from the dead after three days and ascended into heaven. "Now", she continued authoritatively, neither caring nor imagining that she was telling him something which he already knew. Matthew enjoying her enthusiasm, indulged her, so she continued uninterrupted. "The sun is at its lowest point in the sky on December 22nd, effectively dead, and it rises, reborn again, on December 25th. just three days later! Sirius, the star of the east, is over Bethlehem on December 25th and is followed by three stars, interpreted as the three kings, or the three wise men," she took another gulp of wine, warming to her subject she continued, "Christians celebrate Christ's ascension at Easter, three days after his crucifixion, when life begins anew in nature, in other words, the Equinox. Also, all the ancient mythological Gods had twelve disciples too, from the twelve months of the year. The cross is the sign of the zodiac. The day of worship is Sunday--there are so many parallels but the scientific facts about the sun and the constellations no doubt inspired the ancients to accept and worship the sun as their God." She sat back, took a deep breath and another sip of wine.

Matthew, surprised to hear his mother pontificating in this way, humoured her by feigning ignorance.

"So what about the Christian God? How does he fit in with this in your eyes?"

"I don't know," she answered thoughtfully, studying her glass and taking yet another sip of the rich red wine. "Perhaps it is because he is personified through Jesus in our faith; in our love, and it's this which guides our lives. We need an image, a greater being, something to cling to, a belief in better things ahead for all mankind. The concept of a God sustains us in this. However, all races have their own particular Gods and they are all 'jealous Gods'." Her voice and attitude became more forceful, "It's the 'thou shalt have no other God but me' syndrome. This is what causes most problems in the world. Religion imposed in this way is a kind of tyranny and is used to promote and encourage violence. If we all had one God, the God of Love, Peace, and Tolerance, then we could all live in peace and harmony. To me this is what religion is all about." She gave long sigh of satisfaction as one who has captured her audience with her eloquence.

Matthew, was enthralled. He had never heard his mother pontificating in this way before and so obviously enjoying it. He decided to encourage her further.

"Well, mum," he asked "What about 'life-everlasting'?"

"That's a tricky one. I've thought about it a lot recently. Not unnatural at my age I suppose." She suppressed a sigh, "What is our soul? Is it embodied in our thoughts? Maybe our thoughts live on in the ether—in limitless space. I like to think that they do and that when our bodies are no more, then the unique electrical energy transmitted in our thoughts will coalesce and this will represent our soul which will live on forever." She was silent for a while, considering this on a personal level, then added frankly, "It's probably a lot of fanciful nonsense and makes me more of a crank than er, Beth? Oops, sorry! But how much more fanciful is it than believing in a 'Day of Judgement' and 'Ascension to Heaven' or 'Banishment to Hell'?"

Matthew smiled and hugged her, "Hey mum, you're quite a philosopher! Is it the wine that has loosened your tongue? Remind me never to allow you to do the sermons in Church! You'd cause a riot!"

He smiled ironically, then added, "Well, *I* shall continue to believe in life everlasting and do my utmost to convince my congregation of this as no-one can ever prove it right or wrong. It is as Hamlet said, *'The undiscovered country from whose bourne no traveller returns',* and on that note I'm off to bed."

So saying, he hugged his mother again and they both crept up the creaky stairs so as not to disturb Beth.

In the morning Beth asked Matthew to find as many photos of Jo as he could and a map of the whole of the British Isles. These were spread out on the table in the lounge and Beth studied the photos intently and asked many questions about Jo. She listened, scanned the map and began to rule out various places.

"She is a country girl at heart and so we can assume that they will not have chosen major cities and towns. Ireland is a possibility but there are too many logistical problems. I feel drawn towards Scotland –somewhere in the far North. She turned those green eyes upon him and said with conviction, "Yes, I have a strong feeling that Scotland is where they are!"

Chapter 23

Jo was loving her job at the stables and the weather during February half- term had been cold but dry and bright so every day had brought many visitors to experience hacks in the beautiful countryside. The hostel had been busy too with walkers and cyclists and Kate had worked hard alongside Fay to keep things running smoothly. However, the girls knew that they could not stay at the hostel indefinitely and that they would have to find somewhere to rent. Kate needed a job so that they could finance this and James had assured her that come Easter, lots of visitors would arrive at the hotels, cottages and camp-sites and there would be plenty of jobs available. His mother had a holiday cottage which he and his father were working on and he promised her that he would persuade his mother to give her a job taking care of it when the season started which was less than a month away. He and Jo had a very carefree relationship, not too serious yet very good friends. On the other hand, Stuart loved Kate and wanted a closer relationship with her and although she was very fond of him she continued to hold him at arms length. They usually went out in a foursome, James and Jo being the other couple, but whenever Kate was alone with Stuart she always seemed tense. In the cinema he would put his arm round her and she stayed close and relaxed but when he tried to kiss her, she withdrew and turned away giving no explanation other than she was hot, or uncomfortable. When he looked hurt or puzzled, she just smiled, apologised and took his hand.

One night as they were waiting in the 'Drovers' for the girls to arrive, Stuart told James about Kate's apparent frigidity. "She always rejects me when I try to kiss her or get really close but she insists that she likes me." He paused and took a sip of his pint, "I've never forced myself on her. I've never even tried! I've always had a softly, softly approach. I can't understand it. He paused, then said quickly, "Do you think she's a lesbian?"

James laughed out loud, "I very much doubt it. She's far too feminine for that!"

"Not all lesbians have gruff voices and walk with a swagger. Some are as soft and feminine as, er, er, the virgin Mary!" answered Stuart, and they both laughed at this ludicrous analogy.

"Why don't you ask her?"

"Who? The virgin Mary?"

More laughter.

"Don't be daft!" rejoined James, then added teasingly, "Just ask her which team she bats for."

"You're not taking this seriously, are you? If I ask her straight out like that she'll either think I'm joking or be really offended." He quaffed his beer and wiped his hand across his mouth, "Come on, Jim! How can I ask her without offending her? Anyway she may not be sure herself yet. She could be in self-denial which I've heard is quite common, especially in post puberty".

"Well, if she's eighteen she's had plenty of time to come to terms with it."

"Yes, but she's a very young eighteen. Being brought up by her grandmother must have been like being brought up in a convent."

"True, she is very unworldly. I would be patient if I were you and carry on with the softly, softly approach. Remember, mate, 'all comes to him who waits'. And when it does come, Wow! It'll be like you've conquered Everest!"

Stuart gulped his beer as he savoured this prediction. Minutes later the girls arrived breathless and excited their hair and coats covered with thick flakes of snow.

"Did you cycle in?" asked Stuart in surprise.

"Of course, but it looks like we'll be sledging back!"

"Don't worry. If it gets worse you can stay at mine. There's plenty of room. Flora, my sister is away at Uni in Edinburgh.

"What's she studying?" asked Jo.

"Veterinary. She's in her third year and still has two to go."

"I'd love to do that."

"Why don't you then? It's never too late."

"I'm not clever enough and anyway, I hated school."

"Any ideas about what you're going to do instead?"

"Not at the moment. Kate and I both want to travel and see a bit of the world before we settle down."

"And you started with Scotland! Where next?"

"Give us a chance. It takes money and that's what I lack until I win the lottery!" laughed Jo'

"Well, when you do, me and James will come with you!"

"You're on!" she said and they laughed and 'high-fived' in agreement.

They played darts, and chatted and laughed with the locals; some were playing cards, others dominoes, then someone started playing the piano and everyone joined in an impromptu sing-song oblivious of the weather which got worse as the snow fell quietly and continuously. When it came time to leave, everything, including their bikes, was blanketed in snow. In these conditions there was no chance of the girls getting back to the hostel so they rang Fay to tell her they couldn't make it and would be staying at Stuart's house.

When they left the pub the snow was falling thickly and there wasn't a breath of wind. The moon, which was full, tried its best to shine through the thick curtain of snow making a magical glow on the jewelled crystals which covered everything. Happiness and abandonment possessed the youngsters and they rolled like race-horses in the squeaky yielding snow. Then they pelted each other with snowballs laughing and shrieking all the way to Stuart's farm where Andrew and Rhona, Stuart's parents, were anxiously herding sheep into a large barn, ably assisted by two black and white border collies.

Andrew hailed them, "Come and help! There may be some more buried out there. Never thought it would get this bad!"

They followed Andrew through the deep drifting snow driven on by the urgency of the task, uncaring and unaware of their own physical discomfort.

The collies, intent and focussed, began to dig furiously, uncovering any ewes which were buried in the snow and driving them into a corner on the whistle commands of Andrew. When the ewes needed help to move, Jo and Kate pitched in, seizing them and dragging them out of their snowy hideaways. At last Andrew decided that they could do no more. Bess, the keener of the two collies continued digging energetically unearthing nothing, whilst Bridget, her mother, kept vigil over the rescued flock.

Soon they were all back at the farm, the ewes safe and sound in the big barn munching hay as if nothing had happened whilst the humans and dogs sought comfort in the cosy farmhouse.

"Thanks for that," said Andrew kicking the snow off his boots. "God knows how long this will last and some of the flock would have died."

"What about the lambs?" ventured Jo.

"Lambing hasn't started yet and the ewes about to lamb are already in. The ones we got tonight are last year's lambs. Anyway, you must be freezing. Come in and have a drink and a bite to eat. Nice to meet you at last."

They shed their wet clothing and were ushered into the cosy lounge.

Rhona, Stuart's mother, bustled in with warm scones and hot chocolate and they sat chatting in front of a blazing fire whilst the snow continued to fall quietly and relentlessly, intent upon burying the unresisting village. Inevitably the conversation turned to what had brought the girls to this remote area and their plans for the future. Their vague answers were unconvincing and their embarrassment apparent to the astute Rhona who commented again on how young they both looked. Kate tried to lighten the atmosphere and change the subject.

"I've never seen so much snow before. Amazing that anything could survive in these conditions, er," then, trivialising the whole situation, she added with tongue in cheek, "What about the baby haggis? I expect a lot of them die. Is there a name for baby haggis?"

This childish attempt at humour went down like a lead balloon as they all looked at her with puzzled and almost disdainful expressions.

Rhona was the first to speak, "Let's call them 'Haggards'," she said sarcastically, then continued almost aggressively, "And that's how we will all look in the morning if we don't go to bed now. Follow me you two. You can sleep in Flora's room."

Poor Kate squirming with embarrassment followed Rhona and Jo up the stairs.

The 'Good-nights' were said with more politeness than warmth.

The following morning was bright and beautiful and they all set about clearing snow from the doorways and carrying hay to the sheep.

After lunch the girls decided to return to the hostel but James and Stuart would not hear of them attempting it alone. Stuart stayed behind to help his parents on the farm so the girls, clad in borrowed wellies with James as their guide, set out on the five mile trek.

Rhona had been unusually quiet and reserved all morning and when she and Stuart were alone together she confronted him.

"I hope you are not getting too serious about this girl."

"What do you mean?" he demanded, unable to keep the irritation out of his voice."

"You know exactly what I mean. She's far too young for you or anybody else for that matter."

"Here we go again! I'm fed up with people disputing her age just because she happens to look young. I thought the main problem today is that girls try to look older than they are so they can smoke and drink and play around and they *do* look older because they plaster their faces with make-up and dye their hair. Kate doesn't do any of these things and she's led a sheltered life being brought up by her grandmother."

"I wouldn't be too sure of that. Whenever I asked her about her grandparents she was so vague, as if she was making it up. I think she's been in some sort of trouble and is running away."

"Well what if she is? He answered exasperatedly. "Maybe those looking after her were too restrictive and made her life a misery." This was said somewhat pointedly, "Anyway,", he added, "I know her better than you do and as far as I'm concerned she's a great girl and fun to be with."

"I'm asking you to be careful, that's all." There was a warning note in her voice, "I don't think she's even sixteen yet and penalties and punishments for under age sex are harsher now than they've ever been, even for consensual sex."

Stuart exploded, "For God's sake mother—I'm not a child any more!" He leapt up from his chair and began stamping around the room. "Have you never heard of boy and girl *friends?* That's all we are at the moment *friends!* I'm twenty-one years old and I don't need you to dictate moral standards to me."

Rhona kept her voice quiet and her manner calm, "I have a feeling about her that's all. I'm worried that she's going to be bad news for you. I can't explain it, but it's there. Just be very careful. Or better still, give her up."

She had her back to him and her greying hair tied into a bun protruded above the chair. He stifled the urge to grab it and shake her head around. Instead, he clenched his fists and said quietly, "I really don't know what's sparked this off but rest assured that I can take care of myself and make my own decisions." Stiff with anger, he left the room.

"I hope so love. I really hope so." This was said fervently and resignedly in a sad whisper.

Chapter 24

It had been agreed that Beth would stay at the vicarage to help solve the mystery of the whereabouts of the two runaways. She and Matthew decided not to contact the police concerning their theory that the girls could be somewhere in Scotland. The publicity and urgency which had been of paramount importance for the week following their disappearance had now died down and no-one from the press or the police had contacted Matthew during the past couple of weeks to ascertain if he had any news or information. Neither had Julie and although they had not contacted each other personally since the disappearance, Matthew had forwarded letters to her from New Zealand which had been addressed to Tom and Jenny. He was mystified but not surprised by Julie's lack of concern, but shocked by the apparent lack of concern from the authorities. Did no-one care any more? Is this the way it worked? Apathy owing to over-stretched resources?

"The police will have documented the incident in a 'Missing Persons' file and it will remain there until they are alerted or need it to furnish statistics," remarked Beth.

Destiny Obscure

"Very probably," agreed Matthew, "I just wish I could be assured that the girls are both well and not under stress or in danger. What can we do Beth--? I pray for them every day but now I am becoming impatient and want to do something more practical."

"I know", she said gently taking his hand," But all we can do apart from praying is alert the police again which neither of us wants to do and I'm sure the girls would not thank us for that". Her deep green eyes held his and she continued with conviction," I have a feeling that they are coping. Remember what Jo said, 'No news is good news'. That is very true. Had anything happened to them it would have been reported in the press, on TV and radio and the police would certainly have been here." She hesitated then clapped her hands together, "So, let's *do* something practical. Get the large scale map of Scotland out again and we'll pore over every inch to reinforce my original feelings."

Once again they opened up the map on the large dining table and Beth placed the most recent photographs of Jo as she had done before around the edges of the table and and lapsed into a deep trance-like state. Matthew watched but said nothing. Even lively Lulu was transfixed, her head resting on Beth's knee as she gazed adoringly at her new friend. Eventually, without looking up, Beth spoke in quiet, measured tones, "I'm not certain of the exact spot but, as last time, I have a strong inclination towards this area". Her sensitive fingers indicated a location in the north west—a remote and beautiful area opposite the Isle of Skye and overlooked by two hillsides with a lovely loch nestling beneath them.

Matthew stood up and looked over her shoulder. She spoke quietly, "From everything you've told me about Jo, her background, her personality, I am absorbing stronger feelings from this area than from any other. Of course I could be wrong but I don't think it will be far out".

Before he met Beth he would have been sceptical about anyone claiming such extraordinary perception but he did not doubt that she was right. It seemed so obvious to him now. So, what were they going to do about it? Go there of course, find the girls and then try perhaps to persuade them to come back, but in any case they resolved to give them their full support in whatever the two decided what they wanted to do. The problem was,---when?

The following morning there was another letter from New Zealand and written on the back of the envelope was a request to return to sender if undelivered. Matthew pondered for a while. His first instinct was to do the 'proper' thing and re-address it to Julie but he felt that something was not quite right. Why had it been addressed to Bryn Celyn again? Surely Julie would have told Brian and Liz the bad news! Tom had told him all about what good friends they were and how they had pretty well brought up Jenny when her parents were off adventuring and that they had put up the deposit which enabled Tom and Jenny to buy Bryn Celyn. So why----? On a sudden impulse he tore open the envelope.

Dear Tom and Jenny,

We hope all is well with you but we are wondering what has happened as we haven't heard from you since your Christmas card telling us that you were off to Olympia. How did you get on?

We've written to you a couple of times but assume that the letters got lost in the post. Also, we've tried to phone you but again without success. Brian thinks you've gone off on some wild adventure like Mike and Danielle and that you'll turn up on our doorstep! That would be marvellous but I can't see it myself. Seriously though, I am worried about you and hope it's the failure of the postal system. If it is, no worries, we have internet access now and a computer. Our email address is: buggermebert@cob.com

Yes, Bert is still going strong, bless him, and he sends you all his love as do Jack and Janet and baby Graham.

Please get in touch---we are hoping to get over there this summer!

Much love to all of you,
Liz and Brian xxxxx

Matthew was stunned. What had Julie done with the letters he had forwarded to her? He had no idea of her relationship with Liz and Brian but however estranged she could not be excused for ignoring their plea. He resolved to contact them immediately. It is never easy being the bearer of bad news but he decided to use all his tact and experience to soften the blow in an email which he knew would be delivered like lightning and hit them like a thunderbolt! He took the letter into his office and sighed deeply as he sat down to compose the dreadful email. Beth was already in there writing horoscopes for magazines and newspapers. She looked up when he came in and read the letter which he handed to her. She shook her head and sighed in disbelief when Matthew told her how Julie had ignored the previous letters. They sat down together and composed the heart-rending email. There was no way of hiding the facts. They just had to try to present them in a calm and measured way. Not an easy task but eventually they agreed upon the content and pressed the 'send' button.

Matthew then began to compose his sermon for the Sunday Service and they worked in concentrated silence for a while. It struck Matthew that there were similarities between what they were doing. They were both trying to help people to understand and make sense of their lives and sometimes even managing to help them to deal with or even avoid difficulties and problems. Both Beth and Matthew had issues of their own and conceded that ironically, it was easier to help others with counselling and support than to implement this on a personal level. Matthew's approach relied on religious beliefs and he could always consult God and gain help and comfort from communion with Him. Beth had to rely on Astrology for inspiration and this required intuitive sensitivity coupled with belief and immersion in the occult. However, she and Matthew understood and respected each others views. After all, there are so many areas where these ostensibly conflicting beliefs overlap and complement each other.

Beth had been at the vicarage for three weeks now and she and Matthew had developed a bond which had progressed beyond friendship. Megan too had become fond of Beth and they had discovered that they had a lot in common and that their hitherto different liaisons guided them towards the same goals, love, tolerance and peace. Matthew had missed his chess games with Tom but found he had a worthy opponent in Beth and when she was not in deep religious and philosophical discussions with his mother, they would spend whole evenings playing against each other. She also enjoyed helping him at the Wednesday Chess Club in the local school but her relationship with Kate was never revealed to staff or pupils. In spite of all this fulfilment neither could forget what had brought them together and the mystery and stress surrounding the missing girls was a constant cloud in their day to day lives. They knew that they must do something positive to try to find them and now they were both quite convinced that they were somewhere in the Scottish Highlands they began to make plans.

Chapter 25

Easter was just three weeks away and James' mother, Grace, promised that Kate could have the job of cleaning and preparing the holiday cottages for the tourist season as her usual cleaner had decided to move on. This meant that the girls could have the cottage previously tenanted by the cleaner. They were delighted. Independence at last! They both had jobs within easy reach of the cottage and they were becoming accepted by the locals. At last the pressure they felt as guilty runaways living a lie was fading. A new beginning with a future they could control. Exhilaration! They were sad to leave the hostel where they had felt safe and protected and it was a wrench to leave Fay who had been a surrogate mother to them when they most needed it. However, they all accepted that it was for the best and the bond between them would remain.

Setting up home in the small stone built detached cottage, 'Brae Cullen', was an exciting venture for the girls. It seemed a strange almost chilling coincidence that the Gaelic name for the cottage was translated as 'Bryn Celyn' in Welsh and also got its name from the sturdy spiky holly trees which surrounded it. Jo shuddered when she realised this but convinced herself that it was a good omen. They would be as happy here as they had been at first in 'Bryn Celyn'. They would make sure of that and to this end they cast out any negative pessimism. This was a new start. Their hearts and minds were full of youthful hope and optimism. So they harnessed their abundant energy and set about cleaning, clearing, painting and polishing. Upstairs there were two bedrooms and a bathroom while downstairs a porch led into the kitchen which housed an ancient solid fuel stove plus an electric oven and hob, a large ceramic sink and an automatic washing machine. There was an open fire in the lounge and exposed beams which added to the cosy-cottage feel of the place. There was ample furniture, bedding, cutlery, crockery and cooking utensils and an old record player with a collection of vinyl records. They often played these and danced around to the blaring rock and roll music of the sixties, twisting and jiving, exulting in their youth and energy. What more could they ask for—to them it was perfect and perfection became super-perfect when Stuart and James turned up with a small portable television and a radio! They were independent and adult at last. They were earning money and they had their own place to live!

Kate worked hard cleaning and preparing the three nearby holiday cottages and Grace was very pleased with her. However, she made it quite clear that she did not want either James or Stuart or anyone else for that matter to spend the night in 'Brae Cullen' without her express permission. The girls readily agreed to this and James jokingly remarked that she didn't want it to be known as the local 'knocking shop."

"She's very old-fashioned, my mum, and very influenced by *'what the neighbours think'*", this was said in a teasing whine and they all laughed. There was no way that the girls would dream of doing anything to upset Grace and risk losing all this and their new-found freedom. This was a new beginning for them. And the future? Well, they were young and all they wanted to do now was to savour the present. The future could wait.

Easter was a hectic time for all of them. They hardly saw each other. Kate busied herself cleaning and preparing the cottages at weekends whilst during the week she cycled to the hostel and helped Fay. Jo started her day at the stables at 6.30am and immediately set to work mucking out boxes, cleaning tack, brushing horses and taking out rides. Neither of them got back to the cottage before 8pm. As for the boys, Stuart was working flat-out, day and night with lambing whilst James worked alongside his father constructing and repairing houses. All their lives were hectic, happy and fulfilled.

After Easter they decided to have a house-warming dinner, just the four of them, and the girls got very excited planning a menu to make it a really special occasion. They decided on a rib of Aberdeen Angus beef, assured by Fay that this was the best and tastiest cut. They would serve it with roast potatoes, carrots, spring cabbage and of course, Yorkshire pudding!

"I'll make an apple pie with custard for dessert", said Jo.

"And we'll top it off with cheese and biscuits!" added Kate enthusiastically.

"What about starters?"

"Er, I think dips and nibbles would go down well. We could get some white wine as an aperitif and some red to go with the beef."

"Sounds perfect. Good old Fay for tutoring us so well!"

The big day arrived and a large part of it was spent on making themselves beautiful and the house warm and welcoming. Kate slurped rather than sipped the white wine as she bustled round the kitchen checking the food. Jo meanwhile busied herself in the lounge making sure that the laid table looked festive and inviting with an attractive decoration donated by Fay which they adorned with red candles—a perfect match for the blood-red tablecloth bought for the occasion. The open fire, well-fed with logs, spat and sparkled in the hearth and a strategically placed lamp cast a soft warm glow over everything. They were ready! All they needed now was the guests.

"Come and see!", shouted Jo, "Tell me what you think."

"It looks amazing—and so do you! I'm so happy!" and they hugged each other joyfully.

"Pity we have no Champagne to celebrate", observed Jo ruefully.

"No worries!," laughed Kate, "We have Bucks Fizz instead. Let's have quick slurp before the boys arrive!"

They giggled and clinked glasses then jumped as they heard strident tapping on the door.

"Come in if you're good-looking!" shouted Kate, and the two boys appeared, carrying a beautiful bouquet of red roses and more wine.

"Wow, this place looks great!" they enthused, "And you two look so gorgeous!"

Hugs all round and more clinking of glasses as they drank each others and everybody else's health.

"Hey! Guess what I found amongst the books and things that were left here!" announced Kate excitedly, "I remember you saying that you loved the old music of the fifties and sixties".

She rushed over to the old record player and a hissing, crackling sound emerged followed almost at once by, 'One two three o'clock four o'clock rock-Boom-Boom ---' and the the strident tones of Bill Hayley's 'Rock around the Clock', reverberated round the room. They all roared with laughter, and danced and clapped as they shouted out the lyrics intoxicated with wine and Bucks Fizz and exhilarated by youth.

"What next—what else have you got?" urged Stuart, and he laughed and clapped as the companion track 'See you later, Alligator-----' burst forth re-igniting their energy and carefree spirits

The beep -beep of the timer on the oven interrupted their cavortions and Kate, clapping her hands, shouted, "Carry on dancing! Nearly time for dinner! I'll just go and check everything."

The joint of beef which had been resting for a while looked temptingly succulent and gave off a delicious aroma. She picked up the newly sharpened pointed carving knife and began to draw it gently through the meat as instructed by Fay whose words echoed in her head, "No chunks or uneven slices. Smoothly and carefully!" She felt unsteady and clumsy. No doubt she had drunk too much. Potentially fatal for someone who normally didn't drink at all. She felt herself swaying and summoned all her hidden resources in an attempt to regain her self-control. At that moment Stuart came into the kitchen. He stood behind her. "How's it going, love? Come on, let me do that!"

"No, it's all right. I know what I'm doing. I can manage." This was said assertively and a little defensively.

"Oh, 'I can manage---' Little Miss Hoity-toity!" he teased.

He placed his hands around her waist and pulled her bottom towards him thrusting himself against her, then his hands slid upwards and he fondled her breasts.

"No!" she screamed, "Stop it!"

He gyrated his hips gently backwards and forwards and continued fondling her breasts. "That's nice," he breathed, "Oh, that's so nice."

Something inside her snapped. Consumed with horror, anguish and guilt she tore herself around to face him and on a violent impulse without thinking or in control of what she was doing, plunged the knife into his belly.

Pain, shock and terror contorted his features and he emitted a blood-curdling wail as he doubled up and fell, blood gushing from beneath his grasping hands.

The blood-stained knife crashed to the ground. Kate stood stock still momentarily paralysed. Then she too emitted a terror-stricken scream.

Jo and James hearing the commotion ran into the kitchen and gasped with horror as they took in the dreadful scene.

"My God, what's happened! Quick, dial 999 and get a towel!"

James pressed the towel as firmly as he could to the wound in a desperate effort to staunch the flowing blood whilst Jo, trembling uncontrollably called the emergency services.

Kate stood rooted to the spot shaking and wailing, "What have I done! I didn't mean it! Oh God! Please God, I'm sorry! Will he die? Please don't let him die!"

"They're on their way," gasped Jo. Is he breathing? Is he dead?"

James, still kneeling by the blood soaked body choking with emotion yet striving to suppress the panic and fear which were so close to overtaking him demanded that they stopped their commotion and kept calm. Kate, hysterical, ran sobbing out of the house and Jo knelt down next to James closed her eyes and prayed.

They both knew there was nothing else they could do. Stuart was already on his side and his head was in such a position as not to obstruct his airway. Was he breathing? They couldn't tell and even if he wasn't there was no way they could give him mouth to mouth respiration or heart massage. They had to control the blood flow—that was the most vital priority. Moving him around could further damage his internal organs—possibly fatally. Jo could not help thinking of Emily and all that had been done to try to save her life. Alas, to no avail. This situation was different but starkly visible, making it far more horrifying. James reiterated in gasps that all they could do to help Stuart was try to reduce the blood loss, and wait. This they did, in dead silence until the shrill siren rent the air. The paramedics were brilliant. They worked efficiently in unison and within minutes Stuart was in the ambulance attached to the life-support machines and on his way to Casualty. Two police remained behind and demanded an explanation of the incident. Kate was nowhere to be seen so Jo and James told them as much as they knew without accusing Kate of the stabbing. It could have been an accident. They could have been playing around. Sergeant Murphy noticed the empty bottles.

"Have you been drinking?" he asked.

"Yes, we've had a few."

"A few too many by the look of it." he said grimly. "Now where is the other girl? Kate, you called her."

"We don't know. She ran out in a panic. She was so upset."

The policewoman who had been searching outside came in at that moment.

"No sign of anyone in the garden or the immediate vicinity, sir."

"Any idea where she could have gone? Has she any friends round here?"

"Not really. We haven't lived here that long."

More questions followed and Sergeant Murphy took notes whilst the policewoman stared earnestly at Jo and shook her head in disbelief from time to time.

Interview concluded, the police consulted quietly together then Sergeant Murphy said firmly in matter-of-fact tones, "I'm going to ask you both to accompany me to the station."

Jo heard this with sinking dread. So the game was up!

Her hands and dress covered in blood Kate ran away from the cottage in a state of panic and horror. What had she done and how could she have done it!

What had come over her—they had been so happy. Everything was going right for them and now this! Were they beset by some evil spirit that tantalised them then took over their senses? She stopped and retched and retched again and again, choking on the foul rush of alcohol and sour snacks which gushed from her mouth. "Oh please someone help me or let me die! If Stuart dies then I don't want to live any more!" There was only one person who she knew would do her best for her. Only one person she could trust to give comfort and help-- Fay! She half ran and half staggered the five miles in the pitch dark to the youth hostel.

When Fay opened the door she was confronted by a bedraggled Kate wailing and sobbing drenched in blood and vomit. A bolt of shock and dread ran through her as Kate staggered in clutching at her and crying "Help me Fay! Please help me!"

"What's happened? Where's Jo? Oh my God!"

Between sobs and wails Kate told the horrified Fay the grim account of what had happened at their first much-looked-forward-to dinner party with the boys.

As usual, the strong and practical character which personified Fay took over and she soon had Kate in the shower and wrapped up in a warm dressing gown in front of the blazing comfort of the open log fire.

"Now, tell me again from the *very* beginning all that has happened and what brought this on."

Kate, not caring any more about her own perceived guilt and shame, related her whole life story to the silent and attentive Fay. Somehow, for the very first time, it seemed a relief to get it off her chest. The shame was still there but the feeling of guilt was diminished.

Then Kate became more anguished as she said in staggered phrases," I was happy, carving the meat, looking forward to a wonderful evening, all of us together. Stuart was behind me. He started wriggling and pushing his hips against my body. I told him to stop then he put both his hands on my breasts and said,' That's nice. You don't want me to stop. That's nice.' Suddenly it was just like *him* again. Like my father!" These last words were screamed out with choking loathing. Then she continued in a surprised and confused tone, "I don't know what got into me then! I just wanted him to stop! I didn't mean to stab him. It just happened. I didn't mean to do it!" Once again the convulsive sobbing possessed her.

Fay held her close and waited for the powerful emotion to subside. Now at last she understood and was able to put the pieces together. They were two runaways trying to escape from the harsh knocks life had dealt them. But these two were too young to realise that there is no escape. We are all haunted by the harshest realities of our past lives. Time salves but cannot obliterate. Poor, poor kid! All she has had to suffer and now this!

Kate wanted to stay close to Fay and shut out the dreadful reality. She withdrew into herself, her breathing convulsive. Fay stroked her hair and said nothing, waiting for the shock and distress to subside. She did not move until she was obliged to add more logs to the fading fire. Kate snivelled and said in a constrained voice, "What will happen if he dies? Will I be done for murder? Will they lock me up for ever? Please God don't let him die!" The anguish returned and she placed her head between her knees and covered her face with her hands. "If he dies, I want to die too. There's nothing left for me to live for."

Fay looked up from the fire, "Now, now, don't start imagining the worst. He's young and strong and the medics are so good."

"Yes, but I attacked him with a knife! Even if he does survive they can still prosecute me for grievous bodily harm. Will they put me in a juvenile prison?"

"Let's stop this surmising self-torture." This was said calmly but firmly, "You are only fourteen years old and he is twenty-one. Legally he can't prefer charges against you. He could be charged with paedophilia."

This sparked a scream of rage and denial from Kate, "No, he can't! It wasn't his fault. I told him and everyone else that I was eighteen. He believed me. Everyone did!"

"That makes no difference in law. They are only interested in facts."

"Oh no! That's not fair! The facts are that we deceived him---deliberately. He is completely innocent. It *can't* be fair!"

"The law seldom seeks to be fair. There are so many views on what constitutes 'fairness'. The best it can do is to plead extenuating circumstances."

"But what will happen to me now—and Jo?" The despair in her voice prompted Fay to take Kate's chin in her hands. She held the frightened gaze and replied in a calm reassuring tone," I will do my best for you, you know that. Things have not been easy for you and the injury you caused to Stuart was not premeditated. It was an impulsive act engendered by the wrong you have suffered and no doubt sparked off by the alcohol you were drinking." She paused, "That's another thing. Who provided the alcohol? We must make sure that the police know all the facts."

"We bought some—they bought some. What the hell does it matter!" She tore Fay's hands from her face, "Why are we pointing fingers—blaming each other, blaming everybody else! What the hell does it matter? *I* deceived him. *I stabbed him!* He is completely innocent." Then with a whimper in her voice she added, "And he could be dead!" She repeated this with a loud wail, "He could be *dead!*" She was becoming hysterical again. Fay took a firm grip on her shoulders and tried to restrain the violent shaking.

"Come on now. Come on! Calm down. Hysterics will get us nowhere."

A loud banging on the door startled them both. Fay hurried to the door and wrenched it open. It was the police!

There were two of them. The same two who had arrived at the cottage after the stabbing incident.

"Is this Kate Wilson?" asked the policewoman indicating the pale and shaking girl.

"Yes, it is." answered Fay moving protectively towards Kate. "As you can see she's in a state of shock and hardly able to answer any questions coherently. Can't the formal stuff wait until tomorrow?"

"Well she should accompany us to the station," replied the sergeant gravely.

"She has no clothes." protested Fay. "She was in such a state when she arrived that they are all in the washing machine. Anyway she's a minor. What she really needs at the moment is a doctor for her physical and mental state, not being dragged off in a car to some police station to be besieged and browbeaten by strangers."

Fay was aware of the belligerent tone in her voice and hoped that it wouldn't be interpreted as rudeness knowing that if she offended these stalwarts it would be worse for Kate. She continued in a more pleading tone, "Anyway you can't just arrest her without proof. You don't know what happened. You can't be sure of the facts. Maybe they were playing around and it was an accident. Look at her-- she is in a state of shock and in no fit state to be questioned. Can't she stay here for the night? I will accept full responsibility for her. You can stay too, if necessary. She needs caring for at the moment. She's exhausted and distraught and quite unable to cooperate in your enquiries. And as she is a minor, I am willing to take on the full legal and formal responsibilities of a guardian on her behalf."

There was a pause and the two police conferred. Then the senior officer spoke, "Alright, if you are prepared to make a statement and sign it to that effect then she can stay here until the morning."

Fay sighed with relief and the frightened Kate hugged herself harder and buried her head between her knees.

Fay signed the relevant paperwork then plucked up courage to ask the most important question of all. Fearful that it could be bad news she lowered her voice to a whisper to ensure that nothing else must be known by Kate that could add to her torment.

"How is he?"

Sergeant Murphy hesitated, then mumbled, "The last news was that he was in a critical but stable condition."

"Thank God! So there's hope at least."

"He's in the best possible place. The trauma staff in that hospital have successfully treated horrendous incidents from the North Sea oil rigs so he has a fighting chance."

The young policewoman hovered, out of her depth, looking to her superior for guidance. She made as if to approach Kate, presumably to make contact and perhaps try to comfort her. Sergeant Murphy deterred her by a slight shake of his head then said authoritatively, "Time we made tracks. Until tomorrow then. Goodnight." and they left more quietly than they had arrived.

Fay drew the curtains and stared out at the jewelled sky which penetrated all and gave hope to the closeted blackness of the night. She cupped the crescent moon in her right hand and whispered softly, "You're waxing, beginning anew. Please let that be an omen for Stuart!" She knelt down before the window and inspired and chastened by the immense glory of the universe, closed her eyes, bowed her head, put her hands together and prayed fervently. Afterwards she stood up, gathered her strength and said with the same fervour, "Come on Stuart! Fight, fight! You're too young to die!"

Kate was still whimpering and shaking but less so now. "Have they gone? How is he? Is he dead?"

"No, he's a strong boy and he's getting the best possible care. Now what we both need is a nice cup of tea."

Chapter 26

Matthew, Beth and Megan were walking back from church after the Sunday Service in which Matthew had stressed tolerance in religious adherence. 'I thy God am a jealous God' should not be interpreted as 'turn your back on all other religious beliefs'. All the major religions want the same thing--for all mankind to live in peace and harmony. We all have different and unique ways of worshipping and we should respect and understand this. He read extracts from the Koran which he had never done before. His congregation seemed to listen more intently as he compared these doctrines with similar philosophies in the Bible. He went on to stress that we should not blame particular religions for the atrocities carried out in their names by a few murderous misguided groups. In fact, this was the exact opposite of what any of the religions advocated. After the sermon, they sang the hymn, 'All People that on Earth do Dwell' and he exhorted the congregation to regard God as being a God who represents the beliefs of all religions, not just Christians. It was a good sermon, and one which reflected current world-wide events. As the congregation left the church and each one shook his hand, as is the custom, many of them congratulated him and said how much they had enjoyed the sermon. Beth and Megan were still discussing it when they arrived back at the vicarage welcomed by the tantalising aroma of the Sunday joint sizzling in the oven. However, their relaxed enjoyment of the lunch was interrupted by a knock on the door. It was the police.

Although they were shocked to learn the circumstances, at least they now knew the exact whereabouts of the girls and that they were physically unharmed. Matthew and Beth began to make arrangements to drive up to Scotland the very next day. Matthew emailed Liz and Brian in New Zealand to tell them that the girls had been located and were safe but he did not tell them the full story. He also rang Julie but she had already been informed. Her reaction was typical, "I always knew she was a bad lot. Just like her mother!"

"But it wasn't Jo, Julie. Jo has done nothing. It was an unfortunate incident and it's *Kate* who is claiming responsibility."

"Jo probably put her up to it. Anyway, I've washed my hands of her now. I want nothing more to with her. She's nothing to me. Never has been. I will do the right thing for my brother's child and that is that! Oh, and I don't want her smooching round here either, under the pretext of seeing Billy. Make that clear!" And she slammed the phone down.

Matthew shook his head sadly, "Poor miserable Julie."

The very next morning Matthew and Beth set off on the long journey to the Scottish Highlands. As he looked at Beth beside him he couldn't help reflecting that every cloud has a silver lining. Had it not been for Kate's troubled past and Jo's tragedy he would never have met Beth and he knew that he loved her and dared to hope that she was equally fond of him. Their conversation on the long journey centred around the girls and what was to become of them once this latest setback had been resolved. No doubt the law would take a dim view of their running away, even given the extenuating circumstances. But, in the eyes of the law would those circumstances be recognised as extenuating? Probably not. The legal system had already sorted them both out, hadn't it? Done what was best for both of them---in fact, for all concerned. Kate in a kind foster home, Jo with her aunt. Job done! Wash hands. Tap-tap. Next Case!

He and Beth discussed the likely outcome and how it would be viewed in the eyes of the law. Considering the trouble Jo and Kate had caused by turning their backs on 'what was best for them' would they be made an example of and punished by confining them in a young offenders institution? That would be the worst punishment and the best way of alienating them from society, perhaps for ever. And so the discussion went on. But no matter what the authorities decided or wanted to do, Matthew and Beth were determined to stand by the girls and fight for whatever they all agreed was best for them.

Beth was driving through the lovely rolling countryside of the Lake District and they were both absorbing the beauty and tranquillity of this very special landscape. Matthew felt surreal. Beth, who had become so precious to him was transporting him through paradise! He was suffused by a warm wave of emotion and he wanted to tell her he loved her but he felt that to utter these words would somehow break the spell. The lyrics of the song 'And then I go and spoil it all by saying something stupid like I love you' echoed through his mind. But he didn't need to say anything. Beth, sensitive and intuitive as always, absorbed and reciprocated his feelings. She looked at him and smiled.

They stopped near Carlisle and ate lunch in an attractive old coach house pub. The atmosphere in the cosy lounge was warm and friendly, the food wholesome and they basked in the glow of the smiling open fire. They felt an inner warmth and were at peace with the world. Even though the problems of the girls still engulfed them they were able to savour this time together and push aside any feelings of guilt that the happiness and fulfilment they were experiencing had arisen as a direct result of the awful hurt suffered by the two youngsters. Their mutual interest gave them strong bonds of cooperation. They were in it together gaining strength from each other and this gave them confidence to face up to whatever lay ahead. They were sure they could rescue the runaways and bring them safely home.

After lunch they drove through the breathtaking beauty of the Scottish landscape. For mile upon mile they were alongside loch after lovely loch, some framed by mighty mountains rising precipitously with dense forests of Scots pines clinging tenaciously to their near vertical slopes. Above the tree-line snowcapped peaks, even mightier, beckoned North.

Matthew was well-impressed as he absorbed the unspoilt scenery.

"This is truly beautiful!" he breathed, "I've never been to Scotland before."

Beth smiled, "This is only a small part of it," then added, "Pity we're not on holiday."

This chance remark brought home to them both the real reason for their journey so they lapsed into silence, each wondering how the two young girls were at this moment coping with this latest devastating blow.

At 9pm they were within ten miles of the village of Strathkellen and decided to check into a hotel for the night. They were given a pleasant double-bedded room and as it was the first time they had travelled anywhere together it was as if they were on their Honeymoon. It was a bitterly cold clear night and Beth drew back the curtains and gazed at the limitless sky. Matthew joined her and commented on the sheer brightness and splendour of the Scottish heaven.

"Yes, it's the very best place in Britain for star-gazing", she smiled. A northern sky and no pollution." She began to point out different galaxies naming some of the stars within them and lapsing into a lecturing mode. Matthew stood silently beside her, indulging and enjoying her enthusiasm.

"The ancients believed that a living soul is a higher essence of matter and evolves into a star. When I was a little girl I used to wonder how all the dead people, past, present and future, could possibly fit into heaven. I couldn't get my head around the concept of infinity. Then I was told that there were more stars in the universe than grains of sand in the deserts and that if I could imagine this and more besides for ever and ever, that's what infinity is. I began to believe there and then that there was room up there for all humanity for ever and ever--- Amen!" She grinned mischievously and paused. Then she continued in the same grave tone, "Some stars have divine attributes. They evolve into Gods and look down from chaotic violent purity into the world of humanity and invisibly yet powerfully influence the energies of humankind. I suppose this concept of certain souls becoming deities gave rise to the idea of reward and punishment on Judgement Day. Those who fall out of favour break up and shoot down into Hell---shooting stars? Anyway, to get back to Sirius and its influence on the Earth. For instance, in early July in Egypt when Sirius was hidden by the sun's glare, the ancients refused to bury their dead for thirty-five days before and thirty-five days after as they believed Sirius was the guide to the constellation, Argos, the ship, the bridge between heaven and hell."

Matthew was intrigued, "Which is Sirius?" he asked.

"The very bright star you can see is Sirius, known as the dog star. That one, in the constellation, Canis Major. Can you make it out? It's the closest star to the earth after the sun but it's twice as big as the sun and twenty times brighter. It is said that it affects the behaviour of dogs in the hottest days of summer when it is closest to the earth. Hence, 'dog days' It was also reported that the sea boiled, wine turned sour and dogs went mad!"

"There are references to 'dog days' in the King James Bible too," remarked Matthew, "Although not specially related to Sirius. More to the heat from the sun."

"Religion comes into it again," Beth ignoring this allusion to formal religion, continued, "Sirius is the classic 'star of Bethlehem' which led the three wise men to the stable where Jesus was born. Can you make out the three lesser stars behind?" Matthew couldn't but he nodded to reassure her as he wanted her to continue. "Well," she said assertively, "They gave rise to the legend of the three wise men." Matthew smiled as he remembered his mother's discourse on stars the first night Beth had stayed at the vicarage. He moved closer to Beth and put his arm around her waist. She became more animated as she warmed to his touch and her subject. "Even in modern times," she continued assertively, "Sirius is revered as special. For example, on the American dollar bill, the light behind the 'all-seeing eye' comes from Sirius, and there are those who believe that Sirius is 'the sun behind the sun' and therefore the true source of our sun's potency. So, if our sun keeps the physical world alive, Sirius keeps the spiritual world alive." She took a deep breath then continued, "Freemasons too believe that the Sirius is a symbol of deity and it is the sacred place all Masons must ascend to. And even in 'Pinocchio', Gepetto prays to the 'blue fairy' in other words, Sirius, to make Pinocchio into a real boy. Hence Sirius is again represented as a source of life." She paused, earnestly searching for his reaction. Was she boring him, even patronising him?

Matthew, overcome by the love and tenderness which smouldered within him, returned her gaze fondly. He gently stroked her face pushing her hair behind her ears and began to sing, softly, teasingly, "When you wish upon a star---- Your dreams come true-----".

Her reaction, seemingly at odds with his became cocky, "In fact, '*Caruso*'," this a little sarcastically, "Sirius is *two* stars. You can't see the other, Sirius B, as it is much smaller, and it was thought to be the origin of the devil," she chuckled, "I like that. A naughty sibling dogging his big brother!" Matthew laughed too, and they closed the curtains and faced each other.

"Come here, darling---," breathed Matthew. He took her gently, meltingly, into his arms. She shivered ecstatically and they snuggled down together on the soft warm bed.

Matthew and Beth arrived at the Police Station the next morning only to be told that the girls were at the Youth Hostel under the care of the warden until their appearance before the local Magistrate. They were given no more information than that. Thus they set off to Loch-Side Youth Hostel.

Fay, who was half-expecting that Matthew and Beth would eventually arrive had said nothing to the girls as she did not want to raise hopes that could be dashed again if things went wrong. The two girls were absorbed in a game of Chess, the normality of this in their relationship coupled with their deep concentration diluted, temporarily at least, the awful predicament they were in.

Matthew and Beth bumped along the unmade road Beth's car grounding now and again on the roughest areas. When they arrived at Loch-Side Youth Hostel both were struck by the remoteness and beauty.

"This is just the sort of place I imagined them to be." sighed Beth, "No wonder they weren't discovered here."

They approached the door almost tentatively not sure about their reception.

However Fay, true to form, welcomed them with warmth and enthusiasm immediately putting them at their ease, "Matthew, Beth, --so glad to see you—do come in." She took their coats and escorted them into the lounge then called out happily, "Hey girls Look who's come to see you!"

Jo and Kate looked up and for an instant remained rooted to the spot. Then with wild whoops of sheer delight they ran into the arms of Matthew and Beth. They were overwhelmed by mixed emotions as they clung to the people who meant the most to them. Their saviours! They hugged, cried, apologised and thanked.

Fay looked on smiling and deeply contented. Things had to get better for them from now on she thought grimly. Then, her practical side took over.

"Sit down, sit down by the fire. I know you have lots to catch up on. I'll go and make us all some tea." Tea, the ubiquitous British panacea!

The next hour was spent with questions and answers ranging from the time the girls left and leading up to the present grave situation.

Stuart was still seriously ill but responding to treatment and although the hospital refused to give a positive prognosis the seeds of hope were sprouting in all of their minds.

"When can we go to see him?" asked Kate.

"No-one except immediate family is allowed at the moment. When things improve, he will be the one to decide." answered Fay, pausing to pour the tea.

A cold hand clutched at Kate's heart. "Perhaps he will never want to see me again. Perhaps he hates me now."

Reassurance and platitudes seemed futile and would only serve to fuel the guilt and self-pity which threatened to overwhelm her again.

Matthew averted this by saying, "What about this Chess game then! Who's got the upper hand? Why don't we have a foursome? Beth and Kate against me and Jo!"

"Goody, goody!" cried Jo, seizing two pieces and asking Beth to choose from her closed hands.

"Well done, Auntie Beth!" enthused Kate as Beth chose the hand holding the white piece.

"That's not fair!" teased Jo, "I forgot she's psychic!"

The board was cleared, then set up again for the new contest. Soon all four were engrossed in their game.

Fay watched for while so happy to see them reunited, then with a deep sigh of contentment she took up her position by the window and began to paint.

As usual, following the Easter break, the hostel was quiet so Beth and Matthew were given a family room. Jo and Kate pondered about this. Why didn't they ask for separate rooms? They weren't married and he was a 'man of God'. Didn't the Church frown upon such liaisons?

Was it possible that they were a couple? Wouldn't it be marvellous! Neither of them dared ask.

The following day the four of them went for a walk alongside the lovely loch. Conversation at first was limited to the beauty of the location and how fortunate they were in finding it and in meeting Fay. Inevitably, after a while, the problem of their predicament crept to the fore and the two girls lapsed into a glum silence. Kate began to feel guilty that she was here, still alive, with her friends, enjoying herself, whilst Stuart was in hospital fighting for his life and it was her fault. *Everything* was her fault!

Matthew became aware of the change of mood so he stopped walking and turned to face them. "We have something to tell you", he announced, putting an arm around Beth, "We have decided to get married!"

Misery and foreboding were replaced with surprise and excitement as they absorbed this news.

"Really! Whoopee! Fantastic!" Jo and Kate shrieked excitedly. Mutual hugs followed.

"Have you set a date?"

"Not yet, but it will be soon," Matthew replied laconically, "Before she changes her mind." He laughed and hugged Beth who smiled indulgently.

When they got back to the hostel Fay was putting the finishing touches to her painting. "That's really good!" admired Matthew, "It captures the beauty and the mood of this lovely setting."

"The mood and the setting change constantly. I never get fed up of painting it. Today there's a touch of sun behind the clouds. That means hope." She smiled meaningfully then added on a sudden impulse, "Please take it. A gift for you all to remember me by."

They were over-whelmed by this touching gesture.

"This will be a family heirloom for Jo," mused Matthew, "It will be treasured alongside 'Vagabond'."

Chapter 27

Stuart was making a good recovery and was allowed more visitors. His mother, Rhona, did not want Kate to see him nor did she want to set eyes on this troublesome girl.

"I knew that girl was bad news from the time I first met her. It was a feeling I had--- and I never for one moment believed she was eighteen!"

This was said to James' mother Grace, as they were leaving the hospital.

Grace who did not want to be dragged into a dispute with Rhona remarked, "Oh er, The police told me that Jo's guardian is here. Apparently he's a vicar and he would like to see Stuart."

Rhona turned angrily on her friend, "What! What for? What good would that do? He doesn't need prayers now," she added sarcastically.

"Maybe not," responded Grace, "But it might help Stuart to make sense of it all. Stop the lad from feeling like a victim. If he is a vicar he'll be very good at counselling and comforting."

Rhona sighed, feeling deflated as the anger and outrage which sought vengeance began to soften and give way to genuine concern, "Alright then, but I'd like to meet him first."

That same evening Matthew, Beth and Grace went to see Rhona.

The sad and sordid history leading up to the girls' running away was related to the two women. It put things into perspective for them and they saw Jo and Kate in a different light but it did nothing comfort Rhona who felt that whatever had made Kate attack her son in such a violent way, she could never forgive her and no-one should ever excuse or condone it.

"They had all been drinking," said Matthew gravely, "And certainly Jo and Kate were well under the influence. They both admitted that it was the first time that they had drunk wine. I'm pretty sure that it was the alcohol that robbed her of her self-control."

"That's as maybe," retorted Rhona, "But I still can't forgive her for nearly killing my son!" and she broke down.

That was the cue for Matthew and Beth to leave.

The next day James went alone to visit Stuart in hospital. He was in a small side ward sitting up supported by cushions and listening to head phones. James was surprised and pleased to see his friend looking so well. Stuart greeted him warmly and good-humouredly and begged him not make him laugh as the wound would hurt like hell if he did. James smiled. He knew that Stuart's attempt at humour was to make *him* relax and lessen any embarrassment or shock he might feel at seeing his friend in this state. They began to talk about the incident and what was likely to happen next. James related the whole history of Jo and Kate. Stuart listened gravely shaking his head from time to time in disbelief. Then he said through clenched teeth, "The bastard! The selfish, dirty bastard! Five years is not enough for ruining his daughter's life!" He lay back on his raised pillow assimilating the significance of Kate's mental torture then he said quietly and thoughtfully, "This accounts for all her seeming frigidity towards me. She was afraid of where it all might lead if she gave in to me, even a little, and what memories it may bring back." He paused, "Poor Kate! The shame and guilt she feels will probably haunt her for the rest of her life. Maybe she'll never be able to have a normal sexual relationship ever again"

James said nothing at first. Words seemed so superficial. He sought through his mind to find an adequate meaningful response but failed so he shook his head uncomprehendingly from side to side. Then he said, "I'd no idea they were so young, especially Jo. She seems so fearless and confident. They shouldn't be punished for running away though. There was nothing left for them where they were. I quite admire them in a way."

"Me too, but I wonder what will happen to them now."

They were still pondering and discussing this when Grace and Rhona arrived.

Rhona kissed her son, "You look so much better! I've spoken to the doctor and he says that all being well you could be discharged in a week. Those two are appearing before the Magistrates next Wednesday I hope they get what they deserve, little madams!"

"The police were here earlier mum. I told them I don't want to prefer charges against her. I forgive her."

Rhona almost shrieked, "What! She tried to kill you and you don't want her punished! How can you *ever* forgive her for that?"

"Mum, she didn't try to kill me. It was a sudden impulse beyond her control. A spur of the moment thing. She was drunk too. It was my fault!" He faltered, "But I didn't know about her past. I told the police that it was an accident---that we were larking about—that we were drunk---which is true."

"Well *I* am going to tell them that *I* want her punished!"

"I wouldn't do that mother." Remember what you said about paedophilia?"

He buried his head in his hands. The nurse appeared as if from nowhere, "Now now, don't upset him. He's been doing so well. I think he needs to rest now." So they took their leave, somewhat subdued, especially Rhona who wrung her hands in frustration and despair.

Jo continued working at the stables She didn't want to let them down and besides she needed the therapy of being around the horses. Matthew and Beth were introduced to the owners and were again treated to the warm and natural Scottish hospitality.

"No wonder the girls settled here so happily," remarked Matthew. "They made the right choice by choosing this lovely remote place."

Kate, who had been watching Jo riding, came up to them and slipped her hand into Beth's. "I want to go and see Stuart. James said he's much better now and allowed visitors."

"Well," said Beth gently, "His mother doesn't want you or Jo to visit him. She thinks it might upset him."

"I've got to see him. If I don't, he'll think I don't care. Can't we ask *him*? He can make his own decisions can't he. He's not a kid any more even though his mother still treats him like one! Please Aunty Beth, ring the hospital and ask to speak to him."

Matthew intervened, "I think it would be better to talk to Grace first. See if she can do anything. Or, better still to James, so we don't put Grace in an awkward position."

This was agreed to and James rang back and reported that Stuart really wanted to see Kate and a good time would be tomorrow afternoon when his mother would not be visiting.

The four of them arrived at the hospital the following afternoon. Kate was filled with foreboding, wondering how Stuart would greet her. She needn't have worried. He was sitting up watching the door expectantly. Kate controlled her instinct to rush in and hug him so she approached almost reverentially. "Stuart," she whispered tearfully," Forgive me. Please forgive me. I didn't mean it. I'm so, so sorry." She knelt by his bed in abject subservience and he began gently stroking her hair.

"I forgive you, of course I do, but there's nothing to forgive. No-one should blame you." Then, with forced jocularity, "Anyway, no harm done. I'm here to tell the tale and I'm going to be OK."

"No harm done! Nothing to forgive? Look at you! I could've killed you. How can you ever forgive me? I'll never forgive myself." she paused, then added, "I love you" This was said quietly, almost muffled in a sob, as she remained kneeling, grasping his hand and burying her face in it.

He suddenly became aware of the audience witnessing this emotional scene so he released her grasp, and said, a little awkwardly, "Oh, er, Hello Jo. Thank you for coming."

Jo introduced Matthew and Beth whilst Kate stood up and placed chairs round the bed. They chatted amicably until it was time to leave.

Kate kissed Stuart shyly and tenderly and promised to visit again as soon as she could. He smiled and took some time before he released her hand.

They left the hospital quietly, Kate still feeling the warm grasp of his hand and the deep affection in his eyes. Beth was the first to speak,

"What a thoroughly nice boy."

"Yes, he is," agreed Kate, then added with a catch in her voice, "I Never really thought he could forgive me so easily for what I did."

Matthew reflected for a moment then repeated softly, "*'Forgiveness is the fragrance the violet sheds on the heel that crushed it'.*"

Silence, then Jo asked "Who said that?"

"I believe it was Mark Twain", replied Matthew quietly

"That's lovely." breathed Kate.

"And so apt," agreed Beth.

Chapter 28

After much consultation the police and Magistrates agreed on the sentences for the girls. Both would be placed on probation for six months under the supervision of a social worker. Meanwhile foster parents would have to be approved for them. The obvious choice to fulfil this role rested with Matthew and Beth, strengthened by the fact that Beth had family ties with Kate. The legal side could not be formalised until they were all settled back in Wales. Once this was established, plans were made for their return. Neither Jo nor Kate wanted to leave but realised that there was no alternative. It was very hard to say 'Goodbye' to all the friends they had made, especially Fay, and heart-rending for Kate to bid 'farewell' to Stuart. They promised to keep in touch and Kate wept in his arms and promised that she would return as soon as she could. Everyone else was given the usual assurance that there would always be a 'Welcome in the Hillside' of beautiful rural Wales.

The girls were silent for most of the return journey. It seemed that all their hopes and dreams had been dashed just when they were germinating and promising a rich harvest.

Jo compared her situation to that of her parents—a dream fulfilled then shattered before it had borne fruit. It was the same for Kate. She had been dreaming of a new start where her past could be obliterated and the dreadful guilty memories erased. Now they were both returning to the world they had tried to escape from. How would they cope? Especially with imposed surveillance and the stigma attached to that condition which earmarked them as petty criminals, ne'er-do-wells not to be trusted. "And me", observed Kate grimly when they were quietly discussing their plight, "As an attempted murderess!" Jo burst out laughing at this, it seemed so preposterous. Kate laughed too, which caused Matthew and Beth to ask if they may share the joke. "Just a private one," they said guardedly, and left it at that.

As they recognised familiar landmarks they lapsed into silence. Here they were--back where they had started from. What did the future hold now? They sank again into silent introversion bordering on depression.

At the vicarage, nothing had changed except that the trees were beginning to bud as they shook off the dregs of winter. The tremulous beginning of buds bursting shyly through the bark made their branches seem less stark and skeletal as they responded to the onset of spring.

Megan was very happy to see them and hugged them both warmly. Lulu leapt around ecstatically and the aroma of a delicious meal beckoned them indoors.

Matthew, Beth and Megan were so happy and relieved to have the two girls home again. The previous torture of worry and uncertainty they had all endured was now behind them. Give them time to settle. Be patient. Every day was a day further from the dreadful past and impending tomorrows spawned new hopes and aspirations. This was how Matthew and Beth perceived it. However, tucked up in bed at the mercy of their dreams, Jo and Kate's hopes and aspirations seemed futile and full of despair.

During the days that followed, it was agreed that Jo and Kate could have home tuition as neither of them could bear to go back to school. Neither did they want any communication with the people they had known before.

Matthew and Beth went along with this believing that it was a temporary phase and that once they'd settled in and accepted the situation, they would change their minds. Matthew offered to take Jo to see 'Georgie' and was surprised at her violent outburst.

"I can't bear even to think about him, never mind going to see him! What good would it do? I can't have him back. He's part of the worst memories I'm trying to get rid of!" Then added in a peevish angry voice, "Just like everything else around here!" and she fled upstairs.

Kate looked at Matthew, shrugged her shoulders and ran after Jo.

Beth tried to placate Matthew who was hurt and stunned by this angry outburst. "Don't let it get to you. It's early days yet. At least they're both here and safe now. We're going to have to be so patient. It's not going to be easy but it will get better. We just have to learn to listen to them and not try so hard to do what *we* think they need."

For Beth and Matthew, it was time to plan for their dreams and aspirations. Their impending marriage. It seemed a bit rushed to the girls and Megan but nevertheless, Matthew and Beth began to plan their wedding day.

"'Marry in haste, repent at leisure'," teased Jo, "Why the rush?"

"Why prolong the agony of waiting?", laughed Beth, "Anyway, he might change his mind. Strike while the iron is hot!"

"Is Matthew hot? Wow, you surprise me!" quipped Jo.

"Watch this space!" joked Beth, "We're full of surprises. Especially me."

Neither Jo nor Kate read anything into this.

The first priority was the organisation of the wedding. Beth said she wanted to marry in May, at 'apple blossom time' when all life was springing anew.

"May has always been my favourite month. It is so full of promise. Everything recovering from the ravages of winter. I love to see the buds blossoming, garlanding the trees and the leaves opening out to the sun and making food to sustain life-- all life."

"And our lives too will begin anew too, as man and wife." said Matthew sentimentally as he hugged her.

"Aw!" said Jo teasingly, "People of your age aren't supposed to be slushy!"

"Well we are, and it's fun!" laughed Beth, "Now buzz off and leave us in peace!"

The Wedding Day was set for May 1st and the ceremony was to take place at the local church, Matthew's church. He could have done without the fuss and excitement but knew that if he got married anywhere else, his parishioners would never forgive him.

"May 1st," mused Jo, "That's a bit quick. Less than a month!"

"I know." agreed Kate, "There must be a reason. Those two don't do anything without good reason." she pondered for a while then said with a giggle, "Perhaps she's preggers!" and they both fell about laughing.

"Hey, wouldn't that be something! I wonder if God would ever forgive them."

More laughter ensued which was interrupted by Megan calling them for lunch.

The tutor arranged for them was a nice enough woman whose special subjects were maths and science but she assured them that she could cope with the required level in what she pompously referred to as 'the arts' meaning English and History. She was assigned to them for three days a week. This meant that time weighed heavily on their hands and neither of them could bear to visit their old haunts especially Bryn Celyn and the mountain and they still dreaded running into anyone they had known at school. So unless they were taken anywhere by car they were confined to the vicarage grounds. Their social worker visited once a week and tried her best to counsel and advise these two restless teenagers. They were both living from day to day, harking back to their time in Scotland, regretting that it had been so prematurely and cruelly curtailed. At least they still had each other and got comfort from this They were like souls in torment. The only person in Scotland they had kept in touch with was Fay and she gave them what news she could of James and Stuart. She advised them against direct contact with the two boys for the time being although Kate had phoned Stuart a few times but it was always his mother who answered. As soon as she heard Kate's voice she slammed the phone down. Kate told Fay about this and sought her advice. Fay responded with, "Let the wounds, physical and mental, heal. Give it time." This was very hard for Kate who fantasised about Stuart every night as she tried to relax in the groaning over-sprung bed, waiting for sleep.

May 1st dawned and the ceremony was short, simple and well-attended by the villagers. Beth looked beautiful and younger than her forty years, a true 'Queen of the May' in a long white dress with a flowing veil carried by Jo and Kate each clad in lilac. Megan was in her element. Her only son married at last! Dare she hope now for their union to bear fruit? Please God let it be so!

The ceremony concluded with a an extract from Robert Frost's poem, Prayer in Spring,

> *For this is love and nothing else is love*
> *To which it is reserved for God above*
> *To sanctify to what far ends he will*
> *But which it only means that we fulfil.*

There was no honeymoon. They'd had it already in Scotland and Matthew knew he mustn't ask for any more time away from his parish.

Jo and Kate were discussing the day and how well it had gone and reiterating how happy they were that Matthew and Beth were together. They remembered the conversation they'd had during that frightful night in the Lochside forest when they'd wondered about Matthew's sexuality.

"Do you suppose Beth really is pregnant?" asked Kate.

"I hope so. That would be Megan's most fervent prayer answered." replied Jo.

"And she got married in white. I thought only virgins could get married in church wearing white. Didn't they used to say, 'Marry in pink, and your spirits will sink'?" observed Kate.

"That was the rule in the old days when they thought God really cared about conventional trivia." responded Jo, "My great grandma who was an Irish Catholic had to get married in pink. She was pregnant so she couldn't pretend she was a virgin like most of the others did. Her family nearly disowned her. She was branded as a 'scarlet woman' and that shame stayed with her all her life even though you couldn't tell from the wedding photos which were all in black and white in those days. The shame was hers. She knew God knew and hoped he would one day forgive her."

"Poor thing and the man gets away with it again, just like the Adam and Eve saga. Thank goodness we've evolved beyond that, at least in our culture!" observed Kate.

The daily routine in the vicarage was more meaningful for Matthew and Beth following their marriage. They had each found their soul-mate and were blissfully happy.

However, for Jo and Kate the days dragged on. They got fed up of the eternal question, 'What do you want to do in the future?' They had no idea. It all depended on how the present developed and at the moment it was going nowhere. They were literally living from day to day, hoping that something would turn up and free them from this endless non-inspirational sameness.

Beth and Matthew tried to find things for them to do which would fill in the gaps between bouts of tuition and counselling. They were each given a vegetable plot to tend. Jo hated this. The bare soil and the scurrying insects were a dismal reminder of her parents grave in Bluebell Wood so Kate and Beth tended them both whilst Jo moped around pouring her heart out to Lulu. They were encouraged to cook with Megan but somehow it wasn't as much fun as the cooking they had done in the hostel with Fay. Once a week they went shopping with Beth to the nearest town. None of this was enough to satisfy the restless spirits of Jo and Kate. They had lost their erstwhile freedom. It seemed they had no future and still, with insidious regularity, their pasts came creeping back to taunt and torment.

"I feel like a caged animal, said Kate dejectedly, "At the mercy of my captors. Kind as they are, I sometimes feel like biting them."

"Better just keep on snarling," smirked Jo,"It's not their fault. They're trying to do what's best for us. I know what you mean though. I can empathise now with horses confined in their boxes all day. All that frustrated energy! No wonder they weave, crib-bite, boot the door and try to nip their captors as they walk past!"

Kate laughed as she thought of something, "Come on! Let's stand at the window and whinny and weave. It may release some of our frustration."

"Don't be daft! They'll probably put us in a loony bin. Better idea-- three circuits round the garden then you can help me with my homework."

"And if I win, you can weed my rotten veggie plot!"

So saying, they pelted downstairs, helter-skelter releasing their energy and frustration by shrieking and racing round the large vicarage garden hotly pursued by a jubilant Lulu. Then, at last, physically exhausted, they sprawled on the long grass and descanted yet again on their uncertain destiny.

Matthew and Beth although very happy and contented with their marital state were nevertheless aware that the girls were becoming bored and frustrated. Things were not working out as they had hoped. They had been back for four months and at first they had seemed to be settling in, accepting the 'fair cop' situation. Now, however, they were becoming more and more withdrawn and uncommunicative and spent more time together and far less with the rest of the household. Even Lulu felt shunned and spent more time curled up in her bed sighing dejectedly.

"We've been so wrapped up in ourselves that we haven't spent enough time finding out what they want." said Beth, "It's time we had a heart-to-heart with them."

After dinner that evening Matthew challenged the girls directly. He cleared his throat and said authoritatively, "We need to talk. Lately you both seem more unsettled and at times, even unhappy. You must tell us what's wrong. We are here to help but you must talk to us, explain how you feel. Help us to help you."

The girls looked at each other then Jo spoke, "It's just this place, this whole area. We have no future here and we feel like prisoners. The days go on, one after another, and each day feels wasted—like a day less to live. Like we are wasting our lives. We both want to go back to Scotland".

Matthew studied her carefully before he replied, "I can understand that but at the moment it is out of the question. And if you did go back, have you considered what you would do there? You can't just go back there and continue as before. You need an education. You are young and you have your whole lives before you. Have you thought of what you want to do and where you want to be?"

Jo almost choked on her answer, "Anywhere but here! This place was Paradise to me once. I never wanted to be anywhere else. But now it's hell and as long as I'm stuck here I never will be able to forget all the horrible things that happened. I try to push them to the back of my mind, to build a wall as you suggested, but here the memories are all around me, taunting me. It's as if this place is cursed for me. I'm afraid of being happy in case fate steps in and crushes me again. I'm scared something bad will happen to those I love," she choked with emotion, "Like you and Beth and Kate." Shuddering, she added, "I didn't feel like that in Scotland. I felt safe. And in Scotland, in a different environment, I could look forward. The past was behind me!"

He took her hand gently, "I'm so glad you've told me this and I fully understand and appreciate all that you've said. You know that Beth and I love you both very much and we will do anything in our power to make you happy. Neither of us can bear to see you like this. We have to find a solution between us. We must put our heads together and decide what we must do."

Kate who had been listening suddenly piped up, "Can we go back to Scotland—all of us?" A shocked silence whilst they all assimilated this.

Now it was Beth's turn, "Well if that's what everyone wants we won't rule it out, but before we rush into anything we must consider all the emotional and practical considerations"

Megan, who had eavesdropped on everything, stood up from her chair in the corner, head bowed and shoulders slumped. She bade everyone 'Goodnight' and closed the door quietly behind her.

The four looked at each other. Even if they all decided to go back to Scotland, what about Megan? At eighty-two she would certainly not want to move and she couldn't be left here alone. Matthew considered for a moment then ventured thoughtfully, "When we were in Cornwall she expressed a wish to be buried there, in Dad's grave. She wouldn't mind moving there. That's a possibility for all of us, Cornwall."

"It's a hell of a long way from Scotland," moaned Kate.

"Look, we're all jumping the gun here," intervened Beth, "Nothing has been decided. We've all got something to think about so let's go away and do that then pool our ideas and decide what's best for all of us." Then she added almost cryptically, "The world is a big place!"

"Shall we get out the map, or the atlas?" said Matthew, half-teasingly, remembering Beth's intuitive discovery of the whereabouts of the girls.

Chapter 29

At the beginning of July there was a phone call from Brian and Liz confirming their arrival in UK. Their planned itinerary involved visiting friends and family in their home town of Ashbridge followed by a sight-seeing tour which naturally would include visiting North Wales. They enquired about Jo and were concerned to hear about her emotional state.

Matthew gave a deep sigh, "She just can't settle. Not yet anyway. She's hankering after going back to Scotland. She says there are too many painful memories here and she can't escape them. Some of the time she's totally withdrawn and miserable. Other times, for our sakes, she tries to hide it but the pain is always there in her eyes, in her body language."

"Poor Jo!" commiserated Liz, "She's gone through a terrible time. She was such a happy and confident child too. Life can be so cruel sometimes. It does sound as if she needs a complete change." She thought for a moment then added, "How would it be if she came with us? We could take her to all the places she knew as a child round Ashbridge and then she could come with us on our 'tourist bit'. The break might do her good."

"Sounds like a good idea to me. But what about Kate? I doubt she would want to go without Kate but it seems a bit much, imposing both of them on you."

"No problem! It'll be fun having them both and easier for us too. So suggest it to Jo and we'll go from there."

The girls readily agreed and Matthew and Beth drove to their arranged meeting place, a lovely country pub on the edge of the Pennines. It was a happy and emotional reunion for the Johnson family and Jo. Liz and Brian had been like grand-parents to her for all of her childhood and Jan and Jack had been as aunt and uncle. It was good to see 'Bugger-me-Bert' too. He looked well and hadn't changed a bit but he commented that Jo had grown up a lot and he wouldn't have recognised her, "Bugger-me! You're a young woman now!" he quipped.

Baby Graham, hiding shyly behind his mother, made Jo wonder about Billy but she decided it would be better if she didn't go to see him. He was too much a part of the unbearable memories and she was afraid that she would rekindle in him the sense of loss he had felt that fateful Christmas. Also, there was no love lost between Julie and the Johnsons. After all, it was their fault that Tom had met Jenny. Better to steer clear!

After introductions and a pleasant lunch Matthew and Beth took their leave and it was decided that the Johnsons would bring the girls back to Wales in about three weeks.

"They are a lovely family," remarked Matthew in the car on their way home, "Just as Tom and Jenny described them. I think the girls will have a great time and the change of scene will do them good."

"Absolutely," agreed Beth. "Will you miss them?"

"In some ways, No! At least we'll be able to relax now and hopefully when they come back, things will be easier for all of us."

"Yes, and for the first time since our wedding day, we'll be able to do what we want to do together, without worrying about them."

"Yes, true, but it doesn't solve the ultimate problem-- where we go from here. I don't relish a move to Scotland and I have my mother to consider. She's hankering after returning to Cornwall----I could do that to please her as there's nothing left for me here now either!" He paused then added, "Except you, of course."

She took his hand, "I will go to the ends of the earth with you, love."

He sighed deeply then to lighten the atmosphere, remarked teasingly, "I think you'd better look for inspiration in the stars or get out your crystal ball."

She smiled cheekily, "OK. And you can seek inspiration in the Old Testament."

"Touche! Meanwhile, let's live for the present, 'Eat, drink and be Merry, for tomorrow we die', that's a quote from Corinthians."

"Well I prefer this one from Enstein, 'Learn from yesterday, live for today, hope for tomorrow'."

"I'll settle for that." he agreed.

The next few weeks at the vicarage were peaceful and relaxing for Matthew, Beth and Megan. They were relieved to hear that all was going well in Ashbridge and that they were planning family outings and walks in the nearby Peak District, which was another beautiful area that Tom and Jenny had talked about.

The weather was fine and sunny and Matthew felt an urge to show Beth Bryn Celyn and some of the walks he had done with Tom. Accordingly, they drove up to the house and parked the car

The 'FOR SALE' sign was partially obscured by foliage from the over-hanging sycamore and they both wondered how many passers-by would see it. Not that there were many passers-by on this neglected country lane. Matthew, cloaked in nostalgia, began to regret this visit and didn't feel disposed to talk too much about the past. The house and outbuildings seemed sad and uncared for too. Lulu ran eagerly to the stables and the house door. She barked and scratched impatiently. When there was no response she hung her head and slunk back to Matthew and Beth.

"Poor Lulu," murmured Matthew, patting her head, "She doesn't understand."

He wanted to see how much the conker tree they had planted for Emily had grown. He led Beth to the special spot he and Jo had chosen and was pleased to see the tree in full leaf and thriving. He felt that there ought to be some commemorative plaque. He mentioned this to Beth and she agreed.

"We could order something tomorrow and have it in place for when Jo gets back. I'm sure she'd be touched and happy."

"Good! We must choose a fitting epitaph."

As they walked they discussed the plaque and Matthew suggested that it should be made of slate, tough and appropriate as this area had been built around the slate quarries which abounded here.

They were approaching Bluebell Wood.

"We must choose another one too. Something simple for Tom and Jenny."

Beth grasped his hand and they walked in silence. She was moved by the simple beauty of the spot where Tom and Jenny lay. The ginkgo biloba tree looked sturdy and stiff compared to the softer trees surrounding it.

"It looks belligerent, almost as if it's guarding the grave--warding off evil spirits."

Matthew smiled, "Let's hope so. And it should be here for thousands of years if left alone."

Beth stared at the heaving turf, "Lucky things to spend eternity here."

She sighed as she absorbed the soft pervading tranquillity which was all around. "It's really strange, I've never been anywhere where I've felt such an inner peace. Weird-----." She turned to face him, her green eyes soft with yearning, "Hold me Matthew," she whispered. He held her close and kissed her soft hair. They were welded into one as they sank down in the softly yielding grass. The large trees whispered their approval above them whilst the birds trilled and thrilled and the ginkgo biloba stood sentry.

> *The closeness of two bodies intertwined*
> *Inspires the intimacy of each mind,*
> *Gratified lust may satisfy base desires*
> *But true love lasts, rekindling Nature's fires.*

The next few days were spent ordering and installing the plaques.

The epitaphs they had chosen were carved onto the polished slate. For Emily,

> ***Her soul like a star***
> ***Beacons from the abode***
> ***Where the eternal are.***

And for Tom and Jenny:

> ***In the night hope sees a star***
> ***And listening love can hear the rustle of***
> ***a wing***

Now all they had to do was wait for Jo's return and hope for her approval.

Chapter 30

During the three weeks they had spent together Jo, Kate and the Johnsons had become like a family. Liz and Brian had always been the only grandparents Jo had ever known and Jack and Jan had assumed, quite naturally, the role of parents. Jo and Kate were fascinated by the photos and stories about New Zealand.

"So you loved the Scottish Highlands," observed Jack, "Well imagine all that space and beauty magnified a thousandfold and that's New Zealand!"

"It was the best move we made, agreed Jan. "We have a lovely house with land, good jobs and mum and dad next door. Couldn't be better!"

Seeds were sown in the minds of Jo and Kate. Wouldn't it be wonderful if they could go back with them--even just for a holiday? They were very unsettled at the vicarage. They felt like prisoners, especially after the freedom and independence they'd enjoyed in Scotland. One day they would go back there but that 'one day' seemed an age away and would they still be welcome? Also they realised that whilst at the vicarage they were a constant problem for

Matthew and Beth. In the privacy of their bedroom they talked about the possibility of embarking on a new adventure together but neither dared mention it to the adults, not even to Liz. New Zealand! Now that would really be getting away as far as possible from the torments of the past. A completely new start where they could leave everything behind them and look ahead to a brighter future. A young country for young people.

It was all systems go at the vicarage when the Johnsons and Jo and Kate were due back. Spare rooms became bedrooms to accommodate everyone. Megan and Beth made beef casserole and bread and butter pudding to cater for ten. A lot of work done easily and happily to welcome them all.

Jo and Kate arrived bursting with excitement, hugging Matthew, Beth and Megan, recounting many things they had done and many places they had seen during their trip. Lulu, delighted to see them again, rollicked and frolicked her exuberant welcome. Meanwhile, the Johnson family relaxed in the garden planning their itinerary for the rest of their holiday. They wanted to see Bryn Celyn and the surrounding countryside but were anxious about the effect this would have on Jo if she went with them.

"I don't know how she would react," admitted Matthew, "But on the other hand I think she will want to go with you." He clenched his hands and sighed. "It's a difficult one but I think she ought to go with you. She has to accept that she can't go on for ever torturing herself and others. In fact," he added thoughtfully, "It might, or even could, have a positive impact. It may help her to banish the ghosts of the past. She hasn't been anywhere near the place since she got back here. It's as if she's refusing to accept the inevitability of a future without those who meant everything to her. If only she could concentrate on the best times they spent together and rejoice in those treasured memories." He paused, shook his head dejectedly, gave a deep sigh, then added, "If she can't find the strength to face her problems, how can she ever overcome them?"

Beth intervened, "I don't think it's just that. I think she's trying to build that wall she must never look over and every memory jolt smashes it down again. After all, it's barely nine months since her life was turned upside-down. In time she will be strong enough to turn the memories into cement to seal the bricks together."

"I hope so," he said resignedly, then added, "Anyway, she can decide herself whether she wants to come to Bryn Celyn with us or not and we must all suffer the consequences if emotion gets the better of her."

Accordingly, next morning all of them, except Megan and baby Graham, drove up the narrow lane towards Bryn Celyn. The lane, sheltered by the trees on either side and shaded from the glare of the sun by the overhead intertwining branches was splattered by flashes of light switched on and off by the dense foliage.

Jo remembered what her mother had told her of the different impressions Tom and Jenny had formed the first time they drove up this lane to Bryn Celyn.

"Mum said the trees were embracing their neighbours, but Dad said he had a sense of foreboding and to him they were choking the life out of each other." Silence. Then she added with bitter conviction, "Dad was right!"

No-one made any comment.

They drove into the yard the car crushing the weeds which were defiantly pushing their way through the gravel. The house stood alone looking bewildered and neglected. Jo gulped and clenched her hands. Matthew guessed that she wouldn't want to go inside so they left her in the car with Kate.

Lulu jumped out of the car and followed them to the door but then she too seemed confused and reluctant to go any further. Instead she slunk off on a mission of her own, sniffing and digging but without her customary exuberance.

When they emerged, in deference to Jo's fragile mood, no-one offered any opinion about the house but Matthew turned to Jo and said almost conspiratorially, "Come here Jo, I want you to see this."

He took her hand and led her to Emily's tree. He felt her intake of breath so he increased the pressure of his grasp and read aloud the simple inscription on the slate slab.

Her soul like a star
Beacons from the abode
Where the eternal are.

She gulped and turned to him, then said chokingly, "It's perfect! Thank you Matthew," and she hugged him, suppressing the tears which she felt welling up inside her."

No-one else spoke.

The group, headed by Matthew, wandered up the field trampling the long grass which had already overgrown the once well-trodden path.

Matthew mused upon the trite and oft quoted cliché, 'life must go on'. So true! Once you have strutted and fretted your hour upon the stage of life, you are heard no more. But, you do make room for others to make what they will of what is left for them. These opportunistic grasses and weeds once suppressed by constant trampling and now springing up everywhere were testament to that. They too were providing homes food and shelter for myriads of other life forms. Life must and does go on, but at whose expense? He sighed and tried to shed this melancholy mood which he did not want to infect the others, especially Jo, who was being so strong and in control of her emotions. She was trying so hard to summon up this will-power and if she could learn how to martial it now, this would help her to cope with whatever other challenges fate may have in store for her in the future.

Beth, always sensitive to the moods of others, deliberately distracted Matthew by shouting, "Look at Lulu!"

The dog emerged from the stream soaking wet, and began to shake herself vigorously, showering them all amid shrieks and squeals of protest.

"Bugger me, Lulu!" exclaimed Bert, "These pants were clean on this morning!"

They all roared with laughter.

This was welcome light relief and loosened their tongues so that they began to talk about the astonishing view, the lovely August weather and the soft fragrance of the air.

"It's so lovely here!" remarked Jan, "It reminds me of home."

By 'home' she meant New Zealand and her parents noted with some surprise that even after just five years she considered their adopted country as her home.

For Liz and Brian, Britain was and always would be 'home' even though they had no intention ever to return on a permanent basis.

Destiny Obscure

Liz gazed out across the soft green fields and the all-embracing sea to the outline of Anglesey which today was basking in the warm glow of the mid-day sun.

"No wonder Jenny fell in love with this place the first time she saw it." she remarked to Brian who was standing beside her equally impressed with the lovely landscape. "She was always ruled by her heart whilst Tom was much more pragmatic."

"True," agreed Brian, "But he needed to be at times. I think she inherited her impulsive nature from her parents and look what happened to them!"

"Oh don't start that again!" she urged, "We don't know what happened to them. Don't be so glum! Come on---we're getting left behind!"

And they hurried on to catch up with the others.

As they entered Bluebell wood, they all became silent again. This was so hard for Jo. The ultimate test. Kate took her hand and squeezed it, tentatively at first, then releasing and applying gentle pressure like a pulse ensuring the circulation of positive energy. Jo responded by gripping Kate's hand tighter, drawing strength from her friend.

Beth took Matthew's hand too, remembering the love and warmth of their recent visit and their intimacy on the softly yielding grass-------.

They all stood before the grave, heads bowed.

Jo saw the slate slab and with choking emotion read the simple inscription,

'In the night hope sees a star and listening love can hear the rustle of a wing'

"Thank you so much Matthew. That's lovely. It was the only thing missing. I'll remember this every time I think of them. They would have loved it too and it is like mum said, they are here together for eternity. Pity the bluebells aren't in bloom." There was a catch in her voice and she swallowed hard to suppress the choking sobs rising within her.

They stood, a forlorn little group, shuffling uncomfortably wondering what to say next, when Liz looked at Jo and said with fervour, "You are so like your mother. I can see her now at fifteen, running around the yard, riding the horses, full of zest for life. That hasn't gone. She is living on through you. She is and always will be a part of your existence."

Jo stared at her, perplexed, "But what about Tom? He can only live on in my memories."

"Yes, but *his* genes will live on through Billy. I'm sure that you will be reunited with Billy one day. Best that you leave him be now with Julie. She'll take good care of him. She did what she thought was best for Tom."

"She stifled him!"

"Yes, but he escaped in the end and he never stopped loving her because he knew, misguided though it was, that it was done with the best intentions."

"The path to Hell is paved with good intentions." Jo sneered.

Silence again.

Beth changed the subject, "I love this place. It has an air of utter peace and serenity and it's so right that they will spend eternity together here, guarded by the ginkgo biloba." She took one of its leaves, "Look, two lobes, joined together. Concrescence. Just like Tom and Jenny. Joined together for ever."

The others looked and smiled. They were all searching for something other than platitudes to comfort Jo and

Destiny Obscure

to ease their own sense of loss but without becoming too maudlin, and the group mood at that moment was decidedly maudlin.

The August day was warm and windless and they were all feeling drained and dehydrated. As if on cue, Jack opened his rucksack and took out some bottles of water which they accepted gratefully as they made themselves comfortable on the ever-yielding grass. They were all at peace now enjoying the moment, revelling in recollections of happy times spent together. These positive memories slowly overcame the negative ones so that they began to feel relaxed and contented.

Beth stared at the grave and sought inspiration for the future from the spirits of Tom and Jenny which she believed were in there. She wanted them to tell her what would be the best thing for Jo and Kate. But, try as she might, she could not conjure up their spirits. She had never known Tom and Jenny. All her theories were surmised. It is too trite to say 'live for the present'. Horrid things happen in the present then they immediately become the past. Before they happen, they are the future, so how can we categorise precisely the present and the future? The only unalterable one is the past. We all try to shape our future, learn from the past and do what we think is best, but the Damoclesian sword of Destiny wielded by Fate, is for ever above us. She gave a deep sigh of defeat. Her conclusions and predictions, however positive, were all based on surmise.

Jo and Kate had wandered off through the woodland with Lulu, laughing at her doggy exploits and trying to guess if her frantic digging was inspired by rabbit holes or badger sets. Kate laughed and said, "She's trying to dig her way to New Zealand!"

The rest of the group remained behind relaxing in the eternal resting place of Tom and Jenny. Matthew was in animated conversation with the Johnsons. Beth turned to listen.

"It could solve the immediate problem," Liz was saying, "And we all get on so well. Jo has always been like family to us and I think Kate would be happy as long as they're together. They're growing up so fast. In a couple of years they can make up their own minds. Legally, we wouldn't even have to formally adopt them. We could be like foster parents. There are good schools near to where we live. They could continue their education there and when they qualify they can decide whether to stay on and enrol in a New Zealand university or return to UK to study. Perhaps," she added, tongue in cheek, Even back to their beloved Scotland!"

Matthew stared at the mound, the plaque, the ginkgo tree then returned his gaze to Liz and answered assuredly, "I think it's a marvellous idea!"

"So do we!" chorused Jack and Jan.

"Me too!" agreed Beth enthusiastically.

"Bugger me! Will I have to put up with them?" teased Bert, and they all laughed.

Mutual hugs and handshakes all round settled it.

At that moment the girls returned with Lulu and noting the sudden silence, wondered what the adults had been plotting in their absence.

"Sit down, girls!", ordered Brian, but before they had chance to obey, he announced, "We've decided that the best thing for you two tear-aways would be a new start in New Zealand!"

They stared at each other then at the group who were all waiting for their reaction.

"What! Fantastic! We were dreaming about that but hardly dared hope you'd want us." was their wild excited response and they rushed forward, dancing and clapping, to hug the Johnson family.

"Calm down, calm down!" begged Matthew, "Listen now," he added conspiratorially, almost smugly," This is the time and place for good news. Come on Beth, you tell them!"

"Well", ventured Beth, blushing in spite of herself, "Matthew and I are going to have a baby."

Stunned silence then whoops of delight, "Congratulations! Fantastic news!

"When?"

"December!"

"A Christmas baby, lovely!"

This announcement engendered even more hope and happiness in all of them.

"What a fantabulous day!" shrieked Kate.

"Yes!" Agreed Jo. Then with a mischievous look at Matthew, added, "So, there is a God after all!" Matthew made to chase after her amid shrieks of laughter.

Spirits high and hearts full of hope, they made their way back down the hillside. Jo, giggling, couldn't resist whispering in Kate's ear, "Told you! No wonder they were in such a hurry to get married!" And, she added teasingly, "She didn't get married in pink! How about that!"

"Marry in pink and your spirits will sink!" chanted Kate dancing down the hill.

"She married in white so she'll be all right!" rejoined Jo skipping alongside

Then together, they chorused, "New Zealand, New Life. Here we come!"

They held hands and positively leapt and skipped giddily down the field back to the car with the irrepressible Lulu lolloping and leaping alongside.

The adults followed more sedately, relaxed relieved and contented that the day had turned out so well

Life was wonderful again!

The next few weeks were occupied with legal and practical arrangements for the Johnson family to foster Jo and Kate. Passports were obtained and farewells bade to James and Stuart and of course, to Fay. Promises were made and extracted to keep in touch and mutual invitations given all round to visit.

The day before their departure Jo went to see 'Georgie'. Louise was welcoming and understanding. "He is a rising star, like his mother 'Meribel'. She sighed and confided, "I feel he is far too talented for me." Jo knew she would have to be tactful and encouraging. "He's very young yet and he looks so well. You're doing a great job. Thank you so much. I wouldn't trust him to anyone else." They hugged and then Louise left them alone in the box.

As she had done so many times before, she poured out her heart to him and he listened, submitting to her caresses and responding by gently rubbing her with his head.

"I will be back for you one day, I promise." These were her parting words.

Megan doubted that she would ever see the girls again and her farewell hug was particularly poignant. Experience gained through age had taught her that the future was incessantly uncertain. Matthew and Beth were already making tentative plans for when they could visit New Zealand. After the birth of their 'Christmas' baby they would make definite ones. Wonderful—so much again to look forward to!

Lulu was overwhelmed and a little nonplussed by the simultaneous hugs and tears. She lay submissively on her back, melting both the girls' hearts.

Jo had already suggested to Matthew that he should get a passport for Lulu and bring her along too when they visited.

"It's too far for a dog, poor thing." he protested.

"No it isn't", she insisted. "Dad's friends in Brunei brought their two dogs and two cats over and they were perfectly OK after their journey!"

Matthew smiled indulgently, "We'll see," and they had a group hug, Lulu standing on her hind-legs, joined in.

At last the great day came and the girls settled into the cramped seats of the huge jet, buzzing with excited hope on the threshold of this new awesome adventure. Whatever next lay ahead, they felt strong enough--equipped enough--to tackle it together.

The End

*Can the acts of this life determine
the destiny of the next?*